THE VERY NEARLY HONORABLE
LEAGUE OF PIRATES

The Buccaneers' Code

CAROLINE CARLSON

THE VERY NEARLY HONORABLE LEAGUE OF PIRATES

The Buccaneers' Code

Illustrations by DAVE PHILLIPS

HARPER

An Imprint of HarperCollinsPublishers

The Very Nearly Honorable League of Pirates: The Buccaneers' Code
Text copyright © 2015 by Caroline Carlson
Illustrations copyright © 2015 by Dave Phillips

Library of Congress Cataloging-in-Publication Data
Carlson, Caroline.
The Buccaneers' Code / Caroline Carlson ; illustrations by Dave Phillips. —
First edition.
    pages cm. — (The Very Nearly Honorable League of Pirates ; book 3)
 Summary: When Miss Pimm, Enchantress of the Marsh, decides to retire,
she enlists young Hilary Westfield to gather a band of scallywags and prepare
to challenge Captain Blacktooth in an all-out battle for the presidency of the
League in order to save the kingdom.
 ISBN 978-0-06-219440-4
 [1. Pirates—Fiction. 2. Adventure and adventurers—Fiction. 3. Leadership—
Fiction. 4. Magic—Fiction. 5. Sex role—Fiction.] I. Phillips, Dave, illustrator.
II. Title.
PZ7.C21644Buc 2015   2014042510
[Fic]—dc23   CIP
                                                                                  AC

        16 17 18 19 20   CG/OPM   10 9 8 7 6 5 4 3 2 1
                                 ❖
                    First paperback edition, 2016

AUGUSTA

Captain Wolfson's feasting hall

SUMMERSTEAD

Summerstead shipyard

HIGH SEAS

The Ornery Clam

Tilbury Park

NORDHOLM

THE NORTHLANDS

VNHLP Headquarters

HIGH SEAS

GUNPOWDER BAY

Town Square

LITTLE SHEARWATER

GUNPOWDER ISLAND

Gargoyle's quarry

MIDDLEBY

Scallywag's Den

OTTERPOOL

THE SOUTHLANDS

HIGH SEAS

Royal Dungeons

Queen's Palace

Miss Pimm's

Pemberton market

QUEENSPORT

Westfield House

PEMBERTON

The Salty Biscuit

Queensport Harbor

WIMBLY-ON-THE-MARSH

Jasper's house

N W E S

PEMBERTON BAY

Little Herring Cove

Royal Augusta Water Ballet

To the Southern Kingdoms and the Pestilent Home for Foul-Tempered Pirates

THE VERY NEARLY HONORABLE
LEAGUE OF PIRATES

The Buccaneers' Code

CHAPTER ONE

IT WAS SNOWING hard in Queensport, and Hilary thought it might never stop. Snow covered the grounds of Westfield House, drifting against the drawing room's tall glass doors and blocking out every last glimpse of the harbor beyond. When Hilary swung her sword through the air in the figure she'd been practicing all morning, her blade lodged itself once again in the folds of her mother's best velvet drapes, and she felt tempted to leave it there until spring. "This weather," she said, "is entirely unsuitable for piracy."

"I don't like it one bit," the gargoyle agreed. He'd spent the morning perched on the mantel above the drawing-room fireplace, commenting on Hilary's swordplay technique and warming his tail over the embers. "There's no use in digging for treasure when the ground's frozen stiff. Or when half the pirates in the kingdom have anchored their ships for the week and gone to visit their relatives," he added, giving Hilary a look.

"You know I promised Mother I'd visit. It's pleasant for her to have company during the holidays." Hilary pulled her sword out of the drapery and frowned at the holes she'd sliced in the velvet. "Besides, we'll be back at sea as soon as the weather improves."

"Or maybe even sooner," the gargoyle said hopefully, "if your mother finds out you've been carving up her furniture."

There was a knock at the drawing-room door. Hilary dropped her sword, kicked it under an ottoman, and hurried to stand in front of the tattered drapes as Bess, her mother's parlor maid, entered the room. "Excuse me, miss," she said, "but you've got a gentleman caller at the front door."

This sounded entirely unlikely to Hilary. She couldn't imagine what sort of gentleman might be calling on her at Westfield House—or anywhere else, for that matter. "Are you sure he's not here to see Mother?"

"Quite sure, miss," said Bess. "I'm afraid I didn't know what to do with him. It didn't seem proper to invite him in, so I told him to wait on the front step, even though the snow is frightful. But you see, miss, he's not precisely a gentleman." She looked around and lowered her voice. "He's a pirate."

THE VISITOR WAITING on the front step was a pirate indeed, and a damp one at that. Snowflakes dusted his shoulders and laced the brim of his three-cornered hat. Except for the red woolen scarf wrapped around both himself and his parrot, however, he might have been dressed for a summer's day at sea. "Ahoy there," he said to Hilary through chattering teeth. "Are you by any chance the Terror of the Southlands?"

Hilary had never seen this pirate before in her life, but he didn't look threatening; he only looked cold. She took him firmly by the wrists and dragged him through the doorway. "I am," she said, "and you'd better come inside before your parrot catches a chill. I'm sorry Bess kept you waiting, but we don't often receive pirate visitors at Westfield House." She crossed her arms and studied the pirate, who had begun to drip all over the floor. "Now, who are you, and what do you want with me?"

"My name is Partridge," said the pirate, unwinding his scarf. His voice was thin and anxious; he sounded more like a shopkeeper than a scallywag. "I came here as soon as I saw your notice."

"My notice?"

Partridge nodded with great enthusiasm. "The notice you placed in this morning's *Gazette*."

Hilary wondered exactly how long this pirate had been standing in the cold. Perhaps the weather had chilled his brain, for he wasn't making the slightest bit of sense. "But I didn't place a notice in the *Gazette*," she said. "I'm afraid you've made a mistake."

"I have?" said Partridge. "Oh dear. I *am* often mistaken, you know. When I confused the grog with the lantern oil, my mates were horribly ill, and our ship nearly burst into flames." A snowflake dripped from his nose. "Captain Blacktooth dismissed me from the League on account of it. He told me to give up piracy and try my hand at a trade." Partridge wrung out his scarf, which dripped miserably onto the floor below. "He suggested selling jams and chutneys."

Hilary almost felt sorry for him. After all, Captain Blacktooth had dismissed her from the Very Nearly Honorable League of Pirates as well—or, rather, she had dismissed herself. It had all amounted to the same thing in the end: bone-chilling threats from Blacktooth's friends, scathing reviews of her swordplay technique in the League newsletter, and endless reassurances from her mates that a career as a freelance pirate wasn't as grim as it currently seemed. "Did you take Captain Blacktooth's advice?" she asked Partridge.

"I did my best," he said, "but I kept confusing the chutneys with the jams, and no one wants to buy preserves from a pirate, anyway. That's why I answered the notice in the *Gazette*—but I suppose I've got that mixed up as well."

His parrot looked pleadingly at Hilary.

Hilary took Partridge's damp scarf and hung it from the lowest limb of the coatrack, hoping her mother wouldn't spot it there. "I may not be the person you're looking for," she said, "but I won't let you go out into the snow until you've gotten warmed up. I'll ask Bess to bring you some tea." She guided Partridge and his parrot across the hall into the blue parlor, where a fire crackled in the grate. "Oh, and if Mother stumbles across you, do you think you could pretend to be a High Society gentleman? I'm not supposed to let scallywags into the house."

"I suppose I could try." Partridge sounded slightly more hopeful than he had a moment earlier. "Perhaps she'll want to purchase a chutney."

Then he settled himself in Mrs. Westfield's favorite chair, which was sure to smell of wet parrot for the rest of the winter, and Hilary set off to ask Bess about tea.

WHEN SHE RETURNED to the drawing room, Hilary found the gargoyle hopping up and down the length of the mantelpiece. "Tell me everything!" he cried. "I've been stuck up here the whole time you've been gone! Was there really a pirate at the door? Was he one of those nasty sorts from the League? Did you have to challenge him to a duel?"

"Not exactly." Hilary picked up her sword from under the ottoman and polished a tarnished spot with her sleeve.

"There *was* a pirate, but he seems to have come here by accident. Now he's in the blue parlor, drinking tea."

"Well, that's not very exciting," the gargoyle said. "I hope the next one will have something more interesting to say."

Hilary nearly dropped her sword. "The next one?"

"He's coming across the lawn right now." The gargoyle nodded toward the drawing-room windows. On the other side of the glass, a man trudged through the snow. A belt was wrapped around his massive waist, and a glinting, sharp-looking cutlass hung at his side. "You'd better take me with you this time," the gargoyle said. "If there's going to be a duel in your mother's front hall, I don't want to miss it."

Hilary didn't think a duel was likely, but the man with the cutlass had arms and legs as thick and sturdy as the logs in the fireplace. She picked up the gargoyle and tucked him under her arm, just in case.

When they reached the front door, they found Bess with her hands on her hips, giving the second pirate a stern look. "They're multiplying, miss," she said to Hilary. "Shall I tell Mrs. Westfield?"

Hilary shook her head violently.

Bess raised an eyebrow. "I'll put more water on for tea, then."

The second pirate stepped inside without being invited.

He was so wide that he had to turn ever so slightly sideways as he passed through the doorway, and so tall that he had to remove his hat. "The Terror of the Southlands, I presume!" he said. His voice filled every spare inch of the room. When he shook Hilary's hand, he nearly lifted her straight out of her boots. "The name's Flintlock. I'm here on account of the notice you placed in the *Gazette*."

The gargoyle looked up at Hilary. "You placed a notice in the *Gazette*?"

"I didn't!" said Hilary. "I don't know anything about any sort of notice."

"Ah." Flintlock winked. "I understand. You don't care to speak about your treacherous plot in public. That's very wise, Terror—the League's spies might be anywhere." He gave a meaningful sort of nod in the gargoyle's direction.

Hilary could hear Mr. Partridge humming sea chanteys to his parrot in the blue parlor, but she did her best to ignore him. She wasn't sure she could manage more than one outlandish pirate at a time. "If you're looking for treacherous plots," she said to Flintlock, "then you're searching in quite the wrong place. I don't know what the newspaper's printed, and I swear I've got nothing to do with it."

"Quite right." Flintlock winked again and lowered his voice to a rumble. "You're a convincing actress, Terror, but I didn't come here to attend a theatrical performance. Is there a place where we might discuss your plans without being overheard?"

The gargoyle put his snout to Hilary's ear. "What is he talking about?" he whispered. "And why does he keep winking like that?"

Hilary didn't know any more than the gargoyle did, but she could tell that trying to reason with this pirate wasn't likely to do much good. "You may as well wait in the blue parlor," she told Flintlock, pointing to the door. "I'll be there in a moment."

The pirate bowed to her and crossed the hall. When he had closed the parlor door behind him, Hilary set the gargoyle down and began pulling open drawers, overturning trunks, and rifling through closets. "What are you doing?" the gargoyle asked.

"I'm looking for this morning's *Gazette*," said Hilary. "I've got no idea where Mother keeps it." Her former governess, Miss Greyson, had always encouraged her to follow the news of the day, but Hilary had been far more interested in piracy than in current events, and she hadn't seen what use a dull old newspaper could possibly be to her on the High Seas. Now, however, she wished she'd paid a bit more attention during all those blasted lessons. "Finding one strange pirate on one's doorstep is an accident," she said, "but finding two is a pattern. I'd like to read this notice for myself so I can find out why these scallywags are here."

The gargoyle shifted his weight from side to side.

"Actually," he said, "I happen to know exactly where your mother put the *Gazette*."

Hilary flipped through a stack of ancient-looking naval forms. "You do? Where is it?"

"In the drawing-room fireplace," the gargoyle said. "It did an excellent job of warming my tail."

"Oh dear." Hilary stared out the window. "And there's someone else coming up the front steps."

"My goodness!" said Bess, who was crossing the hall toward the blue parlor with a fresh pot of tea. "This house hasn't seen so many visitors since your mother's last masquerade ball. I can't imagine why half the kingdom wants to pay you their respects in this weather."

"Neither can I," said Hilary, "but I'm desperate to find out." She opened the door and studied the person in front of her. "I suppose you're here to respond to my notice as well?"

"Naturally," said the pirate on the doorstep. This one was a young woman. Her hair was pulled back in a short, tidy braid, and her coat and breeches were pressed and spotless. In one gloved hand, she held a snowy scrap of newsprint. "I'm Lucy Worthington," she said. "I'm sorry it took me so long to get here, but I made seven wrong turns and ended up halfway across the city before I'd realized my mistake. I hope I'm not too late to help you, Terror."

Hilary kept her eyes on the scrap of newsprint in Worthington's hand. "I think I know exactly how you can help me," she said, leading the pirate inside. "Is that the notice from the *Gazette*?"

Worthington nodded. "I hope it's all right that I brought it with me. I wanted to be sure of your address." She smiled at Hilary and handed her the newsprint. "It's awfully difficult to remember where you're going once you've started on your way there, don't you think?"

Hilary didn't answer. She stared at the words in front of her, printed in letters as black and dangerous as cannonballs.

NOTICE
TERROR OF THE SOUTHLANDS
SEEKS PIRATE LEAGUE PRESIDENCY

Pirate Hilary Westfield, the Terror of the Southlands, will soon announce her intention to challenge Captain Rupert Blacktooth for command of the Very Nearly Honorable League of Pirates. Captain Blacktooth currently serves as the League's president and has held this position for the past eighteen years. In recent months, however, Captain Blacktooth's connections to villainous activities have raised questions about his ability to serve as the head of an organization that claims to be honorable (or very nearly). The Terror of the Southlands resigned from the League six months ago in protest of Captain Blacktooth's leadership, for she believes that the scallywags of Augusta deserve a captain who is a true pirate—not a cowardly criminal.

All pirates who wish to assist the Terror in her bid for League presidency should demonstrate their support by reporting immediately to Westfield House in Queensport.

Hilary had to read the headline three times before she could believe it. "It says I'm going to challenge Captain Blacktooth," she told the gargoyle, who was craning his neck to get a glimpse of the paper. "It says I want to be the president of the VNHLP."

The gargoyle froze. "Challenge Captain Blacktooth?" he said. "Are you crazy? He'll send his mates after us! They'll slice us up and fry us for supper!" He squeezed his eyes shut. "They'll serve me with potatoes."

"They won't do anything of the sort," said Hilary. "You're far too crunchy. But someone's made an awful mistake, and we've got to fix it at once." She turned on her heel, left Lucy Worthington standing in the hallway, and hurried into the blue parlor without bothering to knock.

In blue velvet armchairs in front of a blue-tiled table, Mr. Flintlock and Mr. Partridge were absorbed in an energetic game of cards. Their teacups had left damp rings on the furniture, and steam rose off the coats they had left to dry in front of the fire. When Hilary laid the notice down on the table in front of them, their playing cards fluttered in all directions. "This is why you're here, isn't it?" she asked. "To help me take over the pirate league?"

Mr. Partridge and his parrot both nodded at once. "Of course," said Partridge. "Ever since Captain Blacktooth ended my career, I've been eager to return the favor."

"So have I," Flintlock boomed. "I was a loyal pirate for nearly fifteen years, but it only took one mishap for Blacktooth to turn me out of the League for good."

The gargoyle hopped in from the hall. "What was the mishap?" he asked.

"I was a human cannonball." Flintlock sighed. "I got stuck in my cannon."

Hilary turned to Worthington, who had come to stand in the doorway. "Did Blacktooth dismiss you, too?"

"He did," said Worthington, "not more than a month ago. I was training as a pirate's apprentice, and he told me there wasn't any place in the League for a navigator who couldn't navigate." She scowled. "We always got where we were going *eventually*."

All three pirates shook their heads.

"It's a good thing the Terror gathered us here," said Flintlock. "When we're done with Blacktooth, he'll be nothing but knucklebones."

"Knucklebones!" said the parrot.

"So, Terror," said Partridge, "when do we start?"

Hilary scuffed her boots across her mother's good

carpet. All three of the pirates seemed so hopeful, so certain that she could help them. "I'm afraid we're not starting anything," she said. "I'm not going to challenge Captain Blacktooth."

The pirates' faces crumpled. Even the kings and queens on the playing cards looked more dejected than usual. "You've changed your plans, then?" Flintlock asked.

"I never had any plans to begin with!" said Hilary. "I don't know where the *Gazette* got that notice. Hardly anything it says is true."

Worthington looked puzzled. "Do you mean to say that Blacktooth *isn't* a villain?"

"Well, no," said Hilary, "that's not what I mean at all. He wants all the kingdom's magic for himself, and he's been completely dishonorable about trying to get his hands on it."

"But you still think he should be in charge of the League?"

"Of course not!" said Hilary. "He should be locked up in the Royal Dungeons!"

Flintlock scratched his chin. "In that case, Terror," he said slowly, "why aren't you challenging him?"

Hilary frowned. "I may want Blacktooth gone," she said, "but that doesn't mean I should be the one to replace him. It would be ridiculous! I don't know a thing about leading an entire league of—"

"Pirates!" said her mother.

Mrs. Westfield stood at the parlor door, with one hand braced against the door frame to keep herself from fainting on the spot. Partridge, Flintlock, and Worthington all offered their own hands for her to shake, but she simply looked from one pirate to the next.

"Hilary, dear," she said, "when I told you that I wished you would be a bit more sociable, this was not precisely what I meant." She looked down at the blue carpet, which was sprinkled with clots of mud from someone's boots, and her face paled. "If only you'd let me know that you were hosting tea for a band of pirates, I could have suggested a more suitable location."

"Pirates?" said Partridge. "I, for one, am a High Society gentleman!"

"Knucklebones!" said his parrot.

"I'm so sorry, Mother." Hilary moved to Mrs. Westfield's side. "These guests arrived unexpectedly, and—well—I didn't want to be an ungracious hostess."

Mrs. Westfield's color improved considerably.

"But they're just about to leave. I'm afraid there was a misunderstanding, and I'm not the scallywag they meant to visit after all."

All three pirates looked thoroughly downcast at this, and Partridge's lower lip began to tremble. Hilary hoped he wouldn't start dripping all over again. "I'm sure they'll find the person they're looking for," she added.

By now, Mrs. Westfield had managed to remove her

hand from the door frame. "I'll have the coachman drive our visitors home," she said, as though that would solve everything. "It wouldn't do for them to walk; the snow is still ferocious."

"That's very good of you, ma'am," said Flintlock. He bowed to Mrs. Westfield and ducked out of the parlor, with Partridge and Worthington at his heels. "If it's acceptable to my new acquaintances," he said, "I'll instruct the coachman to take us to the Salty Biscuit, where we can weather the storm around the grog barrel. You'll find us there, Terror, if you change your mind."

From
The Illustrated Queensport Gazette
YOUR GATEWAY TO THE CIVILIZED WORLD!

MUTINEERS STILL AT LARGE, ENCHANTRESS SAYS

PEMBERTON, AUGUSTA—It has been six months since Miss Eugenia Pimm, Enchantress of the Northlands, disappeared mysteriously from her home in Pemberton and was rescued by the pirate Hilary Westfield. At this time, however, the queen's inspectors have not made any arrests in the case. Miss Pimm still maintains that she was kidnapped by a band of villains calling themselves the Mutineers. "They wanted to replace me as the Enchantress," she told the Gazette. "They hoped to take all the kingdom's magic for themselves, and I must say they came remarkably close to succeeding."

According to Miss Pimm, the Mutineers' ringleaders are the former naval admiral James Westfield; the pirate captain Rupert Blacktooth; his sister, Mrs. Georgiana Tilbury; and Mrs. Tilbury's daughter, Philomena. "The Mutineers specialize in theft and treachery," Miss Pimm told this reporter. "To be perfectly frank, they are not nice people."

So far, however, inspectors have been unable to confirm Miss Pimm's story. Admiral Westfield was arrested nearly two years ago for attempting to steal a sizable stash of magic, and he currently resides in the Royal Dungeons, making it impossible for him to have played a role in the kidnapping. As for Captain Blacktooth and the Tilburys, Inspector John Hastings says there is no evidence linking them to the alleged crime. "Mrs. Tilbury tells us that Miss Pimm fell ill on a visit to Tilbury Park," Inspector Hastings said. "She was in no state to travel home, and she began making up fanciful stories about villains and kidnappings. Now I suppose she believes those stories are true, but I suspect her illness has addled her mind, for I have never heard of the Mutineers, apart from the tales I've been told by Miss Pimm and her friends. I have no reason to believe they exist."

When told of Inspector Hastings's remarks, the Enchantress reacted in a surprisingly unladylike manner. "That man is a dratted fool!" she said. "Of course the Mutineers exist. It's only a matter of time before they make another attempt to control the kingdom's magic, and they're not likely to fail twice. Perhaps Inspector Hastings will finally believe me when the Mutineers blast him into the next kingdom over."

Unfortunately, Captain Blacktooth and the members of the Tilbury family could not be reached for comment. Mrs. Georgiana Tilbury is confined to Tilbury Park under a royal guard's watchful eye after stolen magical items were discovered in her possession, Miss Philomena Tilbury refuses to speak to the press, and Captain Blacktooth fired a volley of cannonballs at this reporter when she tried to approach his pirate ship.

CHAPTER TWO

WHEN THE PIRATES' carriage had disappeared down the lane and Mrs. Westfield had retreated to her private rooms to recover from the morning's excitement, Hilary walked down the long hallway lined with stained-glass windows and pushed open the heavy door of her father's study. No one had dared to use the room since Admiral Westfield had been marched off to the Royal Dungeons; even the maids hadn't been bold enough to enter. Cobwebs dimmed the light that came through the windows, all the nautical instruments lining the walls had wound down ages ago, and the drawers full of charts and maps were preserved under a thick layer of dust. The admiral's chair, however, was pushed back from his desk at an imperfect angle, as though he'd simply stepped out for a moment to stroll in the gardens or chastise his officers. Every so often, a clock in the far corner let out a half-hearted tick.

Admiral Westfield had left his desk unlocked, and Hilary rummaged through it as quickly as she could. In the topmost drawer, behind a small golden spyglass and a thick card pinned with rows of iridescent moths, she found a battered pen, a bottle of ink, and a faded old map of the Southlands coast; they would do, she thought. The admiral would most likely be furious if he discovered the map was missing—but then, Hilary reminded herself, he wouldn't be able to discover any such thing while he was safely imprisoned in the Dungeons. The clock ticked again. "NO VISITORS TODAY," she wrote on the back of the map, doing her best not to smudge the ink. "AND PLEASE, NO MORE PIRATES." Then she signed her name with a flourish, recapped the ink bottle, and slammed the desk drawer shut, sending the spyglass and the moths clattering back into the darkness.

By the time Hilary had slipped out of the study and returned to the front hall, she'd managed to brush most of the cobwebs from her coat. The gargoyle looked on as she tacked her sign to the front door of Westfield House. "What I don't understand," he said, "is who placed that notice in the newspaper. It must have been someone who wants you to lead the VNHLP."

"Or someone who wants to blacken my name even more than it's already been blackened." Hilary stepped back to examine her handiwork. "I hope Captain Blacktooth doesn't subscribe to the *Gazette*. I can't imagine what he'll do if he sees it."

"*I* can imagine," the gargoyle said, "and it's not a pretty sight."

Hilary's makeshift sign seemed to be effective, for no pirates interrupted her lunch or the rest of her sword-fighting practice. When the drapes had become more holes than velvet, she curled up on the drawing-room floor with a thick and discouraging book Miss Greyson had loaned her called *Common-Sense Tips for the Freelance Pirate*. She had barely read past the first page, however, when a commotion rose up from the front hall.

"I'm terribly sorry," she heard Bess say, "but Pirate Westfield isn't accepting visitors. It says so right here on this sign."

"But she'll want to see *us*," someone said with great confidence.

The gargoyle's ears pricked up. "More pirates?" he asked.

There was a flurry of footsteps, followed closely by an enormous bang.

Hilary didn't quite understand what was happening, but she was certain of one thing: the drawing-room door, which had been resting peacefully on its hinges, was now barreling through the air and heading in her direction. She grabbed the gargoyle and ducked under a table as the flying door sailed over them, collided with the wall, and crashed to the floor. "Horsefeathers!" someone cried from the hallway.

Hilary stood up. "That's not pirates," she said to the gargoyle, who was shaking like a small earthquake in her arms. "That's Claire."

Like an actress late for a performance, Claire Dupree hurried into the room. She was wrapped in a long woolen coat and an even longer striped scarf, and she gasped when she saw the door lying in the middle of the room. "Oh, drat," she said. "I *knew* I shouldn't have used that magic piece. I only asked it to lead me to you, Hilary, but I suppose I was a bit too enthusiastic. I haven't squashed you, have I?"

"Not quite," Hilary assured her. "It takes more than a drawing-room door to squash a pirate." She climbed over the wreckage to give Claire a hug. "But what are you doing here? I thought Miss Pimm was keeping you busy with magic lessons over the holidays."

"We had lessons in the coach all the way from Pemberton, though I'm not entirely sure they stuck." Claire poked at the door's bent hinges with the tip of her boot. "And as for Miss Pimm—well, she should be right behind me."

In the doorway, Bess cleared her throat, and Miss Pimm

herself entered the room. She looked as grand as ever, but she walked more slowly than Hilary remembered, and she leaned on a carved wooden cane that Hilary hadn't seen before.

"The Enchantress of the Northlands," said Bess with a curtsy. "I'm sorry I didn't knock, miss, but the door is gone."

"*Gone*," said Miss Pimm, "is a very strong word. I believe the door has merely traveled." She looked across the room at Claire and gave her a thin smile. Then she reached into her handbag and produced a golden sphere the size of an orange. "Magic," she said, "please replace this door in its proper location before someone trips over it at Ophelia Westfield's next luncheon."

As Hilary watched, the door picked itself up, floated across the room, and settled itself obligingly in its frame.

"Much better," said Miss Pimm. "Now, if you don't mind, I'm going to sit down." Without letting go of her cane, she settled herself in an elegant high-backed chair. Like most elegant things, the chair was exceedingly uncomfortable, but Miss Pimm did not seem to mind. "I must apologize for visiting unannounced," she said. "We were in a great hurry, and there wasn't time to send a message."

"That's all right," said Hilary. "We've already had three pirates here today. They didn't bother to announce themselves either."

"They wanted Hilary to be in charge of the pirate league!" said the gargoyle. "What do you think of that?"

Claire and Miss Pimm exchanged a glance. "I thought you told me," Miss Pimm murmured to Claire, "that pirates are never prompt."

"Well, they aren't *usually.*" Claire unwound her scarf. "And I was sure the snow would slow them down. These ones must have been especially persistent."

Hilary stared at her. "Do you mean to say that you knew I'd have pirates on my doorstep?"

"Strictly speaking," said Miss Pimm, "we invited them."

"But they weren't supposed to arrive for days!" said Claire. "Of course, we had no idea the *Gazette* would run our notice early. We hopped in the carriage as soon as we saw—"

"*You* placed the notice?" said Hilary. She almost couldn't believe it. Claire could be silly, but she was never cruel. "And you told everyone in the kingdom that I'm planning to challenge Captain Blacktooth? Did you want him and his mates to come after us with their cutlasses immediately, or did you hope they'd wait until spring?"

The gargoyle shook his head. "You think you can trust people," he said. "You let them scratch you behind the ears. Then they get you in trouble with a band of angry pirates, and before you know it, you're lying at the bottom of the sea with fish swimming up your snout."

Claire knitted her fingers together, looking as uncomfortable as Hilary had ever seen her. Miss Pimm didn't seem entirely comfortable, either, but perhaps that was due to the elegant chair. "I can see I owe you an apology as well as an explanation," Miss Pimm said. "Frankly, however, I've never been much good at the first, so I shall begin with the second." She tapped her carefully clipped fingernails on the handle of her cane. "I am not as young as I used to be—but perhaps you've noticed that."

Truthfully, it had been nearly two centuries since Miss Pimm had been young. Magic, fresh air, and more than a pinch of stubbornness had kept her in good health for two hundred and forty years, however, and she had danced until midnight at her birthday party the month before. "I haven't noticed a thing," Hilary assured her. "You're as vigorous as a swashbuckler."

"And the kingdom must believe nothing else." Miss Pimm looked grave. "I will tell you in confidence, though, that being kidnapped by villains puts quite a damper on one's strength. I have been doing my best to protect the kingdom's magic, but keeping watch over the entire country has been out of the question for months now. Even when I do manage to spot someone misusing magic, I can't cast a simple scolding spell without losing my breath or my balance."

"She's had to mail people chiding letters instead," Claire said. "They're not nearly as impressive as spells are, and the postal courier is starting to complain."

"But you fixed the drawing-room door!" said Hilary.

"And it took nearly all my strength to do it," said Miss Pimm. "The fact of the matter is that it's high time for me to retire. I must let the new Enchantress take over my duties before all the scoundrels and scourges in the kingdom discover I'm no longer a match for them."

At the mention of a new Enchantress, Claire turned pink and looked down at her scarf. Hilary wondered whether Enchantresses were encouraged to blast doors off their hinges in High Society mansions; it didn't seem likely. "You'll be wonderful at the job," she told Claire. "You'll sweep villains out of their boots and toss them into the sea."

But Claire only turned pinker. "I enchanted a cracked pane of glass out of my window last week," she said, "but it snowed overnight and I was thoroughly soaked. Then I tried to warm myself up, and I set fire to my bedsheets—a very *small* fire," she hastened to add. "I suppose I still have a bit to learn."

Miss Pimm looked as though she supposed so, too. "Although Miss Dupree is alarmingly prone to catastrophe," she said, "I believe she is talented enough to be a good Enchantress. When Queen Adelaide asked me which girl should be chosen for the position, I recommended Miss Dupree at once."

"And the queen agreed?" Hilary asked.

Claire buried her face in her scarf.

"Not quite," said Miss Pimm. "When she announced

her plan to appoint Miss Dupree as the next Enchantress, half of High Society flew into an uproar. The Coalition of Overprotective Mothers is even circulating a petition. They believe . . ." She cleared her throat and glanced at Claire. "Ah, they think . . ."

"They think the Enchantress should be a High Society lady," Claire said. "They certainly *don't* think she should be a commoner who grew up on a marsh."

"What's wrong with marshes?" the gargoyle asked. "They're full of interesting bugs."

"And there's no reason why the Enchantress can't be from one if she wants to be," said Hilary. "Those High Society folks will simply have to get used to the idea."

"That's not the worst of it, though." Claire sounded really upset now. "They've offered up a candidate of their own. I'm sure you'll be able to guess whom they've picked."

The gargoyle gasped. "Is it *me*?"

"Oh no," said Hilary. There was only one person in the kingdom who could make Claire so miserable. "It must be Philomena."

The thought of Philomena Tilbury having control of all the magic coins, crochet hooks, and candlesticks in Augusta was enough to make Hilary's toes curl in her boots. Philomena had been the cruelest girl at Miss Pimm's Finishing School for Delicate Ladies, and it seemed that now she was striving to become the cruelest young lady in all of High Society. She wanted nothing more than to be the next Enchantress, and for a moment last summer, after her mother and Captain Blacktooth had kidnapped Miss Pimm, she had nearly accomplished just that. "But surely the queen won't put Philomena in charge," Hilary said. "She's a Mutineer! If she gets to be the Enchantress, she'll take all the magic away from the commoners and give it to her awful friends! She'll let Captain Blacktooth seize the kingdom's treasure! She'll let my father out of the Dungeons!"

"I don't enjoy the thought any more than you do," Miss Pimm said. "Neither does the queen. It can't be proved that Philomena is a villain, but her mother certainly is one, and even Queen Adelaide is wise enough to see that letting that family near the kingdom's stores of magic would be disastrous. However, she may not have much choice in the matter."

Hilary rolled her eyes. "If the queen is so timid that she can't stand up to a few Overprotective Mothers—"

"It's not only High Society that's protesting, you see," said Claire. "That awful Captain Blacktooth has threatened to lead the VNHLP in an attack on Augusta if Philomena isn't made the next Enchantress."

"You're joking." Hilary looked from Claire to Miss Pimm and back, but neither of them looked amused. "Pirates can't attack the kingdom! It's treasonous!"

"And it's not even *close* to honorable," said the gargoyle.

"Which is exactly why we placed our notice." Miss

Pimm sat back in her chair. "The queen says that although she would like to allow Claire to become the Enchantress, she will be forced to appoint Philomena instead unless the High Society protestors and the pirates are dealt with—and she has ordered me to deal with them. I am perfectly capable of handling a gaggle of Overprotective Mothers, but I'm no expert when it comes to pirates."

Hilary sank down into the chair across from Miss Pimm's, hardly minding how uncomfortable it was. "So you want me to handle them instead."

"Precisely!" Miss Pimm clapped her hands as though the matter were settled. "If you replace Captain Black-tooth as League president, the pirates will follow your commands instead of his. No one will be foolish enough to attack the kingdom, the queen will be free to install Claire as the rightful Enchantress, and *I* will be free to retire. We all know you want Blacktooth gone—you've spoken of nothing else for months—and now the time is ripe. Claire and I felt that if we slipped the *Gazette* a few words about your intentions, it might hurry the process along."

Hilary had endured many alarming conversations in the Westfield House drawing room, though most of them hadn't had a thing to do with piracy. She felt nearly as uncomfortable as she had when the Grimshaws had come for a visit and their sweaty-palmed son had invited her to join him for a stroll in the gardens. Unlike young Master

Grimshaw, however, Miss Pimm could not be discouraged by a firm kick to the shins.

"I'd love to help you trounce Captain Blacktooth," Hilary said, "but there are dozens of scallywags more experienced than I am. Shouldn't you be talking to one of them instead?"

Claire brushed the question aside. "Even Captain Blacktooth has loads of experience, and look where that's gotten him! Doesn't everyone always say that what a good leader *really* needs is passion?" She frowned. "Well, even if they don't, I'm saying it now. You, Hilary Westfield, are the most passionate pirate I know. I bet you've dreamed of leading the VNHLP your whole life."

Hilary squirmed. "Perhaps I have," she said. "That still doesn't change the fact that most of the pirates in the League want to run me through."

"Some of them do," Miss Pimm allowed, "but others have already joined you, haven't they?"

It was true that Mr. Twigget, Captain Blacktooth's own first mate, had signed on to Hilary's crew several months earlier. He'd even brought a handful of scallywags with him. All of them had taken more than a few cannonballs to the mainsail from their former crewmates, but they hadn't run back to Blacktooth's ship yet. Then, of course, there were Partridge, Flintlock, and Worthington, waiting for Hilary's word at the Salty Biscuit. Still, earning the loyalty of a dozen pirates was hardly the same as commanding an entire fleet.

Miss Pimm didn't wait for Hilary to reply. "Not only do you have passion," she said, "but you have influence. You've stood up to Captain Blacktooth before, and you've shown you don't fear him. That's more than any other pirate can say for himself."

"And you'll be a wonderful leader!" cried Claire. "Oh, please say yes. I'll pretend to be cheerful if you refuse, of course, but I shall really be absolutely crushed."

The gargoyle looked up at Hilary. "You know," he said, "saving the kingdom from villains does sound thrilling."

Miss Pimm didn't say another word. She simply met Hilary's gaze without blinking once.

"Fine. I'll consider it." Hilary stood up from her chair, feeling entirely outnumbered. "But I'll need a few days to think before I make a decision. If you see any pirates on your way out the door, you'd better tell them I'm not at home."

OVERNIGHT, THE SNOW stopped falling, and the wind changed. A warm breeze blew in from the southern kingdoms, carrying the scent of the sea and melting the ice along the roadways. Early the next morning, before Mrs. Westfield had a chance to prohibit unladylike excursions, Hilary pulled on her boots, tucked the gargoyle into her bag, and walked down to the harbor to watch the ships sail by. Some were narrow-hulled clippers built for speed, and others were gun-laden frigates built for battle, but Hilary kept her eyes on the sturdy, confident ships that flew black flags as they set off to bury treasure or to seek it, keeping the coastline behind them and all manner of adventures in front of them. Those ships were built for piracy.

"I don't know why you're hesitating," the gargoyle remarked. "I can tell you're itching to kick Captain Blacktooth in the trousers."

Hilary raised her eyebrows at him. "Weren't you the one who said that if we challenged him, we'd end up with fish swimming up our snouts?"

"I've changed my mind," the gargoyle said. "Someone needs to protect the kingdom, and I think it should be you. After all, you're very good at protecting me."

Hilary turned away from the harbor and began to crunch through the snow back to Westfield House. "Protecting a gargoyle is one thing," she said, "but protecting a kingdom is another thing altogether. Do you truly think I'm the best pirate for the job?"

"You're certainly not the worst," the gargoyle said cheerfully. "Besides, it will make an excellent chapter in my memoirs."

By the time they returned to Westfield House, the entire household was awake. The gardener was shoveling snow from the paths, and maids were hurrying through the halls with trays and dusting cloths. Hilary slipped through a side door into one of the mansion's long corridors, stamped her feet to shake the snow from her boots, and went along to the breakfast room to say good morning to her mother.

Admiral Westfield sat at the head of the table.

"Hilary!" he said. "How considerate of you to join us. Your mother and I were beginning to worry."

At the other end of the table, Mrs. Westfield sat in front of an empty plate. She didn't argue with the admiral, but her face was tense, and she held her fork like a weapon.

"What's this?" Admiral Westfield said. "No warm welcome from my only daughter? I suppose spending your days on Jasper Fletcher's pirate ship has banished any thought of good manners from your mind."

Hilary was too furious to speak. From her bag, the gargoyle gave the admiral his most terrifying glare.

"You're supposed to be in the Dungeons," she said at last, "not eating eggs at the dining table."

Admiral Westfield lifted his spoon and decapitated his egg in one swift motion. "And yet," he said, "here I am. The Dungeons were terribly dull, and I have so much to do; I couldn't leave matters up to Georgiana Tilbury and her pirate brother any longer. If one wants to take over the kingdom properly, one must do it oneself." He slurped the egg yolk from his spoon. "And that's rather difficult to accomplish from a prison cell."

"I believe that's the point of prison," Hilary said through her teeth. "If you're wise, you'll go back there at once."

"What an absurd suggestion!" said the admiral. "Sit down and eat your breakfast, Hilary. Don't bring that gargoyle to the table, though; I don't care for the look he's giving me." He set down his spoon. "Your mother may have allowed you to run wild while I've been away, but now that I am in charge of this household, you will do as I tell you."

Admiral Westfield gestured toward the empty place at the table, where an egg identical to his own sat quivering in its cup. Hilary didn't move. Her boots seemed to be stuck to the spot.

"The child's as impudent as ever, I see," the admiral said to Hilary's mother. "Never fear, Ophelia. I'll make sure that by the time she's grown, she's a Westfield through and through."

At this, Hilary felt her boots unstick. She walked to the table and picked up her egg cup. "I won't sit down," she said, "and I haven't got time for breakfast. The gargoyle and I are leaving."

"We are?" said the gargoyle.

"Yes. In fact, we're already late."

Admiral Westfield frowned. "And where do you plan to go?"

"To the Salty Biscuit," Hilary said, "and then to the

High Seas. I'm going to lead the pirate league, and you're not going to like it one bit. But there's something I've got to do first." Hilary raised her hand and tipped her egg cup onto her father's head.

"Blast it all!" The admiral sputtered and cursed as streams of yolk cascaded down his nose and gobbets of egg settled into his ears. As Hilary turned to leave, she was almost certain she saw a smile slip across her mother's face.

From
The Augusta Scuttlebutt
WHERE HIGH SOCIETY TURNS FOR SCANDAL

The holiday season may be drawing to a close, but in the halls of High Society, the rumors have just begun! The Scuttlebutt can officially confirm that James Westfield, the famous admiral and infamous villain, has abandoned his prison cell for the cozy comforts of his ancestral home.

"I have given up a life of crime once and for all," Admiral Westfield told the Scuttlebutt in an exclusive interview. "My time in the Dungeons has shown me that true happiness comes not from power and glory, but from the small pleasures of life: giving sweets to children, or darning socks. I feel fortunate that the royal judge was willing to give me a second chance to be a worthy citizen of this great kingdom." The royal judge himself was unwilling to chat with us about the admiral's release, but readers may be interested to learn that in recent months, the judge received many expensive baskets of fruit from Mrs. Georgiana Tilbury, a close friend of Admiral

Westfield. (The judge is said to be particularly fond of oranges.)

What does the future hold for Augusta's favorite gentleman thief? Admiral Westfield is no longer eligible to lead the Royal Navy, but to demonstrate his goodwill to the kingdom, he has volunteered to act as adviser to the current admiral, George Curtis. "I'm not sure this is a terribly wise idea," Admiral Curtis was heard to say before being interrupted by a rather scathing look from Admiral Westfield.

WE ASKED, YOU ANSWERED:
Has Admiral Westfield truly changed his ways?

"I'm so pleased to hear that James Westfield is out of those horrid Dungeons at last. Now that he is reunited with his family, perhaps he'll be able to do something about that daughter of his. She is *not* a proper young lady."—P. TILBURY, NORDHOLM

"What rubbish! You shouldn't believe a word that man says. I'm quite sure he's never darned a sock in his life."
—E. GREYSON, WIMBLY-ON-THE-MARSH

"Admiral Westfield is a true Augustan hero, and I admire his change of heart. He's an inspiration to reformed criminals everywhere."
—O. SANDERSON, QUEENSPORT

"If James Westfield has reformed himself, I'll eat my best pirate hat, feather and all."—J. FLETCHER, WIMBLY-ON-THE-MARSH

Leading the League:
THE OFFICIAL VNHLP GUIDE (FIFTH EDITION)

HOW TO SEEK THE **PRESIDENCY:**

To the ambitious pirate, the prospect of becoming the most dangerous and influential scallywag on the High Seas is even more thrilling than a treasure chest filled with magic coins. As president of the VNHLP, you will be responsible for sending pirates off on quests and adventures, leading your crew into battle, punishing rule-breaking buccaneers, and maintaining the League's fearsome reputation. It is a most exciting opportunity—but it does not present itself often.

Once a pirate becomes president of the VNHLP, he will remain in this role until he is foolish enough to retire or die. This can cause great frustration among pirates who dream of donning the presidential skull-and-crossbones badge. Remember, however, that if the current president shows no signs of budging, you may not simply pursue him with your cutlass. Instead, you must follow the League's official instructions for challenging a pirate in a leadership role:

FIRST: Travel to Gunpowder Square and announce your intention to claim the presidency. You must be accompanied by at least one supporter who is a current member of the VNHLP. If you cannot find a single pirate to support you, we advise you to apologize wholeheartedly, toss your pirate hat into the sea, and seek a new career in dairy farming or music composition.

SECOND: If the current president wishes to remain in charge of the League, he will meet you in Gunpowder Square, accompanied by his own supporters. He will then propose a time and place for a confrontation on the High Seas. If you are wise, you will accept his proposal.

THIRD: During the weeks that follow, you and the current president must each gather twenty crew members to join you in battle. Be warned! If you arrive at the appointed time and place without the required number of allies, you will be forced to forfeit. Choose your mates wisely, and encourage them to show support for your campaign by waving pennants, singing sea chanteys, and performing rousing cheers.

FOURTH: You may not directly attack the president's crew before the battle, nor may he attack you. During the battle itself, however, all forms of weaponry—including magic pieces—are permitted. Lying and cheating are heartily encouraged at all times.

FIFTH: When the battle is over, the winning pirate may assume command of the VNHLP. The losing scallywag must leave Augusta at once. Although he will never be permitted to return to these waters, he will find a welcoming bunk in the southern kingdoms at the Pestilent Home for Foul-Tempered Pirates.

CHAPTER THREE

"I'VE SAILED THE High Seas with plenty of peculiar pirates," said Jasper Fletcher, rubbing his hands
together to warm them, "but I believe this bunch is the
most peculiar yet."

Hilary supposed Jasper had a fair point. At this precise
moment, her good mate Charlie was helping Miss Pimm
out of a rowboat onto the shore of Gunpowder Island,
though Miss Pimm was insisting that Enchantresses did
not need to be helped, even if they *were* two hundred and
forty years old. Jasper's wife, Eloise Greyson, had used her
magic crochet hook to summon a pile of fluffy white mittens, and she was busy handing them out to anyone who

looked the least bit cold. Over by the west gate, Claire was discussing shortbread recipes with the pirate Cannonball Jack. Mr. Twigget and three of his mates stood in a nervous huddle; Partridge, Flintlock, and Worthington looked expectantly at Hilary; and the gargoyle hopped about between everyone's feet, wearing one of Miss Greyson's mittens on his tail.

"They may be peculiar," Hilary said to Jasper, "but I'm awfully glad they're here. Perhaps they'll create such a confusion that Captain Blacktooth will hand over the presidency on the spot."

When Miss Pimm had been freed from the rowboat at last, Charlie made his way across the rocky beach toward Hilary. "What's the plan, Terror?" he asked.

Hilary flipped through the battered old copy of *Leading the League* that Miss Greyson had loaned her from the *Pigeon*'s floating bookshop. Entire chapters kept falling out of the binding, and Hilary wondered if the book's previous owner was living in exile at the Pestilent Home for Foul-Tempered Pirates. "According to the instructions," she said, "we're supposed to go to Gunpowder Square. If Blacktooth wants to accept my challenge, he'll meet me there."

"And if he doesn't, we'll chase him into the sea!" The gargoyle hopped up to them. "Can I ride in your bag, Hilary? There are an awful lot of parrots on this island, and they keep trying to land on my head."

The pirate on duty at the west gate must have been

expecting them, for he swung the gate open without asking to check Hilary's papers. "If it were up to me," he said as she passed, "I wouldn't let the lot of you in, but the League says I'm supposed to give you a fair chance." He frowned as Miss Pimm walked through the gate. "Are you sure all these people are pirates?"

Miss Pimm gave the guard her most imposing look. "This island was my home for many years," she said, "long before the pirate league got hold of it. I assure you that I have every right to be here." She looked down the cobblestone street and shook her head. "I'm afraid a good deal has changed since I was a girl."

In fact, Hilary realized, a good deal had changed since her last visit to Gunpowder Island. Though spring was creeping toward the southernmost parts of the kingdom, winter clung to the Northlands like frost on a windowpane, and the sun hung low in the sky when it bothered to rise at all. On Hilary's previous trips, bustling crowds of pirates had filled the island's lanes and alleys, but today the streets were silent. Even the groggery stood empty. "Perhaps everyone ran away when they heard we were coming," Charlie said.

Hilary peered into the dark windows of the milliner's shop. "You know as well as I do that pirates never run away."

"If anything," said Jasper, "they should be running *toward* us. Ah, here comes someone now."

The person hurrying down the street in their direction had red hair that flew behind her, an emerald green coat of the most fashionable design, a spotless white fur hat, and a dangerous-looking sword strapped around her waist. "Terror!" she called. "I'm so pleased I found you. I was beginning to worry that I'd have to face Blacktooth all by myself, and I'm sure I would have come to a sticky end."

Hilary gave the smaller girl a hug, keeping her arms well clear of the dangerous-looking sword. "This is Alice Feathering," she told the assembled pirates. "Some of you know her already, of course. Her brother, Nicholas, is a Mutineer."

Alice glowered. "I haven't spoken to that bilge rat in months. If he wants to marry Philomena and help her rotten family rule the kingdom, then I want nothing to do with him. When I overheard him talking about coming here to support Captain Blacktooth, I knew I had to be here to support *you*, Hilary, so I hopped on a train, walked a few miles, snuck aboard a ferry, and . . . well, in any case, here I am!"

"I'm surprised your parents approved of such a journey," Miss Greyson said. "They do know you're here, don't they?"

"Of course they don't!" said Alice. "They're dear friends of the Tilburys, and they can't stand the Enchantress." She made an apologetic curtsy in Miss Pimm's direction. "But Mother and Father think I've gone off on an educational tour of the Northlands with my tutor, and my tutor thinks I'm traveling with Mother and Father. They're all so busy with their own dull affairs that it will take them ages to notice I'm gone."

"Alice will be perfectly safe with us," Hilary told Miss Greyson. "I'm sure she'll be a great help against Blacktooth and his mates."

"If they ever show up." The gargoyle shivered. "This island is as empty as Admiral Westfield's heart, and almost as cold. I hope we make it to Gunpowder Square before my snout freezes."

HILARY LED THE way through the island's winding streets, each just as deserted as the last. No buccaneers lurked on the front stoop of the mapmaker's shop or under the striped umbrellas of the ice cream parlor. The farther Hilary walked, the more uneasy she felt. If the pirates of Gunpowder Island weren't anywhere in sight, where in the world could they be?

Then Hilary turned the corner into Gunpowder Square.

"Oh, blast," she whispered.

The square was positively teeming with pirates. Some were jolly and some were grim; some were round and some were spindly; some wore fine cloth coats and some wore thin, patched breeches. They sharpened their swords, checked their pocket watches, and leaned against the square's statues of famous pirates from history. One enterprising scallywag was serving hot grog from a steaming iron kettle.

"Blacktooth hasn't just brought a few supporters with him," said Charlie; "he's brought half the League."

Hilary felt sure he was right. "They may have us outnumbered," she told her mates, "but don't let them intimidate you. Remember, we're just here to announce our intentions; we're not going into battle."

"Yet," said Mr. Partridge, who had turned nearly as green as his parrot. Hilary gave him what she hoped was an encouraging smile. Then she straightened her pirate hat, smoothed her braid, and led her mates out into the square.

All the pirates in the crowd raised their swords.

"Roasted," the gargoyle muttered, "and served with potatoes. I knew it."

Hilary walked down the narrow cobblestone path that ran between the ranks of pirates. She tried not to think about all the shiny steel blades pointed in her direction, or about how very sharp they were sure to be. Some of the pirates jeered as she passed, and others uttered words that Miss Greyson would have described as most unsavory.

"They don't seem to like you very much," Claire whispered in Hilary's ear.

"No," said Hilary, "and I can't imagine that challenging their president to a battle will improve the situation." She gritted her teeth and kept walking, though the crowd of pirates stretched ahead of her like a vast and ill-tempered sea.

At the far end of the square, a small and shivering group of onlookers stood apart from the pirates. The first was Sir Nicholas Feathering, who was bold enough to smile as Hilary passed by. "It's pleasant to see you again, Pirate Westfield," he said. "I'd greet your mates as well, but they seem to be glaring daggers at me, and . . ." He turned as pale as Miss Greyson's mittens. "Alice! What are you doing here? It's far too dangerous! Can't you see these people have *swords*?"

"I'm here to support Hilary," Alice snapped, "and I'm not talking to you. I don't associate with Mutineers."

Nicholas ran a hand through his hair and looked worriedly at Philomena, who stood next to him wrapped in a long woolen cloak. Hilary tried to walk past her as quickly as she could, but that didn't prevent Philomena from grabbing hold of her arm with a surprising amount of strength. "You may think you can ruin Uncle Blacktooth's career, Miss Westfield," she murmured, "but I simply won't have it. Soon I shall be the new Enchantress, and you shall be in exile."

"Please let go of me, Miss Tilbury," Hilary said as calmly as she could manage. "I can't imagine the ladies and gentlemen of High Society think it's polite to grab one's acquaintances. Are you sure your mother would approve?"

Philomena frowned and let go of Hilary's arm as Claire pushed her way through the crowd. "If you touch Hilary again," Claire said furiously, "I shall turn you into a centipede on the spot! Perhaps if you're quick enough, a pirate won't squash you under his boot."

"Exaggeration doesn't suit you, Miss Dupree," said Philomena. "You're not talented enough to do anything of the sort."

Claire clenched her fists, but Hilary put a hand on her shoulder. "Never mind Philomena," she whispered. "Just keep walking."

There had once been a time when Admiral Westfield would have refused to come within fifty yards of a pirate. Now, however, he stood willingly on Gunpowder Island, towering over the other Mutineers and casting a shadow that seemed to stretch the length of the square. Hilary wished he would disappear at once. He didn't say a word as she passed him, but he stared at her intently, which was quite unpleasant enough.

The gentleman on Admiral Westfield's left was young and tall, and Hilary nearly didn't recognize him until she saw the satisfied sneer on his face. "Oliver Sanderson!" she cried. "Aren't you supposed to be at some sort of school for impudent boys?"

"I graduated," said Oliver, "with terribly high marks. When the admiral was released from the Dungeons, he was kind enough to take me back into his employment.

He's been like a father to me, you know."

"Really?" Hilary raised her cutlass. "I wasn't aware he was capable of it."

The sneer on Oliver's face grew broader. "What about you, Miss Westfield? Aren't you supposed to be a proper young lady?"

"If I were a proper young lady, then I wouldn't be permitted to slice off your nose."

Jasper tapped Hilary on the shoulder. "Terror," he said, "I'm not any more fond of Mr. Sanderson's nose than you are, but we have more pressing matters at the moment."

Reluctantly, Hilary lowered her cutlass and turned away from Oliver. There, in front of her, stood Captain Blacktooth, in his grandest coat and a hat so wide that Hilary wondered how he kept it from blowing off his head. Perhaps he'd frightened the wind into obeying his orders. "Hello, Terror," he said. "I believe you have something to tell me."

"You bet she does!" the gargoyle cried.

Hilary put her shoulders back and lifted her chin, for she knew perfectly well that a good pirate doesn't slouch when she issues a formal challenge. "Captain Rupert Blacktooth," she said as loudly as she could, "I am here to seek the presidency of the Very Nearly Honorable League of Pirates."

Admiral Westfield whispered something into Oliver's ear, and Oliver smirked. Hilary glared at them both.

"Therefore," she said, turning back to Captain Blacktooth, "I challenge you to a High Seas battle. Do you accept my challenge, or would you rather leave the kingdom at once?"

This pronouncement had sounded terribly ferocious in Hilary's head, but it must have gotten tangled up in the Gunpowder Island breeze, for Captain Blacktooth didn't even flinch. Instead, he polished his spectacles, looking as exasperated as a governess with a disobedient charge. "I would rather be back in my office at League headquarters," he said, "sitting in my favorite armchair, with a fire in the hearth and an interesting new treasure map to study. But as you've made that impossible, I am here to defend my position." He stepped closer to Hilary. "I am, however, willing to give you a chance to change your mind. I have always thought you were a wise girl, but if I may speak frankly, this challenge of yours seems to me to be the height of foolishness. Are you truly so eager to throw away your promising career for a life in exile?"

"I won't be the one in exile," Hilary said firmly. "I'm not the one who's plotting with a villainous admiral, either. Isn't joining forces with the Royal Navy against nearly every one of the League's rules?"

This time, Hilary knew she had struck a blow, for Blacktooth coughed and fumbled with his spectacles. "My business partners are none of your concern," he said. "In any case, your father merely volunteers for the navy, and I'm quite sure there's no rule against consorting with volunteers." He settled the spectacles back on his nose. "Now, Terror, since you refuse to disappear quietly, I am forced to proceed with the formalities. Where are your supporters?"

"We're right here," Charlie said.

"And we're willing to fight to the death!" Alice added.

"Or very nearly," said Jasper.

Blacktooth smiled. "That's quite noble of you, Mr. Fletcher," he said, "but I'm afraid your support isn't of much use at the moment. The rules specifically state that each candidate must be vouched for by a current member of the League, and I'm certain you don't qualify. In fact," he said, letting his eyes wander over Hilary's mates, "I'm not sure any of these unusual scallywags are League members. Without a qualified supporter, your challenge is—how shall I put it?" Captain Blacktooth smiled. "Dead in the water."

The pirates in the square chortled.

"Oh, honestly," said Hilary, "you needn't be so pleased with yourselves. I'm well acquainted with the rules, and I've brought a League member with me. Mr. Twigget, will you please step forward?"

Blacktooth narrowed his eyes. "Did you say *Twigget*?"

Mr. Twigget had not stepped forward—in fact, he seemed to be trying to hide behind Mr. Flintlock—but Hilary took him by the hand and pulled him in front of Blacktooth. "I'm sure I don't need to introduce you," she said, "since Twigget was your first mate."

Twigget cleared his throat. "I'm here to support the Terror," he said—rather shakily, Hilary thought, but it couldn't be helped.

Blacktooth took one look at Twigget and shook his head. "I expelled this traitor from the League myself. Why are you wasting my time, Mr. Twigget?"

Twigget swayed back and forth until Hilary thought he would swoon like a High Society lady right there on the cobblestones. "It's a funny thing, sir," he said, mostly to his boots. "When you expelled me, you did a lot of blusterin', but you never filled out the paperwork."

"Nonsense." Captain Blacktooth waved his hand, and a short, balding pirate hurried to his side, dragging a long scroll of parchment behind him. Hilary had met this pirate once before; he was Blacktooth's private secretary. "Mr. Gull," said Blacktooth, "please review the membership roll and show Mr. Twigget that his name has been crossed off the list."

Mr. Gull made his way down the parchment, which flapped in the breeze and tangled around his legs. Miss Greyson murmured something about parchment scrolls being entirely impractical in the modern era, and Captain Blacktooth gave her a very dark look indeed.

"Here we are," said Mr. Gull at last, pointing a finger halfway down the list of names. "Eustace Twigget. Expulsion forms have not been filed with the League."

He swallowed. "I believe they're in a jumble on your desk, Captain."

Blacktooth scowled at the membership roll. "The Terror's challenge stands," he said at last, though he sounded as if he regretted it. "Extract yourself from that ridiculous scroll, Mr. Gull."

Mr. Gull did as he was told, and Hilary's crewmates cheered. Captain Blacktooth leaned closer to Hilary. "By the way, Terror," he murmured, "you might remind your mates that gloating is an unappealing quality, particularly in pirates. It tends to attract swords to one's neck."

"Perhaps it does," said Hilary, "but you might remind your own mates that they're not allowed to lay a hand on my crew before our battle."

"Unfortunate, but true." Captain Blacktooth shrugged and stepped forward to address the crowd of pirates in front of him. "I have accepted the Terror's challenge," he announced. "Our fleets shall meet in battle in exactly three months' time, on the High Seas just south of Queensport Harbor. The champion will take charge of the Very Nearly Honorable League of Pirates, and the defeated scallywag will be banished from the kingdom."

All the pirates in the square roared and waved their cutlasses. Claire, who did not have a cutlass to wave, tossed her hat in the air instead. Miss Pimm clapped politely, and Admiral Westfield raised a flagon of grog high in the air, but Philomena drew her woolen cape around her shoulders and looked even more cross than usual.

"Now, Terror," said Blacktooth, "you'd be wise to leave Gunpowder Island at once. I suspect you'll need every moment of those three months to find two hundred pirates willing to support you."

"Two hundred?" The gargoyle nearly leaped out of his bag. "I thought we only had to find twenty! Isn't that right, Hilary?"

"That's what it says in the guidebook." Hilary held up her battered copy of *Leading the League*. "Twenty crew members, and not a scallywag more. As I told you, Captain Blacktooth, I'm quite familiar with the rules."

"May I see that?" Mr. Gull reached for Hilary's book and inspected its spine. He sniffed the pages. He held the book to his ear. Finally, he ran his finger across the cover and touched it to the tip of his tongue. "Just as I thought," he said. "This is a fifth edition. We're up to the seventeenth by now."

Hilary's stomach looped itself into a bowline and pulled itself tight. "And what does it say in the seventeenth edition?"

Mr. Gull looked rather apologetic. "I'm afraid the estimates have been revised due to inflation."

"What does *that* mean?" the gargoyle cried.

"It means you'll need to find two hundred supporters," said Captain Blacktooth. "Two hundred at the very least, or you'll have to forfeit. Isn't that right, Gull?"

Mr. Gull nodded. "That's right, sir."

Captain Blacktooth gestured to the pirates in the square. "As you can see, I've already assembled my crew. I suggest you gather your own at once."

The gargoyle stared at him. "But that's impossible!"

Hilary knew the gargoyle was right. She wasn't even acquainted with two hundred pirates, and most of the ones she had met were sure to be loyal to Captain Blacktooth. If she could barely find one League member willing to vouch for her in Gunpowder Square, however was she supposed to find two hundred who would follow her into battle?

"If you'd prefer," said Captain Blacktooth, "my mates can chase you into the sea right now, and we'll be done with this nonsense once and for all."

Hilary retrieved her book from Mr. Gull and snapped it shut. "That won't be necessary," she said. "There have got to be at least two hundred pirates who dislike the Mutineers as much as I do, and I promise you I'll find them."

Captain Blacktooth raised an eyebrow. "If you and I were still on good terms," he said, "I would wish you luck, for I suspect you'll need it." Then he nodded to Philomena, who hurried to his side. "My dear, could you see that we are transported back to Tilbury Park? We have affairs to arrange with your mother."

"Of course." Philomena reached into the folds of her cloak and pulled out a golden goblet large enough to hold grog for half a dozen pirates. The gargoyle's ears twitched, as they always did when a magical item drew near. "Magic," said Philomena, holding the goblet firmly in both hands, "we five Mutineers would like to leave this uncivilized island before we all catch a chill. Please send us to Tilbury Park as quickly as you can."

One moment Philomena was there, and the next she simply wasn't. In her place was nothing but empty air and cobblestones. The other Mutineers had vanished as well; even Blacktooth's extravagant hat had been whisked away. From the far corners of the square, a few of his mates applauded.

Miss Pimm put her hands on her hips and frowned at the space where Philomena had stood. "Impressive," she said.

The gargoyle rolled his eyes. "Those Mutineers are nothing but show-offs."

Truthfully, Hilary was relieved to see them go, though she wished she hadn't missed her chance to acquaint Oliver with her cutlass. "Show-offs or not," she said, "I'm afraid Captain Blacktooth was right about one thing. If we want to find two hundred pirates who'll lend us their support, we'll have to start searching at once."

A LETTER FROM ROYALTY!

HER ROYAL HIGHNESS

Queen Adelaide of Augusta

Pirate Hilary Westfield, Terror of the Southlands
The Pigeon
The High Seas

Dear Pirate Westfield:

As I read the <u>Queensport Gazette</u> this morning over
my royal breakfast, I learned that you will be facing Captain
Rupert Blacktooth in battle in three months' time. I do not
typically involve myself in the affairs of pirates, for I understand
they prefer to operate ever so slightly outside the law. I believe,
however, that every contest should be judged by a wise and fair
observer, and your battle with Captain Blacktooth is no exception.

The leadership of the Very Nearly Honorable League
of Pirates happens to be a matter of particular interest to
me. Therefore, I shall attend the battle to ensure that all is
"shipshape" and "aboveboard," as I am told you pirates are so
fond of saying. I shall be returning from my annual goodwill

tour of the southern kingdoms on the morning of the battle, but I trust you will not begin to fire your cannons until I have arrived. Needless to say, I would appreciate it if you and your colleagues would keep your cutlasses at a safe distance from my royal person during the skirmish. I have requested this courtesy from Captain Blacktooth as well.

I look forward to seeing you on the High Seas this spring!

Regally yours,

The Queen

Dear Hilary,

I am writing this from our carriage as we speed
south along the road to Pemberton. I hear the
Southlands Hills are quite beautiful at this time of
year, but I've barely been able to glimpse them
through the window, for Miss Pimm has been
keeping me occupied with lessons and exercises
ever since we left Gunpowder Island. I'm afraid
I've been making quite a hash of even the simplest
enchantments: instead of lifting Miss Pimm's
hat off her head, I somehow managed to lift the
entire top of the carriage. The coachman seemed
awfully displeased. Miss Pimm says I must learn
to control myself, and I am trying my best, but
I don't know how much use I shall be to you in
your battle against Captain Blacktooth. Until then,
I shall devote myself to my studies. (Actually,

I shall start devoting myself as soon as Miss
Pimm wakes up from her nap. While she is sleeping,
she cannot point out all the things I am doing
wrong, and I believe she would be sorry to miss the
opportunity.)

You know perfectly well how I feel about
Philomena, but I believe I dislike her more
than ever after the magical display she put on
in Gunpowder Square. I have never managed
anything like it—not intentionally, at least. Do
you think she has gotten more powerful since the
last time she dangled me in the air? Miss Pimm
claims she isn't concerned, but I can tell she is
not being entirely truthful, for she has rarely looked
so impressed during our lessons. (I have, however,
managed to make her look both alarmed and
terrified on a number of occasions.) If Philomena
is truly the better magic user, perhaps all the horrid
High Society folks are right and I don't have any
business trying to be the next Enchantress. It's a
frightfully glum thought, but I shall attempt to
cheer myself by imagining you and your fleet of
pirates chasing Captain Blacktooth's ship all the way
to the edge of the kingdom.

I wish I could join you as you gather the rest of
your crew, but Miss Pimm assures me that I will

be of more use to you in three months' time if I can learn to make things explode on purpose, not just accidentally. I am sure you are having all sorts of thrilling adventures on the High Seas, and I am sorry to miss them. Please hug the others for me, even Charlie, though I am sure he will squirm and declare that he wants nothing to do with hugs from a finishing-school girl. Tell him it is for his own good.

Your fiercest supporter,
Claire

an extract

Leading the League:

THE OFFICIAL VNHLP GUIDE (FIFTH EDITION)

ON CREATING **RULES OF CONDUCT:**

Pirates, by nature, are not fond of rules, but the VNHLP is not a lawless organization. Upon election to the presidency, each League president must create new rules of conduct for his fellow scallywags to follow. These rules allow the president to set forth his expectations for the VNHLP and declare what a true pirate must and must not do. Once written, they will be distributed to every League member, from pirate apprentices and deckhands to ships' captains.

The forward-thinking pirate should begin writing his rules of conduct as soon as he announces his intention to seek the presidency, for coming up with a thorough list of instructions can be a surprisingly difficult process. There are no guidelines: the longest list in VNHLP history contained nearly nine thousand items (including "Pirates must learn to perform a full repertoire of country dances" and "Pirates must write to their mothers once weekly"), while the shortest contained just one ("Pirates must not eat marmalade"). Remember: the rules you create will determine the future of piracy throughout the kingdom, so this task should not be taken lightly.

CHAPTER FOUR

THE CAPTAIN'S CABIN of the *Pigeon* was overflowing
with maps. Diagrams of the coastline covered Jasper's
long table, charts of ocean currents papered the walls,
and sketches of pirate hideaways were scattered on the
floor like debris from an explosive atlas. Charlie sat in the
middle of it all, sorting through the piles of paper while a
lantern sputtered beside him.

Hilary shoved aside her notebook and looked down
at the black-inked map of Augusta that was draped over
the tabletop. To the south lay Queensport and Pemberton,
where Cannonball Jack had sailed that morning to round
up as many supporters as he could gather. He'd agreed to

take Partridge, Flintlock, and Worthington with him on his houseboat, the *Blunderbuss*, once they'd promised to scrub the cooking pots every evening and never refuse dessert. Cannonball Jack had offered to deliver Miss Pimm and Claire back to Pemberton as well, but Miss Pimm had remarked that if the Enchantress of the Northlands and her pupil traveled too frequently on pirate ships, they would find themselves on the front page of the *Scuttlebutt* in no time at all.

To the east, Mr. Twigget and his mates were scouring the coastline for pirates to assist them against Captain Blacktooth. Jasper had written a note to his retired crewmates Marrow, Slaughter, and Stanley, asking them to do the same in the west. That left only the northern coast for the *Pigeon* to cover. Miss Greyson had already started knitting warm woolen socks and hats for everyone, though they all insisted that a true pirate would never dare to wear a striped stocking cap with a tassel at the end. Jasper was searching the ship's treasure storerooms for stray magic coins to hasten their progress, and Charlie was using every map Jasper had stowed on the *Pigeon* to look for groggeries, harbors, and other spots that might serve as gathering places for pirates.

"There's a boardinghouse just north of Nordholm that's supposed to be crawling with pirates," Charlie said, looking up from his maps. "It's called the Ornery Clam. My mam always told me I wasn't allowed to go anywhere near it. She said they used little boys' skulls for lawn bowling and little boys' knucklebones for hopscotch."

"I don't like the sound of that," the gargoyle said, poking his head out from under a map. "It's a good thing I don't have knucklebones."

Hilary wiggled her own fingers experimentally. "I'm not eager to be chopped up and used for sporting events, but a crew of fearsome pirates is exactly what we need. We'd better visit the Ornery Clam tomorrow."

Charlie nodded. "Have you had any luck with your map?"

"Not yet," said Hilary. "I've been working on something else." She looked down at her dog-eared and water-stained notebook. At the top of the first page, she had written one line in her best script.

"'The Buccaneers' Code,'" Charlie read over her shoulder. "What's that?"

"It's for when I defeat Captain Blacktooth. I'll have to come up with new rules of conduct for my League members to follow, so I thought I'd start writing some."

"That's a good idea," said the gargoyle. "I've never liked Blacktooth's rules—especially the one about having to appreciate parrots. You won't write anything silly like that, will you?"

"I'm not sure what I'll write," Hilary admitted. "I've been thinking about it for hours, but all I've come up with so far is the title."

"Well, you'll figure out the rest soon enough." The gargoyle patted her hand with his tail. "How hard can it be to give orders to hundreds of rowdy, sword-wielding scallywags?"

Hilary groaned and buried her face in the notebook. "I'd prefer not to think about it."

When she looked up again, Alice Feathering was coming through the cabin door, swinging a lantern in front of her. Miss Greyson had agreed that Alice could travel with them on the *Pigeon* as long as she kept up with her studies, which Miss Greyson would personally supervise each evening. Alice wore a black-and-white-striped stocking cap embroidered with a skull and crossbones, though her curls were making a courageous attempt to escape. "Your Miss Greyson is even more fearsome than my tutor," she told Hilary. "She wouldn't set me free until I'd read today's newspaper from front to back, and most of the articles were as dull as rocks—no offense to the gargoyle, of course."

"None taken," the gargoyle said. "If you'd ever met my great-uncle Chester, you'd know exactly how dull rocks can be."

"In any case," said Alice, "Jasper's out on the deck, and he'd like to see you for a moment." She passed her lantern to Hilary.

"Thank you," Hilary said. "By the way, if you had to give a band of pirates one rule to follow, what would it be?"

Alice thought about it. "Don't let anyone stick a

stocking cap on your head," she said at last. "You're sure to look ridiculous."

Hɪᴌᴀʀʏ ᴍᴀᴅᴇ ʜᴇʀ way to the foredeck, where Jasper was tossing his magic coin from hand to hand and looking out over the bay. The pirates of Gunpowder Island didn't seem to be the least bit concerned about facing the Terror of the Southlands in battle: bonfires lined the shores, and raucous hornpipe melodies floated on the breeze, though they were frequently drowned out by cannon blasts. "Ahoy, Terror!" said Jasper, turning toward her. "Do you have any need for a magic gravy boat, or perhaps a magic coatrack? I was supposed to hand them out to the good people of Augusta, but everyone kept clamoring for magic coins instead. It's difficult to carry a coatrack about in one's pocket."

"You'd better hold on to it," Hilary said, "and the gravy boat as well. I can barely handle my own magic coins as it is."

"That suits me perfectly," said Jasper. "It's been far too long since I've had any treasure of my own to bury. But I'd better let Eloise take a look at them first. She may be able to use them to speed our travels."

Hilary felt sure that Miss Greyson was capable of taking charge of a magic coatrack. "Is that all you wanted to ask me?" she said.

"Not entirely. I was wondering who you were planning

to put on the night watch. Whoever it is had better be sharp; those Gunpowder Island cannonballs are terribly unpredictable."

"But you're the one who assigns the watch!" said Hilary. "You're the captain!"

"Actually, I've been meaning to discuss that with you." Jasper reached into the pockets of his pirate coat and pulled on a pair of Miss Greyson's fluffy white mittens. To Hilary's surprise, they didn't make him look any less fearsome. "Perhaps you can remind me," he said. "Which of us is the Terror of the Southlands? Which of us was bold enough to issue a challenge to Captain Blacktooth?"

Hilary could feel her cheeks growing warmer. "I suppose that's me."

"Indeed it is," said Jasper. "On top of all that, if you're hoping to attract several hundred pirates to your cause, you'll have to be impressive—and what's more impressive than commanding a ship? Especially a ship owned by the *former* Terror of the Southlands?" He put a mitten-clad hand on his hat and bowed.

"You're giving me the *Pigeon*?"

"I'm *lending* you the *Pigeon*," Jasper said, "and my services on your crew, of course, for the next three months. All I ask is that you take good care of the ship. She's not as young as she once was, and she doesn't enjoy running aground or drawing cannon fire."

Hilary patted the *Pigeon*'s planks, which creaked

agreeably under her hands. "You're very kind," she said to Jasper. "Is there anything I can do in return?"

"As a matter of fact, there is." Jasper's face grew solemn. "You can be careful—and not just with the *Pigeon*. The Mutineers are used to getting whatever they want, however they can get it, and right now they want you gone. Even if you prove that you are the better pirate, Blacktooth won't go quietly into exile."

Across the ship, the gargoyle was attempting to teach Charlie and Alice a sea chantey. Although the three of them sounded more like a cacophony than a chorus, Hilary couldn't imagine having to leave them behind. "Perhaps Blacktooth won't go quietly," she said, "but neither will I. If the Mutineers try anything sneaky, I shall howl and dig in my heels until they surrender."

"I'm glad to hear it." Jasper picked up his lantern. "Now, let us teach our mates how to harmonize properly, or we shall all have splitting headaches by morning."

WHEN THE SUN rose at last over Gunpowder Island, the *Pigeon* sailed north in search of the Ornery Clam and any pirates who might be lodging there. Hilary steered the ship up the coast, past the city of Nordholm with its brightly colored houses, and past Tilbury Park with its windows overlooking the sea. Soon the towns gave way to forests, and the dark outlines of the Northlands Hills rose up behind the trees. Miss Greyson, who never missed an opportunity to deliver an informative lecture, told them all that centuries ago, when the first lumps of magic ore had been found in those very hills, the Northlands had bustled with industry. They certainly weren't bustling anymore, Hilary thought. The *Pigeon* hadn't passed another ship for hours.

"Are you sure we're traveling in the right direction?" she asked. "I don't see anything that looks like a pirate lodging."

Charlie studied the map. "It's awfully hard to tell," he admitted, peering through a ragged hole in the parchment. "*Someone's* taken a bite out of the coastline."

"There's no need to sound so accusing," the gargoyle said from his Nest. "Some of us get hungry every now and then."

"Ahoy!" cried Alice. She was balanced in the rigging high above them, holding a spyglass in one hand and using the other to stop her dress from flying up in a most unladylike fashion. "I think I've spotted something peculiar. You'd better see it for yourself, Terror."

Alice clambered down to the deck, taking care not to snag her petticoats, and handed Hilary the spyglass. In front of them, a large passenger ship lay beached on the rocks at a queasy angle, as though a storm had plucked it from the waves and tossed it inconsiderately on the shore. Although it must have once carried hundreds of elegant ocean travelers, its tattered sails and barnacled hull were in no condition to set out on any sort of voyage. "It's a ship-wreck," Hilary told the others. "It looks as though it's been there for ages."

"How sad," said Miss Greyson. "I do hope no one was hurt."

But Jasper didn't look the least bit concerned. "It's been a while since I've sailed by," he said, "but if I recall cor-rectly . . ." He borrowed the spyglass and took a long look. Then he nodded. "Take us closer, Captain. Pirate Feather-ing has found the Ornery Clam."

Hilary could hardly believe it. As the *Pigeon* approached the shipwreck, however, she saw that Jasper was right. A skull-and-crossbones flag flapped from the crumbling mast, and smoke rose from a woodstove hidden away somewhere in the ship's belly. A section of the hull had been scraped free of barnacles and painted with large bloodred letters identifying the wreck as the Ornery Clam Pirate Lodging, Dining Room, and Dueling Parlor. Under-neath that, a small sign hung from a nail:

> NO ROOMS AVAILABLE.
> GO AWAY.
> WE MEAN IT.

Jasper lowered the *Pigeon*'s anchor, and Hilary and Charlie helped everyone into the dinghy. Then they rowed to shore and climbed up the stacks of wooden crates that someone had placed against the shipwreck's side. "It's not a very friendly sort of place," the gargoyle remarked. "There's no one here to help us with our luggage or fetch us a warm mug of chocolate."

On the Ornery Clam's deck, someone had traced a hopscotch court in chalk. Hilary dearly hoped they wouldn't stumble across any knucklebones. The lounge chairs arranged at the stern of the ship looked as though they hadn't been used in years, but snatches of music rose up from under Hilary's boots, and she could smell something cooking. "There may not be any chocolate," she told the gargoyle, "but I think there's plenty of beef stew."

Miss Greyson sniffed the air. "We must let our noses lead the way," she proclaimed. "If I've learned one thing on the High Seas, it's this: where there is stew, there are sure to be pirates."

They followed the stewing smell belowdecks and passed through a dim, cramped hallway into a long room hung with peeling, gilt-edged wallpaper. Pirates sat at dining tables, swilling stew from chipped china bowls and wiping their beards with the tablecloths. An immense crystal chandelier dangled from the ceiling, looking as though it might crash down at any moment and disturb the dozens of parrots perched on its branches. In the far corner of the room, three pirates played a rousing tune on a sour-noted fiddle, a pennywhistle, and a rusty pail.

Hilary studied the crowd of pirates. "They look

fearsome enough," she whispered to Charlie, "don't you think?"

"Absolutely." Charlie was counting pirates on his fingers. "And there are at least forty of them. Do you think they'll support you?"

"I'm sure it can't hurt to ask." Hilary dragged the nearest empty chair into the center of the room and climbed on top of its embroidered cushion. It squeaked and shifted dangerously under her weight, but she stood as still as she could. "Pirates!" she shouted.

The music stopped, and every sea-weathered face in the room turned toward her.

"I am the Terror of the Southlands," Hilary said, "and I've come to invite you all to join me in battle. Who in this room is brave enough to stand against the villainous Captain Blacktooth?"

Hilary waited, but the pirates didn't cheer. They didn't applaud. They didn't even draw their swords and slice the legs off her chair. They simply turned back to their bowls of stew, and the band began to play as though they had never been interrupted in the first place.

"Pirates!" Hilary tried again. No one paid her the least bit of attention. She even pulled out her cutlass and flashed it in the lantern light, but not one scallywag bothered to raise an eyebrow.

At last, when she couldn't think of anything else to do, she climbed down from the chair. "What's wrong with these pirates?" she whispered to her mates. "I don't believe they'd notice me if I dressed up as the queen and turned cartwheels around the room. Excuse me!" She tried to catch the eye of a passing pirate, but he looked straight ahead and refused to meet her gaze. When she stepped into his path, he simply walked around her on his way out of the room.

"I know pirates don't care to mind their manners," said Miss Greyson, "but this is absurd."

"Perhaps I can get their attention," said Alice. She stepped forward, put two fingers in her mouth, and let loose the most earsplitting whistle Hilary had ever heard.

The chandelier shook, and the band stopped again. "Enough!" the fiddle player shouted. "Get the manager!" A group of nervous-looking pirates scuttled out of the room, being careful to avoid the chandelier.

Alice beamed. "I've been practicing that whistle for ages. Mother and Father simply loathe it. It tends to bring little bits of Feathering Keep toppling down on their heads."

"Well, it seems to have gotten results," said Hilary. The nervous pirates had returned, dragging a well-dressed elderly gentleman along by the elbows. They placed the gentleman in front of her and whispered something in his ear.

"I see," the gentleman said. He looked down at Hilary. "I am Mr. Theodore, the manager of this fine establishment.

My guests tell me that you have been disrupting their meal. Did you not see the sign asking you to go away?"

"I saw it," said Hilary, "but my mates and I don't need a place to stay. We're here to talk to your guests—though they don't seem particularly eager to talk back." She looked Mr. Theodore up and down, from his neatly combed white hair to his impeccably pressed suit. "You're not a pirate, are you, sir?"

"Certainly not!" Mr. Theodore looked rather shocked by the notion. "I was the chief steward on the *Whippoorwill*, the most luxurious ship in this kingdom or any other." He gestured around him. "When our ship was boarded by pirates, the crew ran her aground and guided the passengers to safety. But the pirates asked me to stay on. They had a dream of opening a boardinghouse, you see, and they needed someone to look after the day-to-day operations." Mr. Theodore smoothed a minuscule wrinkle from his suit. "I am responsible for stocking the galley, mopping up after duels, and asking unwanted visitors to leave the premises before my guests grow careless with their swords."

"Are you responsible for speaking for your guests, too?" Charlie asked. "Even their parrots won't talk to us."

"But of course they won't!" said Mr. Theodore. "And they have good reason to hold their tongues. Do you want to send everyone in this room to the bottom of the sea?"

"Of course not!" said Hilary. "What are you talking about?"

Mr. Theodore gave an impatient sniff. "I am talking," he said, "about the notice we received earlier today." He gestured behind him, where a piece of parchment was stuck to the wall with a dagger. Hilary brushed past Mr. Theodore to get a closer look at it.

THE VERY NEARLY HONORABLE LEAGUE OF PIRATES
Servin' the High Seas for 154 Years

ATTENTION PIRATES!

The VNHLP regrets to report that an unscrupulous band of rebels is traveling the kingdom in an attempt to recruit supporters to their cause. They are led by Pirate Hilary Westfield, the Terror of the Southlands, who aims to seize control of the League from its rightful president, Captain Rupert Blacktooth. If she dares to approach you, do not allow her to enlist you in her ranks! According to League regulations, Pirate Westfield may not be harmed, but the VNHLP recommends that all scallywags on the High Seas stay as far from her as possible. Do not talk to Pirate Westfield. Do not look her in the eye. Do not be lured into conversation with her gargoyle. Any pirate who is seen communicating with Pirate Westfield or her friends will be interrogated, stripped of his cutlass, and keelhauled by Captain Blacktooth. And remember: each loyal scallywag who chooses to support the president in his battle against Pirate Westfield will receive a purse of magic coins and a new hat feather of his choice.

"Bribing pirates with magic and hat feathers!" said Jasper, who was reading the notice over Hilary's shoulder. "That's awfully underhanded, even for Blacktooth."

"I'm more concerned about the bit where he says he'll keelhaul anyone who dares to speak to us." Hilary felt rather like keelhauling Blacktooth himself, but she settled instead for glaring at Mr. Theodore. "And I suppose these notices are tacked to the walls of every groggery and pirate lodging in Augusta."

"I expect so," said Mr. Theodore. "My guests tell me that Captain Blacktooth tends to be quite . . . thorough."

"That's one way of putting it," Charlie said. "We'll be lucky if we get two pirates to join us, let alone two hundred."

"Oh, drat." The gargoyle hung his head. "If no one's allowed to talk to me, how will I ever be famous?"

Hilary looked around at the dozens of pirates who were staring resolutely into their bowls of stew. "We can't give up so easily," she told her mates. "We can't let Blacktooth win before we've even begun to fight him! Perhaps some of these pirates will listen to reason."

"I really must insist that you leave," Mr. Theodore said. "I won't have you putting my guests in danger."

"But your guests are pirates!" said Hilary. "They love danger!" She dodged Mr. Theodore and stepped back up on the chair. "Ahoy!" she called.

Some of the pirates in the room groaned. Others

pressed their napkins over their eyes to avoid getting an accidental glimpse of Hilary. One pirate leered at her; his gold teeth shone like doubloons.

"I know you aren't allowed to talk to me," she said, "and I won't ask you to risk your necks on my account. But I'd like you all to know one thing before I leave: if I defeat Captain Blacktooth—I mean, *when* I defeat him—I won't ever punish you just for looking at another scally-wag. Only the most cowardly pirates make those sorts of threats." She jumped down from her chair. "I'm going back to my ship now. If you want to help me stop the VNHLP from turning as rotten as Blacktooth's breath, I hope you'll join me."

The pirates stared at Hilary with their mouths open wide. Mr. Theodore held the door open wider. "Good-bye," he said as she led her mates out of the dining room, "and for heaven's sake, please don't ever come back."

When they reached the main deck, Hilary flopped down in a lounge chair. "I believe I would have preferred it if they'd used my skull for lawn bowling."

Miss Greyson patted her knee with a mittened hand. "Cheer up," she said. "You may have convinced a pirate or two."

The gargoyle tilted his head. "I hear footsteps," he said. "Our supporters must be on their way!"

Hilary scrambled to her feet as the gold-toothed pirate from the dining room crossed the deck toward her. "Hello, matey," she said, holding out her hands to greet him. "I'm glad to see you're braver than your companions. Have you come to join our crew?"

The pirate looked down at Hilary's hands. Then he pulled out his cutlass and pointed it at each of Hilary's fingers, one by one. "Ten fingers," he said. "A good number, ten is. If ye've got ten fingers, then ye've got a few to spare. And if Blacktooth hadn't ordered us not to hurt ye, I'd be takin' 'em fer meself." He grinned, showing every one of his shining teeth. "Ye might say I've got a collection."

Hilary snatched her hands back and reached for her own cutlass. Jasper, Charlie, and Alice had already drawn theirs, and Miss Greyson had pulled her golden crochet hook from her hair. "If you're trying to frighten me," Hilary snapped, "you'd better try harder. The Terror of the Southlands doesn't get frightened."

"Well," said the gargoyle, "not *usually*."

"Excuse me," said Jasper to the pirate, "but hadn't you better leave before someone spots you chatting with us? I'd truly hate to see you keelhauled. You have such admirable counting skills, and such expensive teeth."

"Aye," the pirate said, "I'll leave. I just wanted yer friend to know that Blacktooth's men will never answer to a little girl." He turned and began to walk away, but halfway across the deck he stopped and looked straight back at Hilary. "If yer wise," he said, "ye'll take those ten good fingers back home with ye and leave piratin' matters to pirates."

A HEARTY BLAST
from Cannonball Jack

Dear Terror,

It's been nearly two weeks since I saw ye on Gunpowder Island, an' I hope the Northlands have treated ye kindly. Have ye found a few sturdy pirates to support yer mission against that shifty bilge rat? I dearly hope ye have. I've been searchin' the southern coast fer friendly faces, but Captain Blacktooth's grip on the Queensport pirates be tight as a noose.

Me new mates an' I paid a visit to the Salty Biscuit yesterday an' asked if anyone in the groggery dared to support ye, but the fellows there ran after us with their cutlasses an' chased us away. It were peculiar, Terror: all the pirates had their eyes closed, as if seein' us would be a fate worse than death. Some o' them even ran smack into the walls as they were givin' chase. Miss Worthington an' Mr. Flintlock thought 'twere all rather amusin', but Mr. Partridge were awfully shaken by the whole affair. Now he's gone an' locked himself in his cabin on board the Blunderbuss. Miss Worthington an' I have been tryin' to lure him out with fresh-baked gingersnaps fer the past half hour.

We set sail for Pemberton tomorrow, an' perhaps we'll have better luck there. I hope that when I meet ye back

in Wimbly-on-the-Marsh, I'll have more to show fer me
efforts than a tin o' gingersnaps.

Yers till then,
C. J.

- -

THE VERY NEARLY HONORABLE LEAGUE OF PIRATES
Servin' the High Seas for 154 Years

EUSTACE TWIGGET

~~FIRST MATE OF THE RENEGADE~~
Independent Piracy Professional

✠ ✠ ✠ ✠ ✠

Ahoy, Pirate Westfield,
   I'm writin' to you from the town of Middleby,
where my mates and I have met with more than a
few troubles. We've passed many pirate ships, but
none of them have been eager to drop anchor and
talk with us. In fact, most of them have gone
speedin' off in the opposite direction as soon as
we've announced ourselves. We were hopin' to find
some friendly buccaneers here in Middleby, but the

folks at the Scallywag's Den were unwillin' to talk, and even less willin' to listen. They shooed us out the door and put up a sign that says NO FRIENDS OF HILARY WESTFIELD ALLOWED. One pirate whispered that he's fond of you, Terror, but he has to follow Captain Blacktooth's orders. I know very well how hard it is to disobey Blacktooth, and I'm not sure these pirates have the guts to do it.

When my mates and I returned to the docks, we found a nasty sort named Burly Bruce McCorkle usin' his magic piece to fill our ship from bowsprit to stern with haddock. The poor fish were floppin' about in the wash buckets and cookin' pots, and I found a few more in my blankets this evenin'. My mates tried to show McCorkle just what they thought of his prank, but McCorkle said they weren't allowed to touch him, for he's Blacktooth's man, and he can't be harmed before the battle. Rest assured, Terror, that I'll fill the fellow's breeches with snappin' turtles as soon as I'm permitted. In any case, I hope you and your crew are havin' better luck.

With apologies,
Mr. Twigget

⚓

Marrow, Slaughter & Stanley

PROTECTION • PIRACY • CATERING

Dear Hilary,

I am sorry to write with disheartening news, but our attempts to locate supporters along the western coast of the kingdom have not gone as well as we had hoped. It seems that Captain Blacktooth has sent several of his men to every corner of Augusta to pass out threatening notices and punish any pirates who dare to say a kind word about you—but by now you must have discovered this for yourself.

I admit to being surprised by Blacktooth's tactics. Though his reputation is fearsome, he has never before resorted so openly to threats and bribery in all his years as a pirate. I am convinced, therefore, that his fellow Mutineers are twisting his arm. Mr. Marrow suggested over breakfast that Blacktooth's friends only value his treasure stash and his firepower, and that they shall toss him aside when they have run out of uses for him. I wonder very much if Mr. Marrow is right.

Mr. Marrow, Mr. Slaughter, and I send you our best wishes from Little Shearwater, and we look forward to seeing you in a few weeks' time.

Regards,
Mr. Stanley

CHAPTER FIVE

BY THE TIME the *Pigeon* drew near the town of Summer-stead, Hilary had been ignored, turned down, or chased away by enough pirates to fill all twenty of Westfield House's spare bedrooms. Pirate ships darted into caverns or hid behind trees when they saw the *Pigeon* approaching, and groggeries sent Hilary away without so much as a tip of the hat. Even friends who had come to her aid in the past wrote apologetic notes explaining that although they wished they could help her, they had treasure-hunting engagements and parrot-grooming appointments that they simply couldn't miss.

"Do these pirates truly expect me to believe they've

entered a singing competition that just happens to fall on the same day as the battle?" Hilary crumpled up the letter the postal courier had just delivered from the crew of the dread ship *Matilda* and tossed it across the deck, where a pile of discarded correspondence was growing with remarkable speed. "If Blacktooth doesn't stop terrifying my friends, I shall have to enlist Mother's gardeners to chase after him with their rakes."

The gargoyle looked over from his Nest, which Miss Greyson had lined with warm knitted blankets. Though spring had snuck up on the Northlands at last, Summerstead generally preferred to remain chilly, and its residents complained whenever the temperature rose enough to turn the ice sculptures in the town square to puddles. "At least Blacktooth won't be able to pull any tricks during the battle," the gargoyle said. "The queen will be watching to make sure everything is fair."

"If we can't find any supporters, there won't be any battle for the queen to watch," Hilary pointed out. "She'll simply wave good-bye as I sail off to spend the rest of my days perfecting my embroidery, or whatever it is that pirates do when they go into exile."

"It won't be as bad as all that," said the gargoyle, nestling deeper into his blankets. "If you go into exile, I'll come with you."

"You will?" said Hilary. "Oh, gargoyle, you don't have

to do that. Don't you want to stay here and have adventures? I'm sure Charlie would be happy to carry you in his bag."

"That's kind of him," said the gargoyle, "but I'd rather be with you." He yawned. "The spiders in exile are probably almost as tasty as the ones we have here."

WHEN JASPER CAME to relieve her at the helm, Hilary headed back to her cabin to write a letter to Claire. She had been meaning to start it weeks ago, but every time she tried to begin, she imagined Claire's face crumpling at the news that not a single pirate in the kingdom wanted anything to do with Hilary. Miss Pimm would shake her head and sigh, and the two of them would agree that perhaps Hilary wasn't a very good leader after all. Hilary tried hard not to think about this.

She tried so hard, in fact, that she didn't even notice when Charlie opened his cabin door and stepped directly in front of her. Her forehead connected with his nose, and her hat went flying. "Sorry about that!" she said. "I'm afraid I wasn't paying attention."

"Neither was I," said Charlie, rubbing his nose. "It's a good thing we didn't have our swords drawn." He bent to pick up Hilary's hat, but as he did, something shiny slipped out of his hand and clinked onto the deck. He snatched it up and stuffed it in the pocket of his breeches.

Hilary couldn't have been more surprised if the Royal Augusta Water Ballet had appeared in front of her and dripped all over her boots. "Charlie," she said, "whatever are you doing with a magic coin?"

Charlie squashed his hat lower on his head. Ever since his mam and pa had been sunk for their treasure, he'd refused to use magic himself, and he didn't even care to be around it. He'd certainly never kept a magic piece in his pocket before. "It's Jasper's," he said reluctantly. "He said I could borrow it for a few days."

"But you hate magic!" said Hilary. "Please don't tell me you've decided to enroll in dancing classes as well, or I won't have the slightest idea what's become of you."

"I haven't actually *used* the blasted thing," said Charlie, "and honestly, I'm not sure I will. Just holding on to it makes me itch. I expect I'll give it back to Jasper tonight and tell him to keep it locked as far from me as possible." He lowered his voice. "It's just that I've been thinking about . . . well, about Claire, and what she said to me last summer. That I'm afraid of magic."

"Oh, Charlie, you know she didn't mean it."

"Of course she meant it," Charlie said. "And she was right. A pirate shouldn't be frightened of his own trea-sure—or of anything at all, really."

Hilary nodded. Her mouth went dry every time she thought about the gold-toothed pirate who'd threatened to collect her fingers, but Charlie didn't have to know about that. "There's no use at all in being frightened," she agreed.

"I asked Jasper what he thought I should do about it, and he said that if I carried some magic around with me, I might get used to it." Charlie pulled out the coin and held it at arm's length between two fingers. "So far, though, I haven't."

"At least you haven't thrown it overboard yet," said Hilary. "That's a very good start. And who knows? If you ever do want to learn how to use magic, perhaps Miss Pimm will take you on as a private student."

Charlie barely had time to look horrified before, quite without warning, the *Pigeon* lurched to a stop. The deck heaved up below them, and they went tumbling into a pile of Miss Greyson's knitting.

"Blast!" said Hilary. "What in the world has Jasper crashed us into?"

"A sandbank, I'd bet," said Charlie, pulling bits of yarn from his jacket, "or one of those little islands they always forget to include on maps."

But the *Pigeon* hadn't beached itself on a sandbank or run aground on an inconveniently placed island. When Hilary ran out onto the deck, she found Jasper searching for the spyglass and Fitzwilliam swooping in circles around his head. Miss Greyson clutched the golden gravy boat in both hands, looking as though she might collapse at any moment. Alice, who had been working on her mathematics lesson, was splattered with ink, and her pen lay halfway across the deck. Worst of all, the Gargoyle's Nest had over-turned completely. The gargoyle swung upside down from the bowsprit, held above the waves by a tangle of ropes. His warm blankets had fallen into the sea, and his wings were beating frantically. "Hilary!" he cried. "Help! I'm a damsel in distress!"

Hilary hurried to the gargoyle, grabbed hold of his Nest, and tugged it until it sat right-side up on the bowsprit once more. She could hear the gargoyle's heart thumping as she secured the Nest with the strongest knots she knew how to make. "You're all right now," she said. "Whatever happened?"

"What happened," said the gargoyle, "is that I almost got sent to the briny deep! The abyssal depths! The sea slug's dressing room!" He shuddered.

"I'm terribly sorry, gargoyle." Miss Greyson took a long breath. "I'm sorry to all of you, in fact. I'm afraid this was all my fault. Were any of you hurt?"

Hilary looked beyond her at the books that had flopped onto the deck like mournful fish. "We're fine," she said, "but I can't say the same for the floating bookshop."

"That's all right, then," said Miss Greyson. "Books are more easily repaired than bones, after all. But I never should have used that magic gravy boat; it's far too sensitive." She gave it her most disapproving look. "When I asked it to bring us to a halt, I should have been more specific."

Hilary thought it had been rather bold of the magic to behave so impertinently in Miss Greyson's presence. "But why are we halted?"

"I took the liberty of asking Eloise to slow our course." Jasper pulled the spyglass out from behind a capsized crate of oranges. "The final decision is up to you, of course, Terror, but I presumed you wouldn't want us to sail directly into the middle of a pirate battle."

Hilary had been so busy tending to the gargoyle that she hadn't bothered to look over his head at the long, low pirate ship that floated a quarter of a league in front of them. Its curved bow rose out of the waves like a sea monster's head, and it was doing its best to dodge cannonball blasts from a small but vicious-looking ship with blue and gold pennants flying from its mast. Hilary had watched her father and his naval officers hang those same colors from their battleships hundreds of times—the blue of the sea and the gold of treasure, the two things Admiral Westfield loved most of all. A swarm of hornets would have been a happier sight.

"I thought you said it was a pirate battle." Hilary turned back to Jasper. "You didn't say anything about the Royal Navy."

Though it wasn't an expression he wore often, Jasper managed to look nearly apologetic. "I try not to utter a word about that dreadful institution if I can help it," he said. "I must say, though, they've been far less hostile since they stopped taking orders from your father."

"They look hostile enough at the moment," said Charlie. He was gripping the ship's rail so tightly that Hilary worried it might snap. "They're going to sink those pirates."

The navy sent another shot across the longship's bow, and Hilary flinched. "No, they won't," she said. "We're not going to let them."

"But we're in no position to take on the Royal Navy!" Miss Greyson said. "Our cannon hasn't been fired in years."

"Then we'll use something else," said Hilary. She knew Miss Greyson was right, but she simply couldn't stand there and watch as the Royal Navy blasted a ship to pieces. "We've got to rescue those pirates before they're up to their necks in the sea!"

Jasper nodded. "The Terror's right," he said. "If we don't try to help our fellows, we might as well surrender our cutlasses on the spot. I'll set our course for the battle."

"Very well." Miss Greyson looked grim. "If we must, we must. But please do your best to avoid the cannonballs."

As Jasper steered them toward the skirmish, Hilary, Charlie, and Alice searched the *Pigeon* for anything that might help them ward off the navy ship and its officers. "Remember," said Hilary, "we want to stop them, not sink them."

Charlie frowned. "We do?"

"Sinking ships may be my father's specialty," said

Hilary, "but it won't ever be mine." She dug a handful of magic coins from her pockets and added them to the collection of broomsticks, bedpans, and other makeshift weapons they'd scrounged from all corners of the ship.

Alice looked sideways at the gargoyle. "What about him?" she whispered to Hilary. "Can't we use him to protect the pirates from the navy?"

The gargoyle cleared his throat. "Would *you* enjoy being poked and prodded by people who only want to use your magic?" he asked. "No, I don't think you would. It's not a pleasant experience."

"I promised him ages ago that I'd never ask him for protection," Hilary told Alice, "and in any case, he's had an exhausting day already. Perhaps we can send Fitzwilliam to peck off the officers' buttons instead."

But Fitzwilliam had retired to his cage and refused to leave it—for fear of losing his feathers in battle, Hilary supposed. Charlie came up from the galley with an armload of delicate china plates that he offered to throw at the navy ship, though Miss Greyson winced at the proposal. And Alice suggested reading to the officers from the newspaper until they fell asleep from boredom.

"Whatever you plan to do," called Jasper from the helm, "you'd better do it quickly, or we're likely to receive a shot to the sails." They were close enough now that Hilary could see the pirates, in their sodden fur coats, rushing to bail water out of their sinking ship.

"Ahoy!" she called to them as the naval officers reloaded their cannon. "You scallywags look like you could use some help. I'd be happy to offer it, if you're willing."

One of the pirates looked up at her. His coat was an impressive patchwork of furs, as though every kind of animal in the Northlands forests had donated its pelt to his wardrobe; Hilary wondered if he was the captain. "If you and your mates would care to climb aboard my ship," she said, "we'll toss a rope down to you."

The pirate captain chuckled and shook his head. "I can tell you're not from these waters, pirate," he said. "My name is Captain Wolfson. Every scallywag in the Northlands knows that my mates and I don't fear the Royal Navy, and we don't need to be rescued."

Hilary sighed. Were all pirates so maddeningly stubborn? "I'm sure you're not afraid," she said, "but you're being foolish. At the rate you're taking on water, you'll be sunk in minutes."

Captain Wolfson considered the waves lapping at his ankles. "And you think you can help us?"

"I'm sure of it," said Hilary, "if only you'll give me a chance."

"Take cover!" shouted one of Wolfson's mates. A cannonball splashed down only a few yards from where the captain was standing, drenching him and his crew. Slowly, blinking the salt from his eyes, he wrung out his impressive coat.

"All right," he said at last. "I'll give you that chance. Send down the rope."

Hilary did exactly that, and one by one the northern pirates swung themselves over the *Pigeon*'s starboard rail. They dripped all over the deck, they smelled of wet fur and smoked herring, and they lobbed salty insults at the naval officers despite Miss Greyson's protests. All in all, they seemed to be in much better spirits now that they were no longer ankle-deep in seawater.

"Listen here, pirates!" Jasper called over the din. "I hate to dampen the mood, but I believe that navy ship is preparing to fire on us."

It was true: the cannon that had once pointed at the northern pirates' sinking ship was now aimed directly at the *Pigeon*. "Attention, interlopers!" one officer called out. "Surrender your comrades by the count of ten, or we'll blast the entire lot of you into a thousand bits." He sounded very much as if he meant it.

"Say the word, Captain," said Jasper, "and I'll have the *Pigeon* out of these waters in three beats of a parrot's wing."

"One!" said the naval officer.

Hilary looked over at Charlie, who was still helping pirates in furs climb onto the ship. "We can't leave yet!" she called back. "We've got a few more left to rescue."

"Two!" said the officer.

The gargoyle gave Hilary a look. "All of this counting makes me very uncomfortable."

"Don't worry," Hilary said as confidently as she could. "We're not sunk yet." She leaped over the stack of china plates, kicked aside the pile of newspapers, ran across the ship, and plucked the magic gravy boat from the deck.

"Three!" said the officer.

"Magic," Hilary said, "please bring me . . ." She hesitated. The gravy boat was too small to provide much in the way of weaponry, and Hilary wasn't at all sure she was strong enough to conjure up anything truly fearsome.

"Four!" said the officer.

"Oh, bother!" said Hilary. "Magic, please bring me something that will stop that ship from firing on us—and do it quickly!"

The gravy boat shook in Hilary's hands and drew the strength from her limbs. She squeezed her eyes shut as the naval officer called "Five!" Then a thud shook the deck, and she opened her eyes.

Standing in front of her was an enormous white pitcher that looked as though it belonged to a giant's tea service. It came up to Hilary's waist and was painted with delicate blue cornflower sprigs. Instead of containing something sensible like milk or cream, however, it was filled with a thick, dark liquid that trembled with every passing wave.

With something very much like reverence, the others gathered around the pitcher. "What *is* it?" Alice whispered.

Miss Greyson sniffed the liquid. Then she removed one of her mittens, dipped a finger into the pitcher, and tasted the results. "Molasses," she said. "Blackstrap, to be precise."

Hilary groaned. "I knew I should have been more specific."

"Excuse me," called the naval officer. "Are you pirates paying attention? I said seven!"

"Hold your horses!" said Captain Wolfson. He scowled at the officer. Then he turned back to the pitcher and leaned so far over it that Hilary worried he would tumble inside. She had already rescued him from a sinking ship, and she wasn't sure she had the strength to save him from a vat of molasses as well.

"Hmm," said Captain Wolfson. "We can use this." He drew a handful of gold coins from the pocket of his coat and mumbled a few words.

Without excusing itself or bidding farewell, the pitcher rose up from the deck and floated slowly, but with great determination, toward the navy ship. "Eight!" cried the officer. "Nine! And what in the world is that? Are those *cornflowers*?"

The pitcher picked up speed. It circled the navy ship, settled comfortably a few feet above the deck, and tipped itself over like a gentleman bowing at a High Society ball. A thick stream of molasses poured out of the pitcher, covering the cannon, the ammunition crates, and (judging by his cries of outrage) the boots of the naval officer. His crewmates abandoned the cannon and ran to help him, but they only succeeded in sticking themselves to the deck.

The northern pirates slapped their legs, gripped their sizable stomachs, and laughed uproariously. Jasper was laughing too, and even Miss Greyson let a smile settle on her lips. Captain Wolfson bowed to his mates and turned to Hilary. "I owe you an apology," he said to her. "It seems that even the most fearsome pirates in the Northlands need to be rescued every once in a while."

One of Wolfson's mates tapped him on the shoulder. "Sir," he said, "that's the Terror of the Southlands you're speaking to. Didn't you read Blacktooth's notice?"

The laughter faded away, and Hilary's hopes faded with it. She wondered if the northern pirates would jump over the ship's rails and into the sea now that they knew who she was, or if they'd simply back away and look in every possible direction to avoid meeting her gaze. Either way, she wasn't eager to see it.

"I've read Blacktooth's notice," said Captain Wolfson. Then, to Hilary's amazement, he smiled at her. "I've also decided to ignore it. If the Terror hadn't lent us her assistance, we'd all be halfway to the ocean floor by now. Isn't that right?" He narrowed his eyes at his mate.

"Yes, sir." His mate stood up a bit straighter and held out a hand to Hilary. "Er, thank you, Terror. That was a nice bit of magic you managed."

"You're quite welcome," said Hilary. She shook his

hand, and then she shook Wolfson's. "Thank you for being brave enough to look me in the eye."

Before long, all the pirates on the *Pigeon* were busy making their introductions and trading tales. The gargoyle had just offered to read aloud from his memoirs when he was interrupted by a sharp knock on the ship's hull. "Attention, lawless hooligans!" someone shouted. "I demand to speak with your captain!"

Hilary leaned over the ship's rail and looked down at the naval officer, who floated below her in a blue and gold dinghy. He looked quite annoyed—probably because the bottom half of him was still coated with molasses. "Go get your captain, little girl!" he said.

"I *am* the captain," said Hilary. "And you are a nuisance. What do you want now?"

"I want to complain," the officer said. "You ruined a perfectly good battle. You destroyed a top-of-the-line cannon and several expensive pairs of boots. Your choice of weaponry was thoroughly untraditional, and as if that weren't enough, you've made us fall short of our monthly pirate-capturing quota. I promise you the Royal Navy won't forget this."

Hilary believed him, for her father had often boasted of the navy's ability to hold a grudge. "If you're so concerned about pirates," she said, "why in the world are you sailing about in the Northlands? I hear Captain Blacktooth's men are threatening to attack Queensport; shouldn't you be trying to stop them? Or has the navy decided there's no point in trying to be useful for a change?"

"You clearly know nothing about the Royal Navy's affairs," the officer said. "Typical pirate ignorance. We are all under strict orders not to attack any ship belonging to Captain Blacktooth or his friends." With a molasses-stained hand, he reached into his satchel and pulled out a thick stack of papers. "Any pirate ship on this list may sail freely in the kingdom's waters until Admiral Curtis says otherwise."

"But that makes no sense at all," said Hilary. "Did those orders come from Admiral Curtis himself?"

"Of course they did." The officer held up the papers. "As you can see perfectly plainly, the orders were signed by naval adviser James Westfield on Admiral Curtis's behalf. And I'll warn you, pirate, that your ship is not on his list."

"Of course it isn't," Hilary murmured. "Blast and double blast."

The officer raised his eyebrows. "What did you say?"

"I said that you'd better head back to your ship at once," said Hilary, "before I pour another pitcher of molasses on you."

To her relief, the officer made a hasty retreat, and his ship soon sailed away as fast as the wind could carry it. Captain Wolfson kept an eye on it until it had disappeared over the horizon. "Do you think they're off to badger some other poor scallywags?" he asked.

"I'm sure of it," Hilary replied. Now that Blacktooth's loyal pirates were preparing to fight against her and her father had done nothing except lend them the Royal Navy's assistance, the High Seas suddenly seemed a good deal more perilous than usual.

"Ah well," said Wolfson. "It's fortunate that we pirates enjoy a good battle—as long as we win, of course." He looked wistfully at his longship, which sank farther under the sea with every passing wave.

"I'm sorry about your ship, sir," said Hilary. "Jasper says we've got no hope of repairing it, but I'd be happy to bring you and your mates back to shore."

"Aye," said Wolfson, "that would be grand. You're welcome to join us for dinner, of course. I don't know about you, but all that molasses has put me in the mood for gingerbread."

PIRATE HILARY WESTFIELD
TERROR OF THE SOUTHLANDS

Dear Claire,

I write this sitting in a pirates' feasting hall. A feasting hall, I have discovered, is quite like Westfield House on the cook's day off: the air is filled with panicked shouts and the smell of something burning. Miss Greyson tried to enlist me to tend the fire, but I escaped to a far corner of the hall with my pen and paper before she could make any chiding remarks.

How have your magic lessons been? I haven't heard any reports of vast explosions destroying half of Pemberton, so you must be doing awfully well. I'm afraid things aren't going nearly as smoothly out here on the High Seas. We've made it all the way to the top of the kingdom, but we haven't managed to convince a single pirate to sail into battle against Captain Blacktooth. If these northern pirates refuse to join us as well, I'm not sure what I'll do. We'll have to turn southward soon if we're to have any hope of meeting our mates in Wimbly-on-the-Marsh next month, and I'm beginning to think we'll be a hundred and fifty pirates short when we get there. On top of it all, it seems that Father has managed to trick the entire Royal Navy into following his orders. I'd write a note to the queen if I believed it would do any good, but I'm not sure anyone in the kingdom is capable of stopping the Mutineers from plucking up whatever they want. They are just like the rabbits that live in Jasper's vegetable garden, only with smaller ears and more cannons.

Oh dear. I don't mean to be discouraging. I still have every intention of defeating Captain Blacktooth and seeing you become Enchantress. A good pirate always comes up with a plan, and so will I—even if it doesn't occur to me until I'm lying on my lumpy cot at the Pestilent Home for Foul-Tempered Pirates.

I miss you very much, and the gargoyle tells me he misses you too. I suspect that Charlie sends his regards, though I'm quite sure he'd never admit it.

Arr! and love from
Hilary

———————— ◇ ◇ ◇ ◇ ◇ ————————

What happens when a beloved High Society figure transforms overnight from hostess to hostage? To find out, we visited the Northlands home of Mrs. Georgiana Tilbury. Although Mrs. Tilbury has been kept prisoner in her home since midsummer, she maintains a full social calendar that many law-abiding citizens would envy. "Am I bored? Never!" laughed Mrs. Tilbury from the comfort of her solarium. "Lately, I have been spending time preparing for my daughter's upcoming wedding to Sir Nicholas Feathering. I recently hired several hundred birds from across the kingdom to chirp Mozart's horn concertos during the ceremony. And of course I try to keep up with my charitable works. Why, just yesterday, I hosted a gathering of the Coalition of Overprotective Mothers, of which I am chairwoman. We are concerned by rumors that a common young woman without elegance or taste is next in line for the position of Enchantress, and several of our members are planning to visit the Royal Palace to remind the queen that government posts are most suitably filled by members of High Society."

Under Augustan law, Mrs. Tilbury is not permitted to leave her mansion, and a royal guard is stationed on the grounds at all times. However, we observed a flurry of activity at Tilbury Park on the afternoon we visited. Several friends and family members were in attendance, as was a former admiral of the Royal Navy. Though we tried to learn the nature of their business with Mrs. Tilbury, we learned instead that the doors of Tilbury Park are thick and quite unsuitable for eavesdropping.

WE ASKED, YOU ANSWERED:
What's your opinion of Georgiana Tilbury?

"I greatly admire Georgiana's dedication to the difficult work of preserving our kingdom's values. My friends and I look to her for guidance on every topic from current affairs to hat pins."—L. DEVEREAUX, NORDHOLM

"I don't understand why that woman isn't locked up properly like all the other thieves and conspirators in the kingdom. She claims to be frail and delicate, but I hope you will trust me when I say she is nothing of the sort."—E. PIMM, PEMBERTON

"We may have gotten our magic back, but those in High Society are still treated far better than the rest of us. Someone ought to stand up to that Mrs. Tilbury. I wouldn't be surprised to learn that even the queen herself is afraid of her."—L. REDFERN, PEMBERTON

"If it's all the same to you, I'd prefer not to answer that question."
—N. FEATHERING, QUEENSPORT

CHAPTER SIX

THE FIRE ROARED in the feasting hall, and the night-time sky was streaked with colored light. "You can't see such a sight in the Southlands," Miss Greyson told Hilary as they looked out the window at a green shimmer on the horizon. "Some northerners say the lights have magical properties. It sounds rather unlikely to me, but if magic can burrow under the hills, who's to say it can't stretch across the sky as well?" She shrugged. "I suppose there are a few mysteries even a governess can't unravel."

They walked back toward the fire, where the rest of the pirates had gathered with their drinking bowls and their tales of adventure. The gargoyle was telling the crowd how he had managed to rescue Miss Pimm from the Mutineers' clutches, though his story was more than a bit embellished around the edges. "If you'd truly bitten a sea monster on the nose," said Hilary, "I'm sure I would have noticed it."

The gargoyle gave an embarrassed sort of cough. "You must have been taking a nap."

"Sea monster or no sea monster," said Captain Wolfson, "that battle at Tilbury Park was the most fun I've had in years. My men and I truly enjoyed swinging in through the windows."

"Of course!" said Hilary. Now that Wolfson mentioned it, she distinctly remembered seeing pirates in furs raising their swords against Blacktooth's mates. "You're one of Cannonball Jack's friends, aren't you?"

Wolfson nodded. "We met when my ship was caught in a storm near Pemberton Bay. Cannonball Jack guided me and my crew to safety. When he wrote to me last summer and said that he needed my help in return, I was happy to lend a hand."

Hilary poked at the coals with the tip of her cutlass. As much as she longed to ask the northern pirates for their assistance against Captain Blacktooth, the thought of enduring yet another rejection was almost too humiliating to consider. Still, she thought, it would be more humiliating by far to show up in Queensport Harbor on the day of the battle without any supporters by her side. "I hope you won't think I'm foolish for asking," she said, "but I was wondering if you might be able to help us again. We're looking for pirates who are willing to go into battle against Captain Blacktooth, and we'd be honored if you'd join us."

Wolfson looked around the fire at his mates. Then, to Hilary's dismay, he shook his head. "We're freelance pirates," he said. "We don't have anything to do with the League's affairs, and we generally like it that way. Why should we involve ourselves now?"

"Go on," Charlie whispered. "Tell them why!"

Hilary frowned. She didn't have the slightest idea what was likely to win over Captain Wolfson and his crew. She supposed she might promise to supply them with unsinkable ships and vast stores of herring, but bribery was Blacktooth's strategy, not hers, and she wasn't eager to resort to it. Besides, hadn't Claire once said that all a good leader truly needed was passion? Hilary hoped very much that it was true.

"You might not care for the League right now," she said, "but if I'm in charge of it, I'll do my best to change things. I won't dismiss well-meaning pirates, or force you to help me take over the kingdom. And as for treasure— well, I can't blame Blacktooth for loving it, but I'd give up all the loot in the Royal Treasury in a moment if it would help my crewmates, and I'm quite sure he never would."

Wolfson used his shirtsleeve to wipe the grog from his beard. "Interesting," he said.

One of the other pirates raised his hand. "If ye take Blacktooth's place, Terror, will ye still host the annual picnic? I've always been wantin' to go, but I've never been allowed."

"Of course I'll host it," said Hilary at once. "It's only fair. All pirates on the High Seas should be able to have picnics now and then."

"So they should," said Wolfson, "but trying to replace Captain Blacktooth is a tricky business. There are plenty of scallywags who still remember how Blacktooth came to win his presidency. You're too young to recall it, Terror, but I imagine Mr. Fletcher's told you all about it."

Hilary gave Jasper a look. "As a matter of fact, he hasn't."

Jasper fiddled with the hem of his coat. "I, ah, didn't think the details were relevant."

"They were relevant enough to Pretty Jack Winter!" said one of Wolfson's men, and his crewmates chortled.

"The Terror should hear this tale," said Wolfson firmly. "She deserves to know what she's up against." He set down his drinking bowl and looked down at Hilary.

"Eighteen years ago," he said, "when I was nothing more than an apprentice to my pirate grandfather, a scallywag named Pretty Jack Winter ran the Very Nearly Honorable League of Pirates. He'd been president for almost half a century, but he never once thought of stepping down, and no one dared to challenge him, for he'd never been defeated in battle. My grandfather was a freelance pirate, same as I am, and he knew better than to cross Pretty Jack's path on a moonless night.

"Then Rupert Blacktooth came along. No one thought much of him at first. He was from a family of middling pirates—nothing to write home about, the Blacktooths. But Rupert was orphaned when he was no bigger than a good-sized trout, and the High Society family that adopted his sister didn't care to raise a boy as well. So Rupert showed up on the League's doorstep and devoted his life to piracy. He did well in his studies, and soon enough he was apprenticed to Pretty Jack Winter himself. By the time he was thirty, he held the League records in everything from cannon firing to parrot grooming."

"I myself was a renowned parrot groomer once," Jasper said as Wolfson sipped his grog. "But alas, I haven't had the time to devote to Fitzwilliam's plumage since I left the League."

"It was treasure that Blacktooth loved most, though," said Wolfson. "He'd amassed more treasure than any pirate before him, and he thought he'd earned the right to take over the presidency. Pretty Jack didn't agree, of course, but that didn't stop Blacktooth. He turned up in Gunpowder Square, just as you did, and announced his challenge to his former captain. It was the most scandalous act since Philby Figgins turned in his pirate hat and joined the Royal Navy. Mind you, there weren't many pirates who dared to go up against Pretty Jack's cannons, no matter how many records Blacktooth held. Still, Blacktooth had made a few friends over the years, and he managed to scrape together a crew."

Hilary sighed. "Of course he did."

"He knew, of course, that Pretty Jack Winter was prouder than a parrot and rustier than an old cutlass. Why, he hadn't fought a fellow pirate in forty years! When the battle was over and the smoke had cleared, Pretty Jack's men were clinging to the wreckage of their ship, and Pretty Jack himself was nowhere to be found. They say his peg leg washed up on shore three days later."

"Oh my," said Miss Greyson, turning rather green in the firelight. "How inconsiderate."

"Ever since then," said Wolfson, "Blacktooth's word has been law on the High Seas. Half the scallywags in Augusta are afraid of him, and the other half are downright terri-fied. So you can see, Terror, why they'd be reluctant to join your cause."

"I certainly can," said Hilary. The idea of having bits and pieces of oneself floating about in Queensport Harbor was enough to turn the stomach of even the bravest pirate. "But perhaps Blacktooth is just as proud as Pretty Jack used to be, and just as rusty. Perhaps he won't be prepared."

"And perhaps I'll turn into a cheese sandwich next Thursday," said Jasper. "I'm afraid the odds aren't likely."

Wolfson nodded in agreement. "Blacktooth may be

a scoundrel," he said, "but he's not foolish. If he were, he wouldn't be spending a fortune at the Summerstead shipyard."

Charlie had been leaning against a bench near the fire, but now he sat up straight. "Blacktooth's building a new ship?"

"I don't see why," the gargoyle said. "The *Renegade* is awfully stylish."

"And it's practically unsinkable, isn't it?" Hilary asked. "He can't possibly be abandoning it."

"Unless he's building something even better," Charlie said darkly. "Something that can destroy the *Pigeon* in five seconds flat."

Wolfson shrugged. "No one knows what he's building except the builders themselves," he said, "and they've been paid handsomely not to discuss it. For all the rest of us know, it might not even be a ship. All I can say for sure is that Blacktooth sent a fine treasure chest to the shipbuilders not two days after you delivered your challenge, Terror. Officials from the League have been traveling to the shipyard ever since, although Blacktooth himself hasn't made the journey."

"If you're thinking of sneaking a look," one of Wolfson's mates added, "don't bother. Blacktooth's men are keeping watch. Old Otto here already tried to slip by them, and all he got for his trouble was a nasty lump on the noggin."

Hilary *had* been thinking of sneaking a look, in fact,

but the pirate named Otto wore enough bandages around his head to make her reconsider. In any event, she couldn't afford to linger in Summerstead. "I'd dearly like to know what Blacktooth's up to," she said, "but we've got to make our way back to the Southlands. Our supporters will be waiting for us."

"And they'll be quite lonely until we arrive," Alice said, "since there are only twelve of them."

"Twelve if we're lucky," Hilary corrected her. "If we're not, the only ones who'll greet us at Jasper's bungalow will be the local rabbits, and I don't think they're very good at dueling."

Jasper shook his head sadly. "Indeed they're not," he said. "Their swordplay technique is extremely sloppy."

Wolfson cleared his throat and turned to Hilary. "You're forgetting that I never answered your question, Terror. You asked me if my mates and I would be willing to join you in battle. The fact of the matter is that I like your spirit, and after you were generous enough to rescue us from the navy this afternoon, we can hardly refuse to help you in return. I can only offer twenty pirates to your cause, but I believe we'll be an improvement on the rabbits."

If Hilary hadn't been a pirate, she would have hugged him on the spot. "But you said that challenging Captain Blacktooth was a tricky business!"

"Aye, it is, but pirates are fond of tricks." Wolfson

grinned into the fire. "And if it's a trick played against Rupert Blacktooth and his Mutineer friends, so much the better."

THE NEXT MORNING, after a hearty meal of smoked meat that Hilary didn't care to examine too closely, the *Pigeon* began the long trip back to Wimbly-on-the-Marsh. Since the northern pirates' vessel had been reduced to a few soggy ropes and boards, they had decided to remain in the Northlands until they'd finished repairs on their spare longship. Meanwhile, Wolfson had told Hilary he would do his best to find out exactly what Captain Blacktooth was building at the Summerstead shipyard.

Hilary had hoped that she might encounter a few more friendly pirates on the voyage home, but the North-lands seas were practically deserted, and each pirate ship that came close enough to spot the *Pigeon* soon turned and sailed away as fast as the wind could carry it. The news from the mainland was hardly more encouraging. Charlie swiped a copy of the VNHLP newsletter from a groggery that suddenly became emptier than a plundered treasure chest when Hilary stepped inside, but once they returned to the *Pigeon*, he tore up the paper before she could read it. "It's nothing you'd be interested in," he said, shoving the bits of newsletter into his pocket.

"I don't believe you for a moment," said Hilary. "Even the gargoyle tells better fibs than that." The gargoyle, who was curled up in his Nest, narrowed his eyes at her from under the brim of his hat.

"Well," said Charlie, "if you truly want to know, the *Picaroon*'s been running articles about how cozy the League has gotten with the Navy. Blacktooth's spouting nonsense about a grand new age of cooperation on the High Seas. Pirates and naval officers will soon be sailing side by side, he says, sharing their grog and their gunpowder as they hunt down notorious villains like the Terror of the Southlands. It's enough to make you sick, really."

Hilary had to admit that she felt a little queasy just thinking about it. "I'm surprised at Father," she said. "Everyone knows he hates cooperation nearly as much as he hates pirates."

"But he and Blacktooth both love treasure," the gargoyle pointed out sleepily, "and neither of them likes *you* very much." He gave a dramatic sigh. "It sounds like a beautiful friendship."

"About as beautiful as my old socks," said Charlie.

Hilary quite agreed with him. "I should write a letter to Admiral Curtis," she said. "I'm sure he'd be interested to know that his new adviser is giving out orders behind his back."

"I've already thought of that," said Charlie. "Even if you write to him, he'll never get the letter. Who do you think opens Admiral Curtis's mail?"

As the *Pigeon* sailed south toward Nordholm, Hilary

did her best to squelch all thoughts of plotting pirate captains and villainous admirals. She spent a good deal of time trying to work on her Buccaneers' Code, though her notebook was still mostly empty. "Don't let another pirate frighten you," she murmured, "even if he has two hundred supporters and a penchant for sending his enemies to a watery grave." She tapped her fingers on the ship's wheel. "And don't read the *Picaroon*."

"Also," said the gargoyle, "never let a budgerigar sit on your head. His claws might get stuck in your hat."

Miss Greyson poked her head out from between the bookshop shelves. "May I contribute some advice?" she asked. "Never let a pirate alphabetize your history books, for he's sure to make a mess of things."

"Nonsense," said Jasper. "I've always thought the alphabet was highly overrated."

Hilary frowned. "I don't think I'm going to write any of these down."

"Terror!" called Alice. She was leaning far over the ship's rail, and her petticoats flapped ferociously in the breeze. "Isn't that Tilbury Park ahead?"

Hilary squinted up at the great white house on the hill, with its starched-stiff columns and perfectly clipped hedges. She'd much preferred the way the grounds had looked when they'd been trampled by pirates. "I can sail further out to sea if you'd like," she said. "We don't have to go anywhere near the place."

"But that's not what I'd like at all!" said Alice. "Tilbury Park is where the Mutineers have been meeting, isn't it? I don't know about you, but I'm simply dying to know what Captain Blacktooth is building in that shipyard. If we listen at Mrs. Tilbury's windows, perhaps we can find out what he's got planned."

Hilary had endured far too much time with the Mutineers as it was, and she wasn't sure she wanted to spend one more moment in their company. Still, if she could discover how Blacktooth was planning to defeat her in battle, she'd be far less likely to meet Pretty Jack Winter's fate. "The Mutineers might not even be meeting today," Hilary said, "and we don't have much time to spare. But I suppose if we're lucky, we might learn something useful."

"Oh, good!" Alice performed a twirl that would have drawn rapturous applause from the dance mistress at Miss Pimm's. "I knew you'd agree with me, Terror."

Hilary laughed. "Well, I haven't said yes yet."

"Hold on a moment," said Charlie. He shoved aside the magic coin he'd been staring down for the past half hour. "Aren't the queen's guards watching the house?"

"There's only one guard," said Hilary, "and he's apparently not the crispest wafer in the tin. Miss Pimm complains about him in every letter she writes to me. He's supposed to be keeping an eye on Mrs. Tilbury, but Miss Pimm says he spends most of his time playing dominoes and painting with oils."

"In that case," said Charlie, "I'm all for snooping. It sounds like a grand idea."

"Are you sure it's allowed?" Miss Greyson asked. "By the pirate league, I mean. Will they disqualify you from battle if you're caught spying on your adversary?"

Hilary hadn't consulted the seventeenth edition of *Leading the League*, but she was fairly sure she knew what it had to say on the subject. "I don't think we'll be disqualified," she said. "Lying and cheating are heartily encouraged, after all. Blacktooth's certainly done plenty of both already."

"And we won't get caught," the gargoyle added. "I can hop very quickly when I need to."

"Then it's settled," said Hilary. "We'll spy on Tilbury Park. But we won't be able to stay long, and we mustn't catch the Mutineers' attention. They may not be allowed to harm us before the battle, but if they have a chance to make us thoroughly miserable in the meantime, I'm quite sure they'll take it."

"IT'S NOT FAIR," the gargoyle complained. "When I said I wanted to come along, I didn't realize I'd be up a tree."

"If it's any consolation, we're *all* up a tree," Hilary told him, "and if you don't stop poking me, we might all fall out of it."

"All right." The gargoyle withdrew his tail from Hilary's side. "But I still say that a tree is no place for pirates. I think I just sat on a pinecone."

"I'd prefer that to sitting in the Dungeons," said Charlie, "which is where we'll all end up if the royal guard hears
us. Have you spotted anything yet, Alice? I can hardly see
my own nose from down here."

On the branch above Hilary's, the pine needles rustled
as Alice peered out toward Tilbury Park. "Someone's just
lit a lantern in one of the upstairs rooms," she whispered.
"I suppose it might be a maid, but . . ." Alice scrambled
higher into the tree, sending bits of bark raining down on
Hilary's hat. "Terror, could you pass me your spyglass?"

Alice's hand appeared in front of Hilary's face, and
Hilary stuck the spyglass into it. After a moment, both
the hand and the spyglass vanished up into the branches.
"That's better," said Alice cheerfully. "Yes, there's a maid in
the room, but I think she's talking to someone. . . . Ah! It's
that grumpy old turnip herself."

"You mean Mrs. Tilbury?"

"That's what I said, isn't it? Now the maid's leaving, and
Mrs. Tilbury is taking something from a shelf."

"A magic piece?" the gargoyle asked eagerly. "A stolen
jewel? A fancy hat?"

Alice groaned. "It's a book. And she's settling down
with it. It's probably one of those dreadfully dull Improving Works about budgets or household management."

Charlie shifted on his tree limb. "I'm not spending an
hour in a tree just to learn about the top ten ways to yell
at your servants."

"If Mrs. Tilbury spends her spare evenings reading Improving Works, she's even more villainous than I thought." Hilary's legs were sore from crouching on her branch, and she wished she could move about, but she had one arm around the gargoyle and the other around the tree trunk, and she wasn't about to let go of either one. "In any case, if she's just going to sit there, there's no point in watching her. We might as well head back to the ship before Jasper and Miss Greyson change their minds and decide to join us."

"Wait!" Alice whispered. "Someone's just come in! Quite a few someones, in fact. There's Philomena, and she's got two gentlemen with her. One's that horrid smug boy who sneered at you on Gunpowder Island, Terror."

"Oliver Sanderson." Hilary nearly forgot all about being sore. "Honestly, that boy is as persistent as a cockroach."

"That," said the gargoyle, "is an insult to cockroaches. They can be surprisingly pleasant once you get to know them."

"Then they're a good deal nicer than Oliver." Hilary's legs wobbled beneath her, and she wondered how much longer she could keep her feet balanced on the branch. "Who's the other gentleman, Alice?"

Alice sighed. "My infuriating brother, naturally. Oh, I wish I could hear what they're saying! I don't suppose they'll open the window on an evening as chilly as this one. Perhaps I could shimmy up to the roof somehow, or—"

Quite without warning, Hilary's legs slid out from under her. "Blast!" she cried. She landed hard on the branch below, which made an alarming cracking noise as it met the seat of her breeches. Her hat snagged itself on a pine bough, dangled there for a moment, and fell to the ground.

"Terror!" Charlie whispered. "Are you all right?"

Hilary brushed her hair from her face; her fingers were sticky with sap. "I believe I've scraped my pride," she said, "but at least I didn't drop the gargoyle. Oh, gargoyle, are you hurt?"

The gargoyle wriggled out from under her arm and twitched his ears experimentally. "I'm fine," he said, "considering. But I don't think you should be worrying about me." He jabbed his tail toward Tilbury Park. "You should be worrying about *him*."

"Oh dear." Hilary watched through the branches as a lantern bobbed across the lawn in their direction. "I suppose there's a royal guard attached to the end of that lantern."

The gargoyle nodded. "I told you trees were trouble."

"What's this?" The lantern stopped at the bottom of the tree, and the guard bent over to examine Hilary's hat. "How curious," he said. "I don't believe hats usually grow on trees."

Hilary held her breath and tried her best to be invisible.

"Aha!" cried the guard, peering up at them. "I thought I heard someone shout. What are you all doing up there? A tree is no place for pirates."

"I told them that, sir," the gargoyle said, "but they wouldn't listen."

The guard shielded his eyes with a paint-smudged hand; Hilary supposed Miss Pimm had been right about the oils. "Well," he said, "you'll have to leave. This land is the private property of a convict, you know. She's difficult enough to keep an eye on even when bands of pirates aren't roaming about the place." He scratched his nose with a cadmium-yellow finger. "I really should send you to the Dungeons."

"There's no need to do that," Charlie said quickly. "Just think of all the paperwork you'd have to fill out: arrest forms, transportation forms, and whatever sort of form they've got for finding pirates in trees."

"All that work would distract you from keeping watch over Mrs. Tilbury," Hilary pointed out. "And your job is only to keep her from leaving the property, isn't that right? I'm sure you're not obliged to deal with trespassers as well."

The guard frowned. "Perhaps I should consult Mrs. Tilbury—"

"No!" cried Hilary, Charlie, Alice, and the gargoyle all at once.

"I'd rather not," the guard admitted. "She's terribly critical—always saying there's not enough orange paint in my sunsets. And she cheats at dominoes."

Alice leaned down from her branch and cupped her hand around Hilary's ear. "I thought you ought to know," she whispered, "that I just looked back at Mrs. Tilbury's room. She and Nicholas are still there, but Philomena and Oliver are gone."

Hilary's heart had barely enough time to sink before a door slammed shut somewhere nearby, and two more lanterns appeared on the lawn. "Who's there?" Philomena called out. "Where's that dratted guard?"

The guard stiffened and turned toward Philomena. "I'm over here, Miss Tilbury," he said. "I'm afraid there are pirates in the evergreen border."

It was a shame, Hilary thought, that she couldn't see the face Philomena made in response. "Thank you for informing me," Philomena said at last. "I appreciate your help, but I mustn't keep you from your work. Mr. Sanderson and I are perfectly capable of taking care of pirates."

"Blast," Charlie muttered. "Now we're in for it."

Hilary tucked the gargoyle into her canvas bag and scrambled down out of the tree. "I'll handle Philomena," she told the others, "and Oliver too, if I can manage it. There's no point in all of us getting caught."

Charlie started to say something about not being left behind if he could help it, but Hilary had already plucked up her pirate hat and walked over to Philomena, who was shivering in her silk gown. "It's a beautiful evening, isn't it?" Hilary said. "I was just doing some stargazing. I'd heard the trees at Tilbury Park have remarkable views."

Philomena smiled, not exactly sweetly. "They do," she said, "but they're terribly full of pests. Mother really should tell the gardener to do something about it." She brushed past Hilary and walked toward the tree where Charlie and Alice were hiding. "Don't let Miss Westfield leave, Oliver."

"I wouldn't dream of it." Oliver grabbed Hilary's braid and tugged it hard. "It's been ages since we've had a chat, and we've got so much to discuss. Your father says you've been more of a nuisance than ever."

"Did that school for impudent boys issue an apology to the kingdom when they set you loose?" Hilary asked. "Or did they simply place a warning in the newspaper, the way they do when a wild beast escapes from the carnival?" She reached for her cutlass, but Oliver shook his head.

"You know you're not allowed to harm us, Miss Westfield, just as we're not allowed to harm you. Believe me, I'm as disappointed as you are."

"Then I'd appreciate it if you'd let go of my hair." Hilary pulled her braid loose from Oliver's fist. There was no chance she'd be allowed to linger at Tilbury Park, but if only Charlie and Alice could stay hidden, perhaps they'd still be able to learn something about the Mutineers' plans. "Why don't we come to an agreement?" she asked. "I'll return to my ship, you'll return to your villainous deeds, and we can all spend the rest of the evening in peace."

"Don't be silly, Miss Westfield!" Philomena raised her lantern and peered up into the tree. "You've been thoughtful enough to call on us, and the least we can do is entertain you. Now, where's that dreadful boy you drag about with you wherever you go? I believe I spy his boot."

Charlie jumped down out of the tree, keeping one hand on his cutlass. He looked from Philomena to Oliver and back again. "I'm not surprised you two are friends," he said. "After all, you've got plenty in common."

"If you mean we both have the best interests of the kingdom at heart," said Philomena, "then you're not entirely dull-witted after all." She turned back to Hilary. "Are there any more pirates hidden away on our grounds, Miss West-field? Or haven't you managed to find anyone else to join your crew?"

"It's only me and Charlie," said Hilary, looking up at the top of the tree where Alice was perched, "and we don't need to be entertained for a moment longer. You can walk us to our ship if you'd like."

Philomena cast her lantern light on Hilary's face. "I'd better make sure you're telling the truth," she said. "I know pirates are fond of spinning tales, and Mama will make my life a misery if I let you spin one around me." Philomena held out her hand, and Oliver passed her the golden gob-let she'd had with her on Gunpowder Island. "There's no need to look so accusing, Miss Westfield," she said. "It's a family heirloom. Now, magic, if there are any other spies sneaking around Tilbury Park, please bring them here at once."

"Don't you dare!" said Hilary. She lunged forward and reached out to knock the magic piece from Philomena's hands. Just as her fingers brushed the goblet's rim, however, Oliver stepped in front of her and shoved her to the ground.

"My apologies," he said, though Hilary was sure he didn't mean any such thing. "That wasn't very gentlemanly of me, was it?"

Hilary glared at him and scrambled to her feet, but the goblet was already working its enchantment. A gust of cold wind swirled around them, rustling Philomena's skirts and making the gargoyle shiver. Then the wind shook the branches of the pine tree, its trunk swayed like a ship's mast during a storm, and Alice flew from the treetop, tumbling curls over petticoats. With a shout loud enough to alert half the Northlands, she landed at Philomena's feet.

Charlie cursed, and Hilary ran to Alice's side. "I'm so sorry," Hilary said in a rush; "I couldn't stop her. Are you all right?"

Alice blinked up at her. "I'm not entirely sure about this," she said in a small voice, "but I don't believe one's arm is supposed to snap quite so loudly when one lands on it."

"Blast it all; that doesn't sound good." Hilary tore off her coat and fashioned a sort of sling around Alice's arm, the way she'd once seen Miss Greyson do after Jasper had been injured in a duel. Philomena stood above them with her hands pressed over her mouth; she had dropped the golden goblet, and she didn't seem to be in any hurry to retrieve it. "I hope you're pleased with yourself," Hilary told her.

Oliver looked down at Alice and stuffed his hands in his pockets. "I thought we weren't supposed to hurt them," he said.

"Miss Feathering climbed a tree," Philomena snapped. "The wind knocked her out of it. It had nothing to do with me, and I'll thank you to remember that in front of Mama." Her voice was starting to shake, and with her shoulders hunched against the cold, she didn't look much like a pin-pricked and poisonous High Society lady anymore.

"You know," said Hilary, "your mother may be vile, but that doesn't mean you've got to be horrid as well. You've got a choice in the matter, haven't you? If you left the Mutineers and worked as hard as you could, you might even learn to be kind someday."

Philomena blinked in the lantern light. She stood up straighter. "I assure you, Miss Westfield, that I am perfectly capable of thinking for myself. And unlike you," she said, turning away, "I don't make foolish decisions."

Alice pulled at Hilary's sleeve. "Terror," she said softly, "I want to go back to the ship now."

"Of course." Hilary put her arm around Alice and helped her up from the ground. "I'm sure Miss Tilbury will let us leave without making a fuss." She gave Philomena her most fearsome glare, but Philomena wasn't watching. Instead she was staring up at the lit window of Tilbury Park, where Nicholas Feathering stood with his face pressed against the glass.

"Don't think we'll let you go so easily again," Oliver was saying to Charlie. "Isn't that right, Miss Tilbury?"

"Oh, be quiet!" Philomena shoved Oliver aside and stormed back toward the house.

Charlie shook his head as Oliver hurried away after Philomena. "You know," he said, "I think she knocked the sneer straight off his face."

"And she knocked my stomach straight into my toes." Alice winced. "She's going to be an awful Enchantress."

"She won't be an Enchantress at all," said Hilary firmly. "The next time I see her, I'll let the gargoyle sharpen his teeth on her anklebones, and I don't care who knows it." She looked back up at the mansion window, but someone inside had drawn the curtains. "Now," she said, "let's get back to the ship. Miss Greyson will need plenty of time to give us all a proper scolding."

Dear Hilary,

I'm sorry to hear that the Mutineers are still being so bothersome, though I can't say I'm surprised. If they suddenly abandoned villainy in favor of a more suitable hobby, like carpentry or butterfly collecting, I believe I would faint on the spot. (And you know how awful I am at fainting. When a toad peered out from under the embroidery mistress's skirts last term, I was the only girl in the classroom who didn't fall into a swoon.)

I would like to tell you that my magic lessons have been going well, but I'm afraid that would be an enormous fib. Truthfully, Miss Pimm has lost her patience with me five times in the past five days alone. To make matters worse, when she consulted her magical instruments yesterday evening, she discovered that she is no longer able to get even the

slightest glimpse of the Mutineers or their activities.
(You know how Miss Pimm prides herself on finding
out what everyone is up to, so I'm sure you can
imagine how injured she feels.) She says that trying
to uncover what is happening at Tilbury Park is
like peering into a thick gray fog. Perhaps her ill
health is to blame, but I fear that someone—a very
powerful someone indeed—may be interfering with her
observations. Although I don't have any proof of it,
I am sure Philomena is responsible, and the thought
has made me more flustered than ever. When I tried
to cast an enchantment to harvest plants from the
garden, all the carrots sprouted legs and hurried out
the gate before I had any hope of capturing them.
No wonder Miss Pimm has lost her patience: while
Philomena spends her days creating impressive fogs, I
am busy chasing vegetables through the town square.

 Will you come for tea as soon as you get back to
Little Herring Cove? I can't wait to hear all about
your travels in the Northlands. I know that Miss
Pimm is eager to see you as well, for she has been
saving a special plate of spiders for the gargoyle,
much to the dismay of the housemaids.

 Your friend,
 Claire

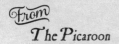

PIRATE REBELS GATHER NEAR PEMBERTON.
Only one month remains until our noble Captain Rupert
Blacktooth faces the treacherous Terror of the Southlands in
battle. The Terror and her supporters have begun to gather in
Wimbly-on-the-Marsh at the home of the freelance pirate Jasper
Fletcher, who is not as bold or as fashionable as he believes
himself to be. Reliable sources whisper that if the people
arriving in Little Herring Cove are the most impressive pirates
the Terror can locate, Captain Blacktooth has no reason to be
worried about the outcome of next month's battle.

☙☙

SHOW YOUR SUPPORT! Have you composed a
rousing chantey in celebration of Captain Blacktooth's brave
deeds? Have you sculpted a flattering likeness of his face or
written a sonnet in his honor? Send your presidential tributes
to the Picaroon! We will share our favorites with Captain
Blacktooth himself. If your submission amuses him, he may
invite you to dine with him on board the *Renegade*.

☙☙

TAKE NOTICE. Captain Blacktooth wishes to remind
all members of the VNHLP that anyone overheard speaking
kindly of Pirate Hilary Westfield or her companions will meet
a most unsavory end.

CHAPTER SEVEN

"**THANK YOU ALL** for coming," Hilary said to the pirates who'd gathered in Jasper's salon. They perched on top of fruit crates, swung in rope hammocks, and wedged themselves into every spare corner of the small room. Mr. Flintlock, who had somehow contrived to look larger than ever, stood outside and peered in through an open window to avoid bumping his head on the rafters. "Are you quite comfortable sitting on that soup tureen?" Hilary asked Mr. Partridge.

Partridge wobbled on his overturned bowl. "Of course, Terror."

"Then we might as well begin." Hilary glanced around

at the pirates' faces; nearly everyone looked nervous. "Cannonball Jack, how many supporters did you and your crewmates gather?"

Cannonball Jack sat up straight in his hammock and mopped his brow with his coat sleeve. "Numbers be a tricky thing, Terror," he said. "Always floppin' about like fish, they be, and ye never know quite how many ye've got—"

"It's three, I'm afraid," Lucy Worthington interrupted. "We only found three people who were willing to join up, Terror. One is a pirate apprentice who's very keen to go into battle, though he doesn't seem to care much which side he's on. Another is an old mate of Cannonball Jack's."

"Nine-Fingered Fergus came out o' retirement just fer us," said Cannonball Jack proudly, "once I promised him a tin o' me famous shortbread."

"And who's the third?" Hilary asked.

"Mr. Partridge's nephew," said Worthington. "I believe his name is Godfrey."

"That's right," said Partridge. "He's a good lad, though he doesn't like loud noises. He gets a terrible twitch whenever there's an explosion nearby."

Jasper raised an eyebrow. "He sounds like just the fellow to fire our cannons."

"I'm very grateful to Godfrey," said Hilary quickly, "and to the others as well. Now, Mr. Twigget, how many pirates did your mates recruit?"

Mr. Twigget looked as though he would prefer to slip

through the cracks in the floorboards. "None, Terror," he said. "All the pirates we met were too frightened to say a word in your favor. We did bring you a bucket of haddock, though."

"That's very kind of you," said Hilary. If the situation didn't improve quickly, she would have to consider sending the haddock into battle. "And Mr. Stanley? I don't suppose you managed to find two hundred eager pirates, did you?"

"Not exactly," said Mr. Stanley. "But one scallywag did agree to join us after we catered his birthday party. Mr. Slaughter produced a scrumptious chocolate torte for the occasion."

Mr. Marrow folded his thin, pale hands. "Gathering supporters was a harder task than we'd expected, Terror," he said. "It's not that the scallywags aren't fond of you—"

"It's just that they're fonder of keeping their heads attached to their necks," said Hilary. "I know. And I can't say I blame them one bit."

"We met plenty of folks who are still grateful to you for giving them their magic pieces," Mr. Slaughter pointed out. "They remember you well. But they're farmers and librarians and banking clerks—not pirates. Captain Blacktooth's warnings have been remarkably effective."

The room grew quiet as each and every pirate tried not to think too hard about Captain Blacktooth.

"Wait a moment!" said Worthington. "The Terror hasn't told us how many pirates she's recruited. I'm sure she had more luck than we did." She smiled up at Hilary. "How many is it, Terror? Eighty? One hundred?"

"Actually," said Hilary, "it's twenty. We had nearly as much trouble as the rest of you. We rescued a band of northern pirates from a naval attack, though, and they'll be joining us from Summerstead as soon as they're able."

"They're very fearsome," Alice added. "They're fortunate, too, for they're allowed to use swords at the moment." She looked glumly at her broken arm and even more glumly at Miss Greyson. To no one's surprise, Miss Greyson had been furious when she'd learned what had happened at Tilbury Park. She had scolded everyone from the gargoyle to the queen as she wrapped Alice's arm in bandages and used her magic crochet hook to encourage the bone to mend. She had even declared that Alice should be sent back to Feathering Keep before any more damage could be done. Alice, however, had proven to be so stubborn that not even a governess could remove her from the *Pigeon*. When they'd finally returned to the cabin they shared, Hilary had given Alice her beloved old copy of *Treasure Island*, though she knew it was hardly enough to make amends for the whole affair.

"Well," said Cannonball Jack at last, "twenty pirates be a good deal better than three." He looked over at Charlie, who was carving tally marks on the bungalow wall. "How many of us are there in all, lad? I see ye've been keepin' count."

Charlie set down his knife and studied the tally marks. "Forty," he said, "not including the Terror, of course. Forty-one if you count the gargoyle."

"Of course you count the gargoyle!" cried the gargoyle. "I'm the most fearsome one of all—or has anyone else here bitten a Mutineer?" He looked around. "I didn't think so."

"Forty," said Miss Greyson, "is a perfectly respectable number. I'm sure most pirates spend half their lifetimes gathering a crew that large."

"It may be respectable, but it's nowhere near two hundred." Hilary slumped lower in her hammock. "Captain Blacktooth won't even get his chance to send us all to the bottom of the sea if we have to forfeit the battle."

"You said the pirates you rescued in the Northlands are loyal to you, Terror," Flintlock mused from outside the window. "What if we attacked other pirate ships and then rescued the sailors on board? I could be the cannonball!"

"Attacking the pirates we want to befriend?" Jasper said drily. "What could possibly go wrong?"

"I'd rather have a sea slug in me ear," said Cannonball Jack.

"We're not going to attack anyone," said Hilary, "and we're certainly not going to trick them into giving us their loyalty. We're supposed to be very nearly honorable, aren't we? Better than Blacktooth and his mates?"

"So we are," said Flintlock hastily. "My apologies, Terror. It was just an idea."

"That's all right, Mr. Flintlock. Ideas are exactly what we need." Hilary looked around the room. "If anyone else has an idea about how to gather up more pirates, I'd very much like to hear it."

Hilary waited, but no one volunteered a suggestion. Fitzwilliam didn't even dare to chirp. "What do ye say we meet again tomorrow?" said Cannonball Jack. "The Terror be sure to have a plan by then."

A hearty round of cheers shook the bungalow, and the other pirates all agreed that the wisest thing to do would be to leave the planning to Hilary. With the matter settled at last, they pulled on their coats and wandered out to the garden to practice their swordplay—all except Charlie. "Do you really think you'll be able to come up with a plan by tomorrow?" he asked quietly.

"Truthfully," Hilary said, "I believe I've got a better chance of convincing Captain Blacktooth to join the Royal Augusta Water Ballet."

Charlie laughed. "If you can manage that," he said, "then you deserve to rule the League."

BY THE TIME Hilary arrived at Miss Pimm's Finishing School for Delicate Ladies that afternoon, she had splattered her breeches with mud and stubbed her toe on a cobblestone, but she still didn't know how in the world she was supposed to convince more than a hundred additional pirates to join her in battle. The gargoyle had tossed out suggestions from the comfort of the canvas bag as she walked, but Hilary didn't think that a lifetime supply of spiders would tempt many scallywags to take up arms against Captain Blacktooth.

The school door opened promptly when Hilary knocked on it, and a girl in a gray woolen dress and a green cardigan gave Hilary a well-rehearsed curtsy. "Welcome to Miss Pimm's," she said. Then she lifted her eyes to Hilary's face. "Oh!" she said, taking a step back. "It's Hilary Westfield!"

"It is," the gargoyle agreed. "Not to mention her gargoyle."

"I'm Rosie Hatter," the girl said. "I'm sure you don't remember me, Miss Westfield, but we used to be classmates. I very much admired how you always stood up for Miss Dupree." Rosie lowered her voice. "Especially on the day we had fish sticks for lunch."

Hilary didn't remember seeing Rosie in the crowd of schoolgirls during the few days she'd spent at Miss Pimm's, but then again, she had spent most of her time attempting to escape. "I haven't been able to eat a fish stick ever since," she told Rosie. "I always worry that Philomena will find out somehow and send it flying into my lap."

"So do I," said Rosie. "I wish Cook wouldn't insist on serving them every Wednesday. In any case, it's lovely to see you—but I heard you were a pirate now." She looked down at Hilary's breeches, then up at her feathered hat.

"And I see you truly are one. What brings you back here?"

"Miss Pimm and Miss Dupree invited me for tea, but I'm afraid I'm late. The roads were muddier than I expected, and a good pirate never arrives anywhere promptly."

"Naturally." Rosie held the door open for Hilary and took her hat and coat. "Should I take your cutlass, too?" she asked. "We won't learn the proper etiquette for weaponry until next term."

"I'd prefer to keep it with me, if you don't mind," said Hilary, "but I'll be sure to take care with it. If I accidentally puncture any schoolgirls, Miss Pimm will be absolutely livid."

Claire was already waiting in Miss Pimm's office when Hilary entered, and she leaped up so energetically that she overturned the sugar cubes. "I'm so glad you've made it back at last," she said, crunching a sugar cube under her shoe as she gave Hilary a hug. "It can be very worrying to have a pirate for a friend. Most of the other people I know don't stumble into battles nearly so often."

Hilary shook Miss Pimm's hand and attempted to balance a steaming cup of tea on its saucer as she settled into her chair. Meanwhile, Claire took the gargoyle from Hilary's bag and placed him in her lap, where he immediately offered up his head to be scratched. "If I hadn't carved him myself," said Miss Pimm, "I'd swear he was part foxhound." She shook her head and placed two plates on her desk next to the tea tray, one piled high with cakes, the other filled with tastefully arranged spiders. "Now, Terror, you must tell us how your work against the Mutineers is progressing. Spare no details, please, for when I don't know absolutely everything, I become quite irritable."

"There's nothing like a good scratch behind the ears to make you feel better," the gargoyle told her. "You should try it sometime."

"Perhaps I shall." Miss Pimm stirred a sugar cube into her tea. "Please begin, Terror."

Hilary would have much preferred to chat about anything other than piracy—the spring weather, for example, or the royal croquet team's recent victory—but Miss Pimm's commands were the sort that couldn't be ignored. She told Miss Pimm and Claire about the Ornery Clam and Captain Wolfson, about Captain Blacktooth's warnings to the pirate league and Admiral Westfield's orders to the Royal Navy. She even reluctantly described the disastrous visit they'd paid to Tilbury Park, for she suspected Miss Pimm would manage to find out about it sooner or later.

Hilary decided not to mention that Charlie had begun to carry a magic coin in his pocket, however, or that he often looked at it as though it might bite off his nose at any moment. That was Charlie's news to tell—or, knowing Charlie, to bury deep in the ground and never speak of again. In any case, it was hardly as noteworthy as the news that the Terror of the Southlands was still several pirates short of an army and likely to be run out of the kingdom in a few weeks' time. "And that's if I'm fortunate," said Hilary. "If I'm not, Captain Blacktooth will do to me exactly what he did to Pretty Jack Winter."

Claire leaned forward in her chair. "What did he do to Pretty Jack Winter?"

"Trust me," said the gargoyle, "you don't want to know. Pass the spiders, please."

"Oh dear." Claire turned pale. "This is all my fault. If Miss Pimm and I hadn't placed that advertisement, you wouldn't be in this mess."

Hilary shook her head. "I was the one who agreed to challenge Blacktooth," she said. "I thought I could help you become the Enchantress and squash the Mutineers once and for all, but I haven't even come close." She kicked off her boots and stared down at her socks. "That horrible scallywag at the Ornery Clam tried to scare me off; perhaps he was right all along. Perhaps I should turn this whole battle over to Jasper and surrender myself to Mother and her dressmaker."

"That," said the gargoyle, "is the silliest thing I've ever heard. If you give up and go home, I'll bite you myself."

"And I won't stop him," Miss Pimm said sternly. "A Miss Pimm's girl does not simply slink away when the situation looks grim, and I suspect a good pirate doesn't either. Is that correct?"

Hilary felt her cheeks flush. "Yes," she said, "it is. I truly don't want to give up or slink away, but I've got a houseful of pirates waiting for me back in Wimbly-on-the-Marsh, and I've got no idea what to tell them. What if we can't defeat the Mutineers? What if they actually manage to take over the kingdom?"

"If we don't try to stop them," said Claire, "then they certainly *will* take over, and your father and his friends will have all the treasure they've ever dreamed of. I know you'll be perfectly miserable if that happens, and from what I know of the Mutineers, the rest of the kingdom is likely to be miserable as well."

"Except for High Society." The gargoyle grimaced. "They'll all be as happy as boulders once the Mutineers are in charge."

"Not everyone in High Society is as unscrupulous as the Tilburys," Miss Pimm reminded him. "I can tell you for a fact that most of the girls here would prefer not to see Philomena become the next Enchantress. Truthfully, they seem quite relieved that she's no longer a student."

Claire nodded. "Besides, I've told them all about your adventures, Hilary, and they've been very encouraging. I believe they like a good pirate yarn almost as much as the gargoyle does. They think you're sure to defeat the Muti-neers."

"That's awfully kind of them," said Hilary. "I wish there

were a few more pirates who thought so. If only I could fill my crew with finishing-school girls, then I wouldn't have to forfeit to Captain Blacktooth."

The gargoyle chewed on a spider. "Why don't you?"

Hilary froze with her hand halfway to the plate of cakes. "What?"

"Why don't you fill your crew with finishing-school girls?" the gargoyle asked. "We've spent the past two months looking for your supporters, and it sounds to me like we've finally found them."

Miss Pimm remarked that this was a ridiculous notion, but Hilary hardly noticed or cared. She thought hard as she bit into a tea cake that tasted alarmingly of lavender. "Perhaps it's not so ridiculous," she said. "All the girls here have magic pieces, don't they?"

"Most of them do," said Claire. She was beginning to sound excited. "They can all use bows and arrows, they're very good swimmers, and they know how to ward off gentlemen with dubious morals—which is exactly what Blacktooth and his mates are." She smiled at Hilary. "They might be exactly the pirates we need."

"Nonsense!" Miss Pimm set down her teacup. "Finishing-school girls are not pirates!"

"Daughters of naval admirals aren't pirates either!" Hilary pointed out. "At least, they aren't traditionally. And neither are gargoyles or governesses—or Enchantresses, for that matter—but I think we've all done well enough for ourselves on the High Seas."

Every inch of Miss Pimm seemed to bristle. "Hilary Westfield," she said, "are you implying that *I* am a pirate?"

"You took everyone's treasure and hid it away for centuries, didn't you?" Hilary asked. "When it was threatened, you set off in your ship to capture the villains. You're terribly fearsome, and you grew up on Gunpowder Island." Hilary crossed her arms. "Miss Pimm, I believe you're the most piratical person I've ever met."

Claire gasped. Miss Pimm, however, said nothing. She peeled the doily from her tea cake with meticulous care and ate the entire pastry in silence, crumb by crumb. When she had finished, she brushed off her fingers and looked straight at Hilary. "It's true that I have been entirely piratical for most of my life," she said, "but I had rather hoped that no one would notice."

Hilary grinned. "Then you'll let your students join our crew?"

"The choice must be up to each of them," Miss Pimm replied. "I won't force any of my girls to go into battle. However, I won't forbid it, either. The fresh air and exercise will be good for them, and I am sure they have the fortitude to stand up to Captain Blacktooth." She gave the smallest of smiles. "If they can survive a term in these halls, they can certainly survive a few days on a pirate ship."

"I'll spread the word at once!" said Claire. "I'll arrange a meeting for tomorrow morning. You can rally the girls to your cause, Hilary, and if they agree to join your crew, we can begin holding piracy lessons right away."

"And making hats," the gargoyle added. "Every pirate needs a good hat."

"I only hope they'll be willing to meet with me," Hilary said. "Most of the scallywags I've met recently won't even look me in the eye."

"I'm sure you'll have nothing to worry about." Claire bent her little finger elegantly as she lifted her teacup to her lips. "You're a very impressive pirate, but it takes more than the Terror of the Southlands to frighten the delicate ladies of Augusta."

A Petition
to all
Young Ladies of Quality!

Protect your Kingdom from the Dangers of
Tyranny, Corruption, and Poor Manners!

Wield your Crochet Hooks against those
who dare to threaten the
Queen and the Rule of Law!

Draw back your Bowstrings
to show your Loyalty
to the Enchantress and the
Terror of the Southlands!

Become a Pirate!

All interested parties shall be gratefully received.
Please gather in the main hallway tomorrow morning at ten o'clock.

QUEEN EMBARKS ON ROYAL VISIT

QUEENSPORT, AUGUSTA—Queen Adelaide departed this morning on her yearly springtime trip to the southern kingdoms, where she will spend the next month discussing everything from treaties to table tennis with foreign rulers and other frightfully important individuals. Traditionally, this trip allows Augusta to improve its relationships with other kingdoms while also giving the queen and her advisers a pleasant vacation from the mud and slush of Queensport. In previous years, Queen Adelaide has been thoughtful enough to bring back crates of foreign treats to share with her loyal subjects, though no one has forgotten the scandal that erupted only four years ago when a greedy royal adviser devoured an entire crate of chocolates during the voyage home.

Queen Adelaide and her staff are reported to be traveling on her personal ship, HMS *Benevolence*. Several senior naval commanders, including Admiral George Curtis, are also accompanying the queen to ensure her safety. Some people fear that Queensport Harbor will be left open to a pirate attack while Admiral Curtis is away, but the admiral's adviser, James Westfield, says that there is no cause for concern. "The city of Queensport is safer than ever," Westfield told reporters earlier today. "In fact, I shall be keeping a close eye on the harbor myself until Admiral Curtis returns."

Westfield also shrugged aside rumors that the Very Nearly Honorable League of Pirates has threatened to attack the royal city if the queen does not agree to its demands. "I doubt the rumors are true," he said, "and if they are, I'm confident that the queen will make wise decisions to prevent an attack from happening. The only real danger comes from freelance pirates, who are well known to be both untrustworthy and unpredictable."

Queen Adelaide will return to Augusta next month, when she will judge the upcoming battle between Captain Rupert Blacktooth and Pirate Hilary Westfield—an event sure to be the high point of the spring social calendar.

CHAPTER EIGHT

"**D**O YOU REALLY think this is a good idea?" Charlie asked for the third time that morning. He had asked it the first time when the carriage from Miss Pimm's pulled up at Jasper's bungalow, causing all the pirates in residence to draw their swords and advance upon the trembling driver until Hilary rushed outside to stop them. And he had asked it for a second time as the carriage carried them up the Pemberton road, making their teeth chatter as they bounced over the paving stones. Now that they were finally standing in front of Miss Pimm's, he sounded less certain than ever.

"It *is* a good idea," said Hilary as she made her way

through the gate and up the front path. "You'll see for yourself in a moment. When we step into the hall, there are sure to be dozens of girls just waiting for their chance to become pirates." She looked back at Charlie, who was still standing on the other side of the gate. "Aren't you coming?"

"Maybe I should wait outside," said Charlie. "You don't really need me here, do you, Terror?"

"Of course I need you!" said Hilary. "You may be the only pirate on the High Seas who can teach a gaggle of schoolgirls to wield cutlasses without shredding their skirts to ribbons."

Charlie looked around as though he was searching for an argument, but Hilary knew he wouldn't find one. He was the finest swordsman on the *Pigeon*, after all, and even some of the more barnacled old pirates in the kingdom had begun to write to him for dueling advice. "Can't the gargoyle teach them instead?" he asked.

"I can't," said the gargoyle, poking his head out of Hilary's bag. "I'm going to teach the shouting lessons."

Charlie wrinkled his brow. "Shouting lessons?"

"That's right," said the gargoyle. "How to say 'Arr!' and 'Shiver me timbers!' That sort of thing."

"He's very enthusiastic about it," Hilary said. "I know you're not, Charlie, but I'd be grateful to have my first mate by my side. After all, finishing school can be awfully dangerous. What if the embroidery mistress captures me and makes me sew my initials onto all my handkerchiefs?"

At last, Charlie smiled. "All right," he said. "I'm sure I can manage to fend off an embroidery mistress."

Hilary knocked on the door, as she always did when she paid Miss Pimm a visit. This time, however, the door didn't open promptly. In fact, it didn't open at all, not even when Hilary knocked a second time. She tried to peer through the windows into the main hall, but all she could see was a good deal of dust that refused to come off the glass when she rubbed at it with her sleeve. "Perhaps we're early," she said, though the clock in the market square had just struck ten.

"Or maybe the schoolgirls have forgotten our visit," said Charlie—a bit too hopefully, Hilary thought.

Before she could knock again, however, the door creaked open halfway and Claire stuck her head out. "I'm so sorry to have kept you waiting!" she said. "Miss Pimm would be horrified if she knew. I've been trying to gather up your audience, but we've run into a sort of snag, and— oh!" She curtsied to Charlie. "Hello, Pirate Dove! Hilary didn't tell me you'd be coming, but I'm very glad you did."

Charlie looked down at his knees, which seemed to be locked in place. "Thank you," he said, mostly to his kneecaps. "Er, how's the Enchantressing going?"

"It's a bit dull at the moment," Claire admitted. "Miss Pimm is making me read Good King Albert's treatise on magical oversight. I expect I'll perish of boredom before the week is out."

Hilary, meanwhile, was trying her best to look over Claire's shoulder. "I'm sorry to interrupt," she said, "but exactly what sort of snag have you run into?"

"Well," said Claire, "to put it simply . . ." She pulled the door open wider, and Hilary stepped into the hall. It was full of stone and sunlight, but it was entirely empty of people.

The gargoyle blinked. "Where are all the schoolgirls?"

"They're not here," said Hilary with a sigh, "and I suspect they're not coming." Her boots echoed in the empty hallway, and the grand carvings and oil paintings were beginning to make her feel very small. She hadn't truly thought she'd be greeted by hundreds of would-be pirates, but to be greeted by no one at all was even worse than she'd feared.

"I was sure they'd come," Claire was saying. "I made pamphlets! I papered every inch of the dormitory staircase with them last night. I even enchanted a few to float in the air, but I had to pull those down after they started chasing people through the halls. I think some of the younger girls were quite frightened."

"I don't understand it," said the gargoyle. "Why don't they want to be pirates? Don't they know they'd get to wear hats?"

"Blast it all, Terror, I'm sorry about this," said Charlie. "If only they'd let you talk to them—"

"I don't think talking is likely to do me much good,"

said Hilary. "It certainly didn't convince the pirates at the Ornery Clam."

"If we wait a few minutes," said Claire hesitantly, "perhaps a few girls will come by."

The thought of standing in the vast, empty hallway, listening to someone banging out a waltz on the harpsichord in the dancing classroom, made Hilary squirm. "I can't simply wait for my crewmates to appear," she said. "Just think what would have happened if we'd waited for Captain Wolfson and his mates to find us and volunteer their help. They'd have been sunk by the navy!" She took a breath, trying to think less like a nervous scallywag and more like the leader of the pirate league. "If I'm going to persuade these girls to join us, I've got to show them exactly what a good pirate can do."

The gargoyle looked concerned. "You're going to conjure up another pitcher of molasses?"

"I hope not," said Charlie. "I can't bear to eat one more piece of gingerbread."

The harpsichord music grew louder as Hilary reached for her cutlass. "Don't worry," she said. "I believe I've got a plan that's not nearly as sticky."

IN THE DANCING classroom, pairs of girls waltzed gracefully across the floor, wearing gray woolen dresses and somber expressions. While the music mistress plunked away on the harpsichord, the dancing mistress passed from girl to girl, straightening shoulders, lifting chins, and calling out instructions. "Confidence, my dears!" she cried. "Remember: a true lady waltzes with confidence!"

The pirates watched all this from the shadows just outside the doorway. When the dancing mistress had turned her attention to a student's wrinkled stockings, Claire gave Hilary's hand a squeeze and stepped into the room. With all the confidence befitting a true lady, she put two fingers in her mouth and whistled.

The harpsichord stopped plunking, and the girls stumbled to a halt.

"Thank you for your attention," said Claire. "You're all lovely dancers, but I've brought some guests along who will help you sharpen your talents. Please join me in welcoming the fearsome pirates Hilary Westfield and Charlie Dove!"

The girls gasped, and there was a mad rush toward the back of the classroom. Some girls hid under chairs; others pressed themselves against the walls. "Someone alert Miss Pimm!" cried the dancing mistress from behind an ottoman. "Inform her at once that pirates have invaded my classroom!"

In the midst of the commotion, Hilary and Charlie marched into the room with their weapons drawn and their heads as high as they could hold them. The music mistress, who seemed intent on providing the proper melody for any occasion, played a few suspenseful notes on the harpsichord.

"On your guard, Pirate Dove," said Hilary. She pointed her cutlass at Charlie. "I've been practicing my swordplay all winter, so please don't insult me by allowing me to win."

Charlie bowed to her and nearly sliced the buttons from her coat. "Of course not, Terror," he said. "I've got more honor than that."

Hilary had battled up and down the decks of the *Pigeon* with Charlie hundreds of time before, but this was the first time she had faced him in a real duel—even if it *was* a duel at a finishing school. He was quick enough to dodge her cutlass and clever enough to guess her next moves, and once he was caught up in battle, not even a room full of schoolgirls could unnerve him. In fact, his only fault as a swordsman was that he had never taken up ballroom dancing. As they made their way across the classroom, Hilary kept time with the lively tune coming from the harpsichord. She twirled away from Charlie's sword, extended her arm as gracefully as she could to parry his attacks, and even managed to curtsy as she carved up his bootlaces.

"Arr!" cried the gargoyle, swinging back and forth in Hilary's bag. "Grab his nose! Pull on his toes! Use his ears to swab the deck!"

Some of the schoolgirls had begun to crawl out from under their chairs, and a few of them applauded whenever Charlie landed a crucial blow or Hilary made an impressive riposte. Better yet, as they dueled their way toward the front of the room, Hilary saw that more girls were gathering in the doorway. The handwriting students were still clutching their ink bottles, the fainting students waved their smelling salts under their noses, and the music students had flutes and piccolos tucked under their arms. Rosie Hatter, who must have come from water-ballet practice, was wearing her embroidered bathing cap and dripping all over the floor.

"I think your plan is working," Charlie said as he swatted Hilary's cutlass away for the hundredth time. "You've definitely got their attention."

It was growing warm in the dancing classroom, though, and Hilary had to dig a handkerchief from her pocket to wipe the sweat from her brow. As she did, Charlie swung his sword dangerously close to her shoulder. "Is that a white flag of surrender, Terror?" he asked. "Are you giving up so easily?"

"Never!" Hilary tossed the handkerchief aside. As much as she hated to admit it, this wasn't a battle she was likely to win, but if she could manage to keep dueling for long enough to impress the schoolgirls—

"Stop this bedlam at once!" someone shouted from the doorway. The crowd of schoolgirls parted as a tall, muscular young woman strode into the classroom. She wore a quiver of arrows strapped to her back, a vicious-looking collection of hairpins, and an expression as hard-hearted as any pirate's.

"Oh dear," Hilary whispered. "It's the archery mistress."

The archery mistress crossed the floor at an astonishing pace. Before Hilary and Charlie could dodge her, she had seized them both by the collars and held them at arm's length. "Pirates in the ballroom!" she boomed. "Disrupting our lessons and frightening our students!"

"We're not terribly frightened, actually," said a small girl in a woolen bathing costume.

But the archery mistress barreled on. "I've never seen anything so improper!" she said. "What do you two have to say for yourselves?"

Hilary tried to pull herself free from the archery mistress's grip, but it was no use; she would simply have to do her best to look dignified. "We've come to teach your students to be pirates," she said. "We thought we'd begin with a swordplay demonstration."

At this, some of the schoolgirls began to murmur. "Whyever would they want to be *pirates*?" said the dancing mistress, who had crawled out from behind her ottoman. "They are young ladies of quality!"

"And young ladies of quality should be able to protect themselves from danger," said Hilary. She twisted her head to look up at the archery mistress. "Don't you agree?"

"Certainly." The archery mistress didn't relax her grip. "I assure you, however, that the halls of Miss Pimm's are not usually swarming with scoundrels." She glared at Hilary. "Today seems to be an exception."

"*We're* not scoundrels!" the gargoyle cried.

"My friend is right about that," said Hilary. "We'd never plot against you, but not everyone in the kingdom can say the same. Has anyone here heard of the Mutineers?"

The schoolgirls exchanged looks. A few of them raised their hands. "They're the ones who kidnapped Miss Pimm, aren't they?" asked Rosie Hatter. "The ones who stole all those magic bowls and vases and things?"

"That's right," said Hilary. "They're trying to control all the kingdom's magic, and they don't mind breaking every rule in the etiquette book in order to do it. They've even threatened to attack Augusta."

The room fell silent. Even the music mistress couldn't seem to think of a suitable tune to accompany the news. "How dreadful," the dancing mistress murmured.

"Dreadful it may be," said the archery mistress, "but that's no excuse for—"

"Wait a moment," said a girl with long, dark braids. "Will these Mutineers try to take *our* magic?"

"I don't see why not," said Charlie. "They're trying to take everyone else's."

Hilary nodded as well as she could with the archery mistress holding on to her collar. "My friends and I can stop them," she said, "but we'll need your help to do it. If enough of you are willing to join my pirate crew, I'm sure we'll be able to put a stop to the Mutineers once and for all."

All the girls were staring at her now. "We saw the

pamphlets," Rosie said, "but we never dreamed they could be serious. Do you truly want us to be pirates?"

"Of course I do!" Hilary grinned at her. "I can't promise it will be easy work, but I shall always be honest with you, and you shall always have my respect."

"And hats!" said the gargoyle. "Don't forget the hats."

The small girl in the woolen bathing costume looked doubtful. "We're finishing-school girls," she said. "I don't think we can learn to be scallywags."

"Nonsense," said Hilary. "I was a finishing-school girl myself, so I know exactly how formidable you all can be. If you can learn to waltz, you can learn to duel—it's nearly the same thing, and far more practical." She looked around the room. "How many of you have poked yourselves with an embroidery needle?"

All the girls raised their hands, though most of them looked embarrassed to admit it.

"Then you can poke your enemies with a cutlass," Hilary said. "If you can perform water ballet, you're perfectly capable of swimming to safety if it's required, and if you can use magic to starch your petticoats, you can use it just as well to send a Mutineer flying head over heels. Besides," she added, "I'm sure most of you are already as brave and as loyal as any good pirate. You wouldn't last a month at Miss Pimm's if you weren't."

Some of the girls giggled at this, which only made the archery mistress frown more deeply than ever. "Enough!"

she said sharply, raising her arm until Hilary's toes were barely touching the floor. "There is a limit to the amount of nonsense I can abide, and you, Miss Westfield, have reached it. I'm sure none of our students are interested in setting sail on the High Seas."

"I'm interested." Rosie Hatter stepped out of the crowd. Hilary could have hugged her. "I'd like to learn how to duel like that."

"So would I," said the girl with her hair in braids.

"And so would I." The music mistress stood up from her harpsichord bench. "I thought that pirate battle was terribly thrilling; didn't you, Pauline?"

The dancing mistress wrung her hands. "It *was* rather graceful," she said grudgingly.

By now, nearly thirty girls had stepped forward to join Rosie. In their petticoats and cardigans, they didn't look much like any pirates Hilary had met before, but she didn't mind one bit. In the corner of the room, Claire was practically bouncing with joy. Even Charlie looked pleased. "Would you mind letting us go?" Hilary asked the archery mistress. "We've got lessons to teach, and I'm eager to get started."

Reluctantly, the archery mistress released her grip. "I won't have you girls catching yellow fever or forgetting to bathe, do you understand?"

The schoolgirls curtsied prettily. "Yes, miss," they said all together.

"Hmm," said the gargoyle, studying them. "Teaching these people to shout might be more difficult than I thought."

Hilary laughed, though she suspected the gargoyle was right. "We've got loads of work ahead of us," she said, "but it will be entirely worth it to see the look on Captain Blacktooth's face when our crew arrives in Queensport Harbor."

WESTFIELD HOUSE
QUEENSPORT, AUGUSTA

Dear Hilary,

It seems as though it has been ages since your last visit. The gray weather has dragged on interminably, and I find myself rather lonely without you here to tear up the drapery and reduce the drawing room to rubble. I quite miss your funny little gargoyle as well, for Westfield House has been crawling with spiders since he departed.

So many people do not seem to care for honesty these days, but I hope you will not mind if I am honest with you, Hilary. When your father was first sent to the Royal Dungeons, naturally I hoped for his release. As the months wore on, however, I began to enjoy my perch at the top of the household. My busy schedule of hosting parties, performing charitable works, and visiting with friends left me very little time to miss your father—and I must admit that eventually, I did not miss him at all. My fainting fits had become far more rare during his absence, and I had only locked myself in my wardrobe three times in the past year. In short, my dear, I found myself enjoying life without James Westfield far more than I ever enjoyed it with him.

As I suspect you noticed, I was quite furious on the morning of your father's return, and I have been wrapped in a gloom ever since. How wise you were to leave the house at once! Since that day, your father has been sharper and more demanding than ever, and he behaves quite rudely when he is home. More and more, however, he is not home at all. His volunteer work with the Royal Navy requires him to travel often to Tilbury Park, though I cannot see quite what the Tilburys have to do with the navy. I would ask your father about it if I had any hope at all of receiving a truthful answer.

I have been reminiscing about our own visit to Tilbury Park last summer, and while I cannot say that I enjoyed the pirate battle that occurred there, I did feel proud of myself for leading all those poor guests to safety. I believe it was a real accomplishment! Lately, I have caught myself thinking that it might be pleasant to accomplish something else one day.

I hope you will keep my silly thoughts in confidence,

Hilary, for I would never dare mention them to the High Society families of my acquaintance. I suspect, however, that you may be able to lend a sympathetic ear.

Your loving
Mother

PIRATE HILARY WESTFIELD
TERROR OF THE SOUTHLANDS

Dear Mother,

I recently received your letter, and I have an idea that I hope will improve both your circumstances and your mood. Before I propose it, however, I think you should find a comfortable chair to sit in —the divan in the blue parlor, perhaps? Ask Bess to stand nearby with a pot of tea and a tray of smelling salts. You should probably keep your folding fan close at hand as well. If there are any visitors staying at Westfield House, please ask them to leave for a moment or two. (I'm sure you won't want them to be disturbed if you begin to shriek.)

Are you prepared? Very well. Here is my idea:

Have you ever considered becoming a pirate?

Love,
Hilary

———————————— ◇ ◇ ◇ ◇ ◇ ————————————

CHAPTER NINE

BEFORE LONG, THE classrooms and corridors of Miss Pimm's finishing school were filled with all sorts of unladylike activities. Girls whistled sea chanteys on the way to breakfast and sat in the hallways mending the holes they'd torn in their stockings during swordplay lessons. With Miss Pimm's blessing, Cannonball Jack led daily excursions to the *Blunderbuss*, where he instructed a small but determined group of girls on the finer points of cannon firing. With the archery mistress's reluctant approval, Mr. Partridge oversaw extra rounds of target practice that lasted until dusk; only once did he return from the pitch with an arrow lodged in his hat. The gargoyle's students worked diligently on their seafaring language, though they still said "Excuse me!" after every "Arr!" or "Blast!" Miss Greyson and Mr. Stanley conducted magic tutorials for those who weren't yet comfortable with their golden crochet hooks, and Claire spent every spare moment buried in textbooks of magical theory.

Even Charlie had become considerably more cheerful. He still grew tense every morning before leaving Wimbly-on-the-Marsh, but his nerves seemed to fall away as soon as he began to explain the difference between a cutlass and a broadsword, or the etiquette of dueling. His lessons proved to be so popular that Hilary could hardly make her way up the school staircases without running into pairs of girls fencing up and down the steps.

Most of the girls who'd stepped forward in the dancing classroom took part in the piracy lessons, and each day they brought a few more of their friends along with them. Even those girls who preferred not to go into battle volunteered to sew pirate clothing, mend their classmates' cuts and bruises, strategize over maps of Queensport Harbor, or prepare Miss Pimm's ship, the *Dancing Sheep*, for battle. The embroidery mistress remarked to anyone who would listen that she had never seen anything so shocking in her life, but even she had stitched a furtive skull and crossbones onto her handkerchief. "It seems that piracy has become something of a fad," Miss Pimm remarked drily. "I wonder if it will linger as long as last year's craze for opera."

Even if it didn't, Hilary hoped it would last at least a few more weeks. Her crew was growing by the day, but she still didn't have nearly enough supporters to challenge Captain Blacktooth. She spent each morning overseeing lessons at Miss Pimm's and working on her Buccaneers' Code, but in the afternoons she left the school grounds and tried to muster up as many potential pirates as she could.

One sunny Thursday, she and the gargoyle ventured to the Pemberton market to talk with would-be scally-wags. She assured the fishmonger that as president of the VNHLP, she would stop the League's ships from attacking his trawlers, and she promised to negotiate fairer prices with the greengrocer, who sold most of his oranges to pirates fearful of scurvy. After a whispered conversation behind a towering stack of lettuces, both men agreed to join Hilary's crew. The weavers and jam makers claimed that a life on the High Seas left very little time for weaving or jam making, and the butcher seemed far more interested in Hilary's cutlass than he did in Hilary, but the baker confided that she had always longed to abandon her flours and yeasts for a more adventurous career. To Hilary's delight, she vowed to become a pirate on the spot.

"Who knows?" Hilary remarked to the gargoyle as they left the market. "We may recruit two hundred pirates yet."

"I'm not sure I liked the way that butcher was looking at me," the gargoyle said. "I'm sure his mouth was watering. By this time tomorrow, he'll be making a fortune selling juicy gargoyle steaks to all the cooks in Pemberton."

"He'd better not!" said Hilary. "If he so much as lifts his cleaver in your direction, I'll warn him off."

"I'd appreciate that," the gargoyle said. "Where are we going next?"

Hilary turned down a skinny lane that led in the opposite direction from Miss Pimm's. According to the rusted signpost, it bore the unfortunate name of Ankle-bone Alley. She wasn't entirely familiar with this part of Pemberton, where the air smelled of cooking meat, damp earth, and sharp, sour things she preferred not to identify. "I thought we'd walk down to the bay," she said, "to inquire if any members of the Royal Augusta Water Ballet are interested in becoming pirates."

"That's a good idea," said the gargoyle. "They're already excellent at treading water." He looked around at the moss-covered stone buildings that lined the alley. "Are you sure you're headed in the right direction?"

"Of course! A good pirate always knows which way is north—or south, in this case." Hilary squinted up at the sun, which hung in the sky over the right-hand row of buildings. "It's just a matter of observing one's surroundings."

"Oh, well, I can do *that*," the gargoyle said. "I can see there's a tasty-looking patch of stinging nettles by the side of the lane. I can see you're going to refuse to let me have them for a snack. And I can see a suspicious-looking gentleman lurking behind that cottage, even though he thinks I can't."

Hilary stopped walking. "What did you say?"

Before the gargoyle had a chance to repeat himself, a pair of black-gloved hands reached out from behind her, took hold of her arms, and pulled her out of the alley.

"Drat and blast!" cried Hilary. "Let me go!"

She tried to reach for her cutlass, but the hands held her fast; she couldn't even twist around to catch a glimpse of her attacker. In her bag, the gargoyle snapped his jaws together. "I'm trying to bite him," he called up to Hilary, "but he's not cooperating! He won't even let me have a nibble!"

The gentleman sounded as though he was trying to say something, but Hilary wasn't interested in listening. Instead, she raised her right leg in front of her, swung it backward as hard as she could, and kicked him squarely in the knees. With a shout, the gentleman let go of Hilary's arms, lost his balance, and tumbled into the patch of stinging nettles.

"I think," the gargoyle said shakily, "he might have overheard me."

"I think you're right." Hilary walked over to the nettles and looked down at the gentleman. He lay facedown in the dirt, and his elegant suit looked rather the worse for wear. "I also think his clothes are far too fine for a common cutpurse."

"Maybe he stole them," the gargoyle suggested.

"Ow!" said the gentleman, who was still being stung by nettles. "I'm not a cutpurse!"

"Then what are you?" Hilary asked. "Get up and explain yourself before I let my gargoyle chomp on your earlobes."

The gentleman rolled out of the nettles, saying "Ow!" several more times as he did so. Hilary drew her cutlass in case he tried to run away, but he did no such thing; instead he scrambled to his feet and gave her a miserable little bow. "Hello, Terror," he said. "I suppose I should have sent my calling card in advance."

"Sir Nicholas Feathering." Hilary eyed his scratches and stings, but she didn't lower her cutlass. "I hoped you'd put your kidnapping days behind you. If your fellow Mutineers have sent you here to snatch me, I assure you I won't be snatched."

"You've got it entirely wrong," Nicholas protested. "The others didn't send me; they don't even know I'm here." He put a hand to his cheek and flinched. "What the devil did you push me into, a hornet's nest?"

"I wish I had," said Hilary. "However did you find me?"

"The Terror of the Southlands isn't exactly difficult to track down. I made some inquiries—and once I reached Pemberton, I used this." Nicholas pulled a polished golden ball from his pocket.

Hilary lifted her cutlass to his chin. "Put that down immediately."

"Sorry!" Nicholas yelped. He backed away and set the magic piece down at his feet. "I didn't mean to alarm you, Terror. I only wanted to help. That is, I still *do* want to help, but your cutlass is making it rather difficult."

The gargoyle was glaring at Nicholas and showed no intention of stopping. "I don't trust him," he said. "Do you trust him, Hilary?"

"Not even a bit." Hilary lowered her sword a fraction of an inch. "But I *am* interested in what he has to say. I suppose we should let him explain himself before we have him shipped to the Dungeons."

"Thank you," said Nicholas. He sounded truly relieved. "I should have known you wouldn't be happy to see me, but I had to speak to you at once. You see, I . . . well, I'm not sure I want to be a Mutineer anymore."

Hilary stared at him. "Whyever not? Don't you want to rule the kingdom?"

"Not particularly," said Nicholas. "I never have, really; the whole idea of ruling doesn't appeal to me. It seems like quite a lot of work, to tell you the truth." He shoved his hands in his pockets. "It appeals to Philomena, though, and when she asked for my help, of course I agreed. I didn't know there'd be kidnappings or battles."

"But you've been a Mutineer for ages now," said Hilary.

"If you disapprove so heartily of kidnappings and battles, why didn't you leave the group at once?"

"I couldn't! Mrs. Tilbury said she'd ruin me—ruin the good name of all the Featherings. She can do that, you know. That group of hers, the Coalition of Overprotective Mothers, they spread rumors faster than the *Scuttlebutt* can print them. And I couldn't leave Philomena. No one should have to face Mrs. Tilbury alone." Nicholas shuddered. "She's not a pleasant woman."

"So I've gathered," said Hilary. Her arm was growing sore from holding up her cutlass, but she didn't dare put it down. "Go on. Don't you want to explain why you've had such a convenient change of heart?"

Nicholas hesitated. "I was there," he said. "That night at Tilbury Park. I saw Philomena launch Alice out of that tree."

From the look on Nicholas's face, Hilary guessed that being pushed into a patch of nettles was the nicest thing that had happened to him in quite some time. "I thought I saw you at the window," she said carefully.

"I knew Philomena had a temper, but I never imagined she'd truly harm anyone. She swore to me that Alice wasn't hurt, but—well—is she all right, Terror?"

"Her arm is broken," Hilary said. "You needn't look so horrified; she'll be perfectly all right in a few weeks. If you're fortunate, perhaps she won't have to wear bandages at your wedding."

"I don't know if there's going to be a wedding." Nicholas slumped against the cottage wall. "I used to think I could rescue Philomena from her wretched mother, but now I'm not sure she's the rescuing type." He sighed. "I can't bear to tell her, though. She's been in a sour mood for months, and I suspect that if I break our engagement, she'll leave me in the path of an oncoming train."

"So you ran away?" the gargoyle asked. "I don't blame you. If I had to marry a Mutineer, I'd run away too—or at least I'd hop."

But Nicholas shook his head. "Running away won't do me much good. If I don't want Georgiana Tilbury chasing me across the kingdom with her antique magic shoehorn clutched in her fist, I have to pretend that I'm perfectly happy with the Mutineers' plans. I don't speak much to the others on the best of days, and I believe they prefer it that way. I watch them, though, and I listen. That's why I've come to see you, Terror." Nicholas looked from one end of the alley to the other. "I thought you might be interested in making a deal."

Hilary narrowed her eyes. "In that case, I'm sorry you've gone to so much trouble. I don't deal with villains."

"Not even villains who hope to reform themselves?"

"*Especially* not them," said Hilary. "I'm acquainted with a few of them already, and they simply can't be trusted."

Nicholas wiped his glove across his face, leaving a smudge of dirt and dust on his brow. "I could tell you what

Captain Blacktooth is planning," he said. "I could tell you how to defeat him. Don't you think that information is worth having?"

"Well, yes," Hilary admitted. "Despite what you may have heard from my father, I'm not entirely foolish. But I'm sure you'll be wanting something in return."

"Only a bit of protection. I'll need your word that you and your crew will defend me from any Mutineers who find out about our arrangement."

"That's all you want?" Hilary frowned. "You really aren't very good at villainy, are you?"

"Well," said Nicholas, "there *is* one more thing. Could you put in a good word for me with Alice? She hasn't spoken to me for months, and I'm starting to miss her ridiculous stories. I know she'll do whatever you advise, Terror."

Hilary was familiar with lies, for pirates lied frequently and well. She didn't think Nicholas was being untruthful, but she had trusted him once before, and he had tried to send her to the bottom of the sea as a result. She lowered her sword, but just to be cautious, she put her foot firmly on top of the ball of magic.

"How can I be sure that you're not only here to find out what I'm up to?" she asked. "For all I know, you'll tell me a pack of tales and run back to Captain Blacktooth with everything you've learned about my plans."

"I won't!" said Nicholas, standing up straighter. "And

I'll prove it. I can tell you right now that your father and Captain Blacktooth are working together to take control of the High Seas. They think that if the only ships left in Augustan waters are loyal to the pirate league or the Royal Navy, there won't be anyone left to stop them from defeating you and threatening the queen."

None of this came as a surprise to Hilary, but at least Nicholas seemed to be telling the truth. "I've already learned all that from an unpleasant gentleman covered in molasses," she told him. "Would you mind coming up with something a bit more useful?"

Nicholas turned rather pink around his freckles. "Perhaps you'd better tell me what you'd like to know."

"You said you could tell us what Captain Blacktooth is planning," the gargoyle said. "Why don't you do that?"

"Ah," said Nicholas, turning even pinker. "Well. To be perfectly honest, that was just an example of something I *might* be able to tell you."

"You mean you don't have any idea what Blacktooth is planning, or how to defeat him?" Hilary crossed her arms. "Philomena might break off your engagement herself when she sees that a gargoyle has bitten off your toes."

"The big ones," the gargoyle said happily. "Both of them."

"I can find out!" Nicholas said. He sounded very eager to keep his toes. "Captain Blacktooth is coming to see Mrs. Tilbury next week. I'm not usually invited to their meetings, but I'm sure I can find a way to overhear their conversation. Will you give me a few more days?"

Hilary glared at him. "All right," she said at last, "but make sure to overhear something useful, please. If you give me information that's more than fluff and nonsense, I'll protect you from the Mutineers in return. I suppose I can talk to Alice, too, though I can't promise she'll forgive you. Being related to a scoundrel isn't exactly a pleasant experience."

Nicholas gave a solemn nod and extended his gloved hand. "Shall we shake on it?"

"Pirates generally prefer not to," Hilary told him, "on account of the hooks. But if it would make you feel better, I suppose we can." She shook his hand, and quite a bit of his arm as well. "By the way, the next time you want to pay me a visit, please don't leap out at me from the shadows. It's not a polite way to greet anyone at all—not even a pirate."

"I'm sorry about that, Terror. I'm still getting accustomed to being a spy." Nicholas reached down and retrieved his magic piece from under Hilary's foot. "I'm afraid I have a train to Nordholm to catch. Are you heading toward the station?"

"Not today," said Hilary. "The gargoyle and I are on our way to watch the water ballet perform. Aren't we, gargoyle?"

"That's right." The gargoyle grinned, showing most of

his teeth. "Have a nice trip, Sir Nicholas, and give my best to the Mutineers."

IT WAS OFTEN said in the halls of High Society that attending a performance of the Royal Augusta Water Ballet required patience, optimism, and extremely sharp eyesight. The troupe swam in Pemberton Bay in every sort of weather, donning extra layers of woolen bathing costumes in the winter and holding umbrellas over their heads during summer downpours. Because they splashed, flipped, and kicked their way from one side of the bay to the other, it was occasionally difficult for their audience to spot them from the wooden chairs arranged in thoughtful rows at the water's edge. The ballet director had placed a pair of opera glasses next to each seat so that guests could scan the sea for an exquisite swan dive or a tantalizing glimpse of pointed toes, but many ballet goers gave up and went home long before the troupe had floated close to shore.

Hilary wasn't very fond of water ballet, and the mere thought of a woolen bathing costume made her itch. She had seen the swimmers several times before, however, for they often sprang up without warning alongside the *Pigeon*. Now, as a tinny gramophone played selections from *Swan Lake*, she settled herself in one of the wooden chairs and waited for the ballet to appear on the horizon.

"I hope they swim over here soon," the gargoyle said. All the other chairs along the shoreline were empty, and the gargoyle was practicing hopping from seat to seat. "I love it when they twirl." He performed a twirl of his own as an illustration.

"That's very beautiful," Hilary told him. "I know you don't want to learn water ballet, but I believe you have natural talent."

"You know perfectly well how I feel about waves," the gargoyle replied, "and about bathing caps." He twirled again, nearly toppling off his chair. "Do you really think we can trust Sir Nicholas Feathering?"

Hilary had spent the past hour wondering much the same thing. "I'm not entirely sure," she said. "I don't intend to tell him anything about our own plans, but who knows how long he's spent following me around Pemberton? If I learn he's been spying on us through the bars of Miss Pimm's, he'll wish the Mutineers had tossed him in the Dungeons long ago." She shrugged. "There's a good chance he's dangerous, but if we're going to defeat Captain Blacktooth, we can't afford to be safe. Pirates don't have much regard for safety, you know."

"I know," said the gargoyle. He launched himself across the gap between two chairs, but even though he fluttered his wings as rapidly as he could, he landed on the beach with a most undignified thump. "I just hope we don't all end up with sand in our snouts."

They hadn't been waiting more than a quarter of an

hour before the Royal Augusta Water Ballet splashed elegantly into sight. The swimmers seemed pleased to have an audience; when the gramophone sputtered to a halt halfway through the musical recording, they came out of the water to say hello to Hilary and the gargoyle, whom they recognized at once as the *Pigeon*'s figurehead.

As Hilary explained why she'd come, the swimmers pulled off their embroidered bathing caps and shook the water out of their ears. They had all heard of Captain Blacktooth, and none of them were fond of him. "He's always sailing his ship directly through our water-ballet routines," the troupe leader explained to Hilary. "He and his mates have been doing it for years now, and they never make any apology. Can you do anything to stop them?"

"I certainly plan to," said Hilary. "As far as I'm concerned, pirates and water-ballet dancers should be able to work together. If you help me fight against Blacktooth, I'll make sure you aren't squashed during your rehearsals. Perhaps you can even give a performance at the League picnic."

The troupe leader smiled. "In that case," she said, "it would be my pleasure to support you."

The rest of the troupe soon agreed, and Hilary walked back to Jasper's house with ten more pirates in her crew and a spring in her step. From the depths of her bag, the gargoyle warbled *Swan Lake*. "Perhaps it's foolish of me," she said to him when he paused for breath, "but I'm starting to think we might actually be able to win this battle after all. Captain Blacktooth's tried terribly hard to make me forfeit, but I don't believe there's anything more he can possibly do to ruin our chances."

As they turned into Little Herring Cove, the air filled with shouts, squawks, and a sound very much like a pirate overturning a china cabinet. "I wonder what all the commotion is about," the gargoyle said. "Do you think Clumsy-Hands Mortmain is baking hardtack again?"

"I hope not," said Hilary. "His house nearly went up in flames the last time he tried it." She began to walk faster, and then to run. When she reached Jasper's bungalow, however, she stopped so suddenly that the gargoyle nearly flew out of her bag.

"Hey!" he cried. "What's going on?"

"Jasper's got houseguests," Hilary said, setting her bag down beside her, "and they don't look friendly."

PIRATE BENEFACTOR GIVES GIFT
TO SUMMERSTEAD

SUMMERSTEAD, AUGUSTA—Town councillor Henrietta Thaxter-Thwaite announced today that funds have been raised for a new, state-of-the-art skating pond and toboggan hill in the center of Summerstead. The construction of this facility, which is sure to bring years of outdoor fun to every citizen in this charming yet chilly town, would not be possible without the generous financial support of Captain Rupert Blacktooth, president of the Very Nearly Honorable League of Pirates. According to Mrs. Thaxter-Thwaite, Captain Blacktooth has provided these funds in gratitude for the excellent and speedy work that the laborers in Summerstead's shipyard have performed for him in recent months.

"I have no idea what Captain Blacktooth is building in that shipyard," said Mrs. Thaxter-Thwaite, "but now is not the proper time to be raising questions about the captain's activities or his motives. I am currently devoting most of my energy to perfecting my toboggan technique, for I plan to challenge our council secretary to a race as soon as the new park opens next winter."

When asked about Captain Blacktooth's connection to

the Summerstead shipyard, five hundred laborers refused to discuss the captain's mysterious project in detail. They did report, however, that construction will be complete by early next week. Pirates who have overseen the project over the past two months responded to our reporters' inquiries by waving their cutlasses and shouting certain phrases that cannot be reproduced in the pages of this well-regarded newspaper.

An ice sculpture of Captain Blacktooth himself will be displayed in the Summerstead town square next month, though viewers should plan to arrive early if they hope to see the pirate's shimmering likeness before it melts.

CHAPTER TEN

IN ALL THE time Hilary had been paying visits to 25 Little Herring Cove, she'd never seen so much commotion. Jasper was pacing up and down the front path, wearing an enormous scowl and making frequent exclamations to Fitzwilliam, who flew around his head like a small orbiting moon. Mr. Partridge stood on the grass shivering in his stocking feet, and Hilary thought she spied Mr. Twigget's elbow peeking out from behind a tree. Most of her other mates were huddled in front of the bungalow door, looking on as Miss Greyson stood on the front step and waved her knitting needles furiously at Captain Blacktooth. No one paid any attention to Hilary.

"You've done quite enough damage already!" Miss Greyson was saying. "Attacking a pirate ship is one thing, but destroying one's home is quite another, and I simply won't allow it to continue. Please gather your men and depart at once!"

Captain Blacktooth looked thoroughly uninterested in what Miss Greyson had to say, though he did step back when her knitting needles came perilously close to his nose. "I apologize for the inconvenience, madam," he said, "but I had to investigate whether the rumors I've been hearing are true."

A half-dozen rusty cutlasses, three tins of oatmeal, a corset, and a lacy petticoat flew out of the bungalow's front window in quick succession. Then a pirate stuck his head out and looked around for Captain Blacktooth. "We've found plenty o' odds an' ends, Captain," he called, "but we haven't turned up any schoolgirls yet."

"Keep looking," Blacktooth replied. From deep inside the bungalow, something let out a long, dejected wheeze.

"Curses!" cried Jasper. "That's my concertina!"

He still hadn't caught sight of Hilary standing by the mailbox, so she planted herself in his path. "What's happened?" she asked. "Why are pirates throwing Miss Greyson's underthings out the window?"

"It seems," said Jasper darkly, "that the VNHLP has learned about our plan to recruit schoolgirls to our crew. As you can see, our friend Blacktooth doesn't care for the idea, and he's decided to put his usual charms on display." A chamber pot flew out the window and landed by Jasper's left boot. "He seems to be under the misconception that these girls are living in our wardrobes and cutlery drawers."

"How foolish!" said Hilary. "Why in the world hasn't anyone stopped him?" She frowned. "And where's your sword?"

"Locked in a treasure chest, blast it all," said Jasper, "along with all the other cutlasses, cannons, daggers, mousetraps, and magic pieces we've got." He nodded toward an enormous wooden box at the edge of the property. "One moment we were running swordplay drills in the garden, and the next our swords had flown from our hands and our magic coins had fled from our pockets. Blacktooth must have had twenty men working the enchantment." He stopped pacing to let Fitzwilliam settle on the brim of his hat. "They weren't clever enough to whisk away Eloise's knitting needles, though. If you want to know the truth, I believe she's quite enjoying herself."

"Well, I've still got my sword, and I intend to keep it." Hilary made her way through the crowd and stomped up the bungalow steps. "Thank you, Miss Greyson," she said. "I think I can handle matters from here." She held out her magic coin. "Perhaps you can use this to pick the lock on that treasure chest."

With great reluctance, Miss Greyson tucked her

knitting needles away and accepted Hilary's magic piece. "Very well," she said. "I shall turn our visitors over to you, Terror. If I discover that they've touched a single piece of my grandmama's good china, however, I won't hesitate to pull out my sewing shears."

As Miss Greyson and her knitting needles retreated, Captain Blacktooth seemed to relax. "I see the Terror's returned at last," he said. "We've been wondering where you were. Enlisting more dainty little schoolgirls in your pirate crew, I suppose?"

"Not at all," said Hilary. "The finishing-school girls joined the crew last week. Today I enlisted water-ballet performers."

Captain Blacktooth raised his eyebrows. "So the rumors are true," he said. "You *are* turning schoolgirls into pirates."

"I can't see that it's any of your business," said Hilary. "Who's been spreading information about my plans?" A horrid thought occurred to her. "Have you been talking to Sir Nicholas Feathering?"

Blacktooth chuckled. "You can't truly expect to keep secrets in a kingdom this small, can you, Terror?"

Hilary reached for her cutlass. "I didn't expect that my friends' house would be ransacked by scoundrels, either," she snapped, "but I see I was wrong about that as well. You might as well call your mates off; all the finishing-school girls are safely behind the gates of Miss Pimm's."

"I suppose that's fair," said Blacktooth. He opened the bungalow door and leaned inside. "Avast, mateys! That's enough pillaging for today. It's back to the *Renegade* with the lot of you, and no dawdling!"

"Aye, aye!" shouted the pirates. They stomped out of the bungalow, leaving piles of shattered pottery and splintered wood in their wake. The walls were splattered with jam and scored with cutlass marks. Ink flowed from overturned bottles and made miniature jet-black seas on the floorboards. Even Fitzwilliam's birdcage was battered beyond recognition. One pirate was covered from head to toe in dirt; Hilary guessed he had been searching for schoolgirls in the garden bed.

The last pirate out of the bungalow was Mr. Gull, Captain Blacktooth's private secretary. He lingered in the doorway. "Captain," he said, "why have you called off the search? We're still in need of evidence."

"Evidence?" said Hilary. "Whatever are you talking about?"

"I don't like the sound of that," the gargoyle muttered from her bag.

"Never fear, my dear Horatio," said Captain Blacktooth, clapping Mr. Gull on the back. "Pirate Westfield herself has admitted to recruiting schoolgirls to her cause. Even if we don't have the girls themselves, I believe the Terror's confession is all the evidence we need."

"Quite right," said Mr. Gull. He nodded to Hilary.

"Come along, Terror. The captain hates dallying, and time grows short."

"You're mistaken," Hilary told him. "I'm not going anywhere, and I'm certainly not going anywhere with *you*."

"Then you may as well pack your bags for the Pestilent Home for Foul-Tempered Pirates," Captain Blacktooth said. "Mr. Gull is the arbiter of our friendly competition, and we must both abide by his rules. Isn't that right, Mr. Gull?"

"Indeed." Mr. Gull pulled out his copy of *Leading the League* and tapped his fingers briskly against the cover. "We're only going to the *Renegade*, Terror. If you answer my questions in a satisfactory manner, you'll be back here in three taps of a peg leg."

"And you won't kidnap me? Or run me through?"

"Certainly not!" Mr. Gull looked horrified. "As I hope you're aware, contest rules don't permit anything of the sort. I must insist that both you and Captain Blacktooth keep your weapons to yourselves during our discussion."

All of Hilary's mates were looking up at her with concern. Even Mr. Twigget was peering out from behind his tree. "Oh, very well," she said to Mr. Gull. "I'll come with you, but I don't see what we have to discuss."

THE *RENEGADE* WAITED in Little Herring Cove, dwarfing the other boats at anchor and casting long shadows across the shoreline. Mr. Gull escorted Hilary in one of the dinghies, but he proved to be such a poor rower that Hilary longed to seize the oars out of his hands and do the job herself. She wondered if he was truly as weak as he seemed, or if he was merely trying to annoy her. By the time they reached the ship at last, all the other pirates were already on board.

"I won't be climbing the mast again," Hilary told Mr. Gull, "so don't even think about asking." The last time she had been called to the *Renegade* for a scolding, Blacktooth had insisted on holding their conversation in the crow's nest—but that had been ages ago, before Hilary had learned there wasn't any point in agreeing to his ridiculous requests.

"I didn't have anything of the sort in mind," Mr. Gull assured her. "We will be meeting in the captain's personal quarters."

As they made their way through the crowd of pirates gathered on the deck, a peculiar sound surrounded them, low and rumbling like far-off thunder. There wasn't a storm anywhere in sight, however; the sky was clear and streaked with sunset. "What's that noise?" Hilary whispered to the gargoyle. "Can you hear it too?"

The gargoyle wriggled halfway out of her bag and adjusted his ears. "That's strange," he said. "It sounds like someone's humming."

"That's correct," said Mr. Gull, overhearing them. "Captain Blacktooth always asks his mates to hum in a menacing sort of way whenever an enemy boards the ship.

He believes it makes the atmosphere more ominous."

It seemed to Hilary that the atmosphere was quite ominous enough without all the humming. The deck creaked and groaned under her boots, and an enormous Jolly Roger billowed overhead. Torches burned on either side of the door leading to Blacktooth's quarters, making the tip of Hilary's braid curl. The door itself was branded with a skull and crossbones, under which someone had carved a few words with a sharp dagger:

ABANDON ALL HOPE, YE WHO ENTER HERE

The gargoyle studied the words and yawned. "The skull and crossbones is a nice touch," he said, "but the motto is awfully theatrical."

"Captain Blacktooth plundered it from his favorite book," said Mr. Gull. "Like all great pirate captains, he is extremely well read." He rapped three times on the door and held it open for Hilary.

Inside Blacktooth's quarters, the light was dim and the air was smoky. Candles burned in polished sconces. A vast, velvet-draped window overlooked the sea, though the squares of window glass were so warped and rippled that Hilary could barely make out more than a faint impression of sky and waves. Most of the cabin, however, was occupied by a table that bore an uncanny resemblance to the one in Jasper's cabin on the *Pigeon*. Hilary wondered if there were regulations governing the sorts of furniture a pirate captain could own.

At one end of the table, Captain Blacktooth sat rigidly in his armchair. He was looking down at a ship's compass and watching the needle twitch. "Welcome, Terror," he said without looking up. "Please take a seat."

Hilary pulled out the chair at the opposite end of the table, as far away from Blacktooth as she could get. Mr. Gull gave her a nod of approval and seated himself halfway between the two of them. "May I sit on the table?" the gargoyle asked from Hilary's lap. "I can't see anything from down here."

Hilary bit her lip. "All right," she said reluctantly, "but you mustn't hop away from me. I don't want anyone to snatch you up."

Captain Blacktooth raised his gaze from the compass. "You must think I'm terribly dishonorable, Pirate Westfield," he said.

Hilary blinked. "Yes," she said, "I do."

"I, however, am not the pirate who stands accused of breaking League rules," he said. "Please read the charges against the Terror aloud, Mr. Gull. I want her to understand exactly why she is here."

"Certainly," said Mr. Gull. He unfolded an ink-splattered sheet of parchment and cleared his throat. "Hilary Westfield, Terror of the Southlands and candidate for president of the Very Nearly Honorable League of Pirates, has violated the guidelines set forth in *Leading the League*, seventeenth edition, by inviting non-pirates to join her crew. As a result, her candidacy will be considered null and void, and she will be sent into exile within the hour." He set down the parchment and looked at Hilary. "It's all rather straightforward, Terror. Do you wish to challenge these charges, or shall we prepare a ship for your departure from the kingdom?"

Hilary felt as though she were viewing the entire room through the warped and rippled window glass. "Of course I wish to challenge the charges!" she said. "I'd like you to show me the precise place in *Leading the League* where it says that finishing-school girls aren't allowed to join a pirate crew."

"Really, Terror," said Captain Blacktooth, "there's no need to waste Mr. Gull's time. It doesn't matter how long you drag out this conversation; you'll still be banished at the end of it."

"Have patience, Captain," Mr. Gull said calmly. "The Terror has every right to issue a challenge, and I'm bound to honor her request. It won't take more than a moment." He placed his heavy, gold-stamped volume of *Leading the League* on the tabletop. Unlike Hilary's copy, this one seemed to have most of its pages; they didn't even threaten to fall out as Mr. Gull thumbed through them. "Here we are," he said after a moment. "Page seven hundred thirty-three, appendix Q, clause five. 'Each candidate for the presidency must be supported in battle by no fewer than two hundred pirates. Wild beasts, enchanted household objects, and other non-pirates do not qualify as supporters and may not be recruited. The penalty for breaking this rule shall be disqualification and exile.'" He passed the open book to Hilary and tapped the page. "The requirement is quite clear."

"That's right," said Blacktooth. "No finishing-school girls—and no water-ballet performers, either. It's right there in the text."

Hilary scanned the page that Mr. Gull had pointed to. Then she shut the book. "I'm afraid I don't agree," she said.

Blacktooth folded his hands over his stomach. "It's really not a matter of agreement."

"The book says that only pirates may support me," Hilary continued, "but it doesn't say anywhere on this page that a finishing-school girl is not a pirate. In fact, I'd wager it doesn't say such a thing anywhere in this entire volume. Does it, Mr. Gull?"

Mr. Gull wrinkled his brow and leafed through *Leading the League* once more. "As a matter of fact," he said, "I don't believe it does. It doesn't mention finishing-school girls at all."

"Have you lost your wits, Terror?" Captain Blacktooth demanded. "Of course finishing-school girls aren't pirates! Any fool can see that."

"Then you must be a fool," said Hilary. "I don't think your secretary is as foolish as you are, though. Do the rules say that pirates must be League members, Mr. Gull?"

Mr. Gull scratched his head. "No," he said, "but—"

"Good," said Hilary. "Must pirates carry swords?"

"Well," said Mr. Gull, glancing at Captain Blacktooth, "the book doesn't discuss it one way or the other."

"Must they drink grog? Must they grow beards? If they wear petticoats, must they walk the plank?"

Mr. Gull looked rather embarrassed. "I'm afraid the rules don't specify."

"Of course they don't!" Blacktooth seemed to be starting to overheat. He unbuttoned his coat and loosened his cravat. Hilary expected that in a few more moments, he would begin to produce steam and whistle like Miss Greyson's teakettle. "Everyone in the blasted kingdom knows what a pirate *is* and what a pirate *isn't*. This entire conversation is absurd!"

"As far as I'm concerned," said Hilary, "if a schoolgirl says she's a pirate, then so she is—and that goes for waterballet performers, bakers, and fishmongers as well."

"And gargoyles!" said the gargoyle.

"Precisely." Hilary patted his wings. "I used to believe that the VNHLP had the power to make me a pirate, but perhaps I was actually a pirate all along." She kicked her feet up onto the table. "What do you say to that, gentlemen?"

Blacktooth rolled his eyes. "I say it's utter nonsense. And furthermore, Mr. Gull should have required you to remove your boots before boarding my ship." He narrowed his eyes at Mr. Gull. "I'm starting to wonder if my secretary is losing his touch."

"My apologies, Captain." Mr. Gull was still squinting into the pages of *Leading the League*. "It seems to me," he said, "that both of you present compelling arguments. The Terror is quite right that the rules don't prohibit finishing-school girls from acting as pirates, and I don't believe it would be appropriate to punish her."

The gargoyle began to cheer, but Mr. Gull held up a finger to silence him. "However," he said, "I am sure Captain Blacktooth is correct that the pirates who wrote these documents didn't intend for anyone to assemble such an unconventional crew. The idea probably never occurred to them, and if it had, they would certainly have outlawed it." He frowned into the book and rubbed his forehead. "Oh dear. I don't see what can be done."

Captain Blacktooth looked down at his compass, which seemed to be pointing in every direction other than north. He looked across the table toward Hilary. Then, to her alarm, he began to smile. "If I may make a suggestion," he said, "how about a compromise?"

Mr. Gull perked up. "I like the sound of that, Captain."

"I don't." Hilary glared at Blacktooth. "I wasn't aware that League members were allowed to make compromises."

"For heaven's sake, Terror, I'm not completely unreasonable. I'm willing to let you bring your peculiar crewmates into battle if that's what you truly want—but I'll need you to agree to my condition first."

The thought of agreeing with Blacktooth made Hilary's stomach churn, but being put on the next ship to the Pestilent Home without a chance to say good-bye to her mates would be even worse. "Fine," she said. "What do you want? It'll be treasure, I suppose; you Mutineers are awfully predictable."

"Not exactly." Captain Blacktooth leaned forward. "If I win our battle, I want you to give me the gargoyle."

At first, Hilary thought she hadn't heard him properly. The words hardly made sense. "You want the gargoyle?" she repeated. "*My* gargoyle?"

"Is there any other?" said Blacktooth. "Whoever triumphs in battle wins the gargoyle. That is my condition."

Mr. Gull beamed. "An excellent compromise, Captain."

Nothing about it seemed at all excellent to Hilary. She took her feet off the table and wrapped the gargoyle in her arms. "He's not a trophy to be won," she said. "He's my friend, and I won't let you have him. You don't even like him!"

"As a pirate's companion, he is highly unsuitable," Blacktooth agreed, "but his magic intrigues me." He looked at the gargoyle. "The Enchantress ensured that you could only be used for protection, did she not?"

The gargoyle showed his teeth. "That's right."

"Well, when you are mine, I'll have my niece examine you. Perhaps she'll be able to crack that particular enchantment. Even if she can't, I'm sure you'll be able to make yourself useful protecting me from my enemies."

Hilary stood up. "Mr. Gull," she said, "please escort me off this ship. I'll never agree to your captain's demand, and I'm sure he knows it."

"Then you'll forfeit the battle?" said Mr. Gull. "You'll withdraw your challenge and go willingly into exile?"

This must have been what Blacktooth had wanted all along; he'd never truly intended to compromise. He stared at Hilary, daring her to answer. Even Mr. Gull was on the edge of his seat. Hilary could almost feel the rusty bedsprings at the Pestilent Home digging into her back, and she could almost hear the Mutineers clinking their champagne glasses together with glee when they learned what she was about to do. Perhaps Charlie and Claire and the others would still find a way to defeat them, even if Hilary wasn't there to see it. She steeled her nerves and met Blacktooth's stare.

"I agree," said the gargoyle suddenly. "I accept Captain Blacktooth's terms."

The cabin fell silent. Even the candles stopped flickering. If the look on Blacktooth's face was any indication, he was almost as stunned as Hilary was. "You do?" he asked.

"Yes." The gargoyle raised his snout nobly. "Whoever wins the pirate battle wins me as well. Go on, Hilary; tell them."

"No!" she whispered. "What are you doing? I won't let Blacktooth take you!"

"And I won't let you forfeit," the gargoyle replied. "Anyway, it doesn't matter. Blacktooth won't take me."

"Of course he will! You heard what he said. He'll force you to protect him!"

"He won't," said the gargoyle, "because he's not going to win."

The gargoyle sounded so confident of this that Hilary hardly knew what to say. "That's very sweet of you, but we really can't be sure—"

"Just tell him you accept his compromise," the gargoyle said, "or I'll chomp on your thumbs. I've been eyeing the left one for years."

"Oh, all right." Hilary moved her thumbs farther away from the gargoyle's teeth. "Captain Blacktooth has made the most odious suggestion I've ever heard," she told Mr. Gull, "but the gargoyle wants me to agree to it, and I won't let him down." She took a breath. "I accept Blacktooth's compromise."

"Splendid!" said Mr. Gull, clapping his hands. "If you'll give me a few moments, I'll draw up an amendment to the rules, and both of you may sign it." He crossed the cabin and began to rustle through piles of parchment and ink bottles.

Captain Blacktooth remained in his seat. Hilary could tell he was furious, for he looked just the way the archery mistress at Miss Pimm's had looked on the first day of piracy lessons. "I know you don't care for our agreement," she told him. "Neither do I. But you have more of a right to be cross than I do, because even if you *do* win our battle, the gargoyle will make a snack of you."

"I shall do my best to avoid his jaws," said Blacktooth drily. "Do all of you Westfields have a knack for being infuriating, or are you and your father the only ones who possess it?"

Hilary felt all her muscles grow tense. "If I were anything like my father," she said, "I'd have tossed you overboard already. How can you bear to help him take over the kingdom? Can't you see he'll betray you as soon as he's finished with you?"

Blacktooth shrugged. "Not if I betray him first."

"If you don't mind my saying so," the gargoyle said, "I think you could use some better friends."

"Here we are," said Mr. Gull, placing a freshly inked sheet of parchment on the table. "I've written out your compromise in the most official-sounding words I could think of. Sign here, please." He handed one pen to Hilary and another to Blacktooth. When they had both signed the document, he pressed it against a blotting paper and tucked it neatly inside his copy of *Leading the League*. "Thank you both," he said. "Will you be staying for dinner, Terror?"

"Absolutely not," said Hilary. "Please take me to the dinghy at once, Mr. Gull."

Mr. Gull rowed Hilary back to shore, and he tipped his hat as she stepped onto the sand. "I shall see you in two weeks, Terror," he said, "unless you plan to run away before then."

"I certainly don't," said Hilary. "If you can't spot me when you sail into Queensport Harbor, don't be alarmed. I'll be arriving fashionably late."

THE VERY NEARLY HONORABLE LEAGUE OF PIRATES
Servin' the High Seas for 154 Years

THE RENEGADE
CABIN OF THE PRESIDENT

✠ ✠ ✠ ✠ ✠

Let it be noted to one and all that the pirate Rupert
Blacktooth and the pirate Hilary Westfield have agreed to
the following Amendment to the Very Nearly Honorable
League of Pirates' rules of battle (originally set forth in
Leading the League, Seventeenth Edition):

FIRST, for the purposes of this battle, the term "pirate" shall
apply to any individual who wishes to be one, even if she is a
student at Miss Pimm's Finishing School for Delicate Ladies.

SECOND, the pirate captain who emerges victorious
in battle shall be granted possession of a magical and
opinionated stone beast known as the Gargoyle.

This contract was made aboard the most majestic pirate
galleon on the High Seas, the *Renegade*. It shall remain valid
until the unfortunate day when the Jolly Roger no longer
flies over the golden shores of Augusta.

Signed,

Captain Rupert Blacktooth, PRESIDENT, VNHLP

Pirate Hilary Westfield, TERROR OF THE SOUTHLANDS

Pirate Horatio Gull, WITNESS

PIRATE HILARY WESTFIELD
TERROR OF THE SOUTHLANDS

◇ ◇ ◇ ◇ ◇

Sir Nicholas Feathering:

It is well past midnight. I have sipped a glass of warm milk, balanced on my head, and counted exactly five hundred dancing sheep, but I have not yet fallen asleep. You see, Sir Nicholas, I am far too furious to relax. More specifically, I am furious with you.

Not more than a few hours after you so rudely approached me and attempted to gain my trust, Captain Blacktooth and his men ransacked Jasper's house and nearly succeeded in sending me out of the kingdom. You will be disappointed, I think, when I assure you that I am still here. (Despite my crew's best tidying efforts, the pirates' mess remains here as well.) It seems Captain Blacktooth discovered that I have been instructing Miss Pimm's students in piracy—but you already know this, of course, because you must be the black-hearted double-crosser who gave him this information.

There's no use in denying it. How long did you spend following me through the streets of Pemberton before I spotted you? Did you spy a sword-fighting lesson through the finishing-school window, perhaps? Or did you overhear my conversations with the gargoyle? He is my dearest friend, Sir Nicholas, and thanks to you, I may lose him forever. I hope you are decent enough to feel a twinge of remorse.

Obviously, our arrangement is canceled. You needn't worry about giving me any information about Blacktooth's plans, for I'm sure whatever you tell me will be a falsehood. If the Mutineers ever do turn on you, I won't lift a finger to help you—and as for Alice, I am sure she is better off staying as far away from her deceitful brother as possible.

I am still furious, but now that I have written you this letter, perhaps I'll finally be able to get a few hours of sleep. If you contact me again, I shall push you back into the stinging nettles without a second thought, so please don't bother.

With outrage,
Hilary Westfield

◇ ◇ ◇ ◇ ◇

CHAPTER ELEVEN

"**C**APTAIN BLACKTOOTH WANTS to take the gargoyle?" cried Claire from behind a towering pile of pirate coats. "And the gargoyle's going to *let* him?" The coats swayed in her arms, threatening to fall to the floor in a jumble as she hurried through the hallways of Miss Pimm's. "But that's awful! Why didn't you tell me ages ago?"

"You were busy." Hilary was doing her best to keep up, but the bundle of crisp linen shirts she was carrying was cumbersome, and she had to keep stopping to adjust her grip. "We all were." It had taken three full days to clean the bungalow after Blacktooth's men had pillaged it, though Hilary had discovered that scrubbing jam off the walls was surprisingly quick work when one was furious. In the middle of it all, Captain Wolfson and his mates had arrived from Summerstead, singing hearty northern songs late into the night and devouring meat pies as quickly as Mr. Marrow could bake them. Hilary was grateful they'd come, but they were starting to get underfoot.

"Busy or not, you should have told me immediately," said Claire. "I would have filled Blacktooth's boots with pond scum—and I shall do it anyway as soon as I have the chance. Do you really have to go through with the agreement?"

"I don't think I have a choice," Hilary said glumly. "Mr. Gull had us both sign a horrid contract, and if I break it— well, you know what pirates are like. I'll be lucky if I have a full set of knucklebones left for them to put on display at League headquarters. But the gargoyle keeps telling everyone not to worry, that he won't be going anywhere because I'm sure to defeat the Mutineers. I wish he'd lend me a bit of his confidence." She paused at the foot of the dormitory staircase and looked back over her shoulder. "Where *is* the gargoyle, by the way?"

"I'm coming!" called the gargoyle. Although Hilary had told him that she and Claire could manage perfectly well on their own, he had insisted on carrying the hats. Now he followed them down the hall with a stack of stately black tricornes balanced on his head. The bottommost one had slipped over his eyes, and several more escaped from the top of the stack each time he hopped; a trail of hats lay scattered in his wake. "I'm just taking my time," he said solemnly, "because hats are very particular about the way they're carried. They don't enjoy being rushed."

Hilary set down her armload of shirts and retrieved the hats from the gargoyle's head before he could crash into a door frame. "In that case," she said, "why don't we leave them here at the bottom of the stairs and come back for them later?"

The gargoyle looked distinctly relieved. "I think the hats would like that," he said.

They made their way up the dormitory staircase, stopping on nearly every landing to deliver their bundles of pirate clothing to the girls who had promised to join them on the High Seas. The sewing mistress and her pupils had pieced together green coats for the cannon tenders, crimson coats for the sword fighters, purple coats for the older girls who'd been appointed ships' officers, and orange coats for the girls who'd volunteered to perform sea chanteys during the battle. With the extra scraps of fabric, they had even fashioned a handsome cape for the gargoyle; now he hopped up and down the stairs showing off his new finery to anyone willing to admire it.

"We've got nearly enough supporters now," Hilary confided to Claire as they collected the last few scattered hats from the floor. "Charlie's keeping count on the bungalow wall. I checked last night, and he'd carved one hundred ninety-five marks."

"That's good news," said Claire. "Isn't it? You look about as cheerful as a thundercloud."

"I've been feeling a little peculiar ever since I met with Blacktooth," Hilary said. "My stomach has been leaping about, my mouth is too dry, my hands are too damp, and every time I close my eyes, I see the *Renegade* firing its cannons. It's all very unsettling." She sat down on the staircase. "Do you think I'm ill?"

Claire sat down next to her. "I think you're nervous," she said kindly. "It's perfectly normal."

Hilary groaned. "I was afraid of that. And it isn't normal, not for pirates. The Terror of the Southlands isn't supposed to be nervous!"

"Nonsense. I'll bet even Captain Blacktooth himself is chewing his fingernails to nubbins at this very moment."

Hilary thought about it. "I'm not sure Blacktooth is the nail-chewing type."

"Perhaps he isn't," Claire admitted. "Still, you should try to look on the bright side of things. It's been days since anything's gone disastrously wrong!"

"Er, Terror?" Charlie came through the doorway, looking grim and pale. "I'm sorry to interrupt, but there's a sort of commotion going on outside, and I thought you ought to know about it."

Hilary sprang up from the steps and reached for her cutlass. "What's happening?" she said. "Is it the Mutineers?"

"Actually," said Charlie, "it's your mother."

BY THE TIME Hilary reached the finishing school's front gates, Miss Pimm was already standing there. So were five black carriages, five bored-looking coachmen, twenty of the kingdom's most well-bred horses, a passel of servants, and, in front of them all, five High Society ladies dressed in long coats and wide-brimmed hats. The widest hat of all sat atop the head of Hilary's mother. Ophelia Westfield was deep in conversation with Miss Pimm, waving her parasol for emphasis, while Miss Pimm frowned and occasionally took a few steps back to avoid a blow from the parasol.

"Mother!" said Hilary, running up to her. "I wasn't expecting you!"

"Neither was I." Miss Pimm raised her eyebrows at Hilary.

"Oh dear," said Mrs. Westfield. "Didn't you receive the letter I sent? I gave it to the postal courier ages ago."

The postal courier had been turning up on Jasper's doorstep each morning for the past few days, delivering a persistent stream of letters from Nicholas Feathering. The handwriting on the cream-colored envelopes had grown increasingly frantic as the week wore on, but Hilary had tossed each letter into the fire without even bothering to open it. Now she suspected that she'd accidentally roasted Mrs. Westfield's correspondence as well. "Don't worry, Mother," she said hastily. "I'm sure Miss Pimm is pleased to have you here." Miss Pimm didn't look anything close to pleased, but Hilary charged on nonetheless. "What are you doing in Pemberton?"

"I hope she's not here to try to make us act ladylike," said the gargoyle. He hopped down the path behind Hilary, doing his best to keep his new cape out of the mud. "It won't work, you know."

"The gargoyle's right, Mother," said Hilary. "I know you don't like it when I put myself in danger, and I'm sorry if you're concerned about the battle, but I've got to stop the Mutineers."

"I *am* concerned," said Mrs. Westfield, "and so are my friends. That's precisely why we are here." She beckoned to a cluster of footmen. "Retrieve the parcel, please."

The footmen scurried off behind the row of carriages and returned a few moments later pushing a large, heavy-looking object in front of them. It was draped in a cloth and balanced on wheels that shuddered, squealed, and threatened to fall off altogether as the footmen strained to move the object over the cobblestones. Finally, the footmen gave up pushing. They bowed to Mrs. Westfield and whisked away the cloth to reveal a massive and ancient-looking iron cannon.

Even the youngest finishing-school students had been

taught that a proper lady never raises her voice in anger, but Miss Pimm chose this moment to abandon any notion of propriety. "Mrs. Westfield!" she boomed. "I don't enjoy unexpected visitors, and I enjoy them even less when they arrive with cannons packed in their luggage. Why have you aimed this infernal device at my school?"

"Is your mother really going to blow up Miss Pimm's?" the gargoyle whispered to Hilary. "I'd never have guessed she had it in her."

"She's gone round the bend at last," Hilary said. "I can't believe it." Now Mrs. Westfield was beaming proudly at the cannon as if it were a prize oil painting in her vast collection. "Mother," said Hilary as calmly as she could, "have you brought along any more weapons we should know about?"

"Unfortunately not," said Mrs. Westfield. "The cannon was the best we could manage on such short notice. It's been gathering dust in Mrs. Cathcart's mansion for centuries." She gestured to one of the other ladies in wide-brimmed hats, who gave Hilary an apologetic sort of curtsy. "Still, it should work perfectly well."

One of the footmen rolled a small iron cannonball to Mrs. Westfield's side, and she frowned at it. "I can never remember," she said. "Does this go in before or after the gunpowder?"

Mrs. Westfield never received her answer, however, for the doors of Miss Pimm's finishing school burst open and a pack of young ladies in pirate coats and hats ran out. "Arr!"

they cried with passion as they waved their swords at the visitors. The servants shrieked and ran to hide behind their carriages, and at least one High Society lady swooned on the spot.

"Good heavens!" said Miss Pimm. "Are those my students?"

"They're good shouters, aren't they?" The gargoyle beamed with pride. "Just look how far they've come."

Dressed in a crimson coat, Rosie Hatter squeezed through the crowd and held her sword close to Mrs. Westfield's ribs. "Stand down, villain," she shouted, "and turn your weapon away from our school! If you please," she added for good measure.

Mrs. Westfield's eyes went wide. Her knees buckled, and she began to tip perilously toward the point of Rosie's sword. "Stop!" cried Hilary, running into the crowd. She dodged the sharp edges of the schoolgirls' cutlasses and caught her mother before she toppled over. "You've done a fine job, pirates, but I'm sure this has all been a misunderstanding. Isn't that right, Mother? Did you really intend to blow up Miss Pimm's?"

"Of course not!" Mrs. Westfield struggled to her feet. "What a barbaric idea! My friends and I traveled here to lend you our support against the Mutineers—and our cannon, if you'd like it."

The schoolgirls lowered their weapons and backed away as Hilary stared at her mother. "Do you mean to say that you've decided to be pirates?"

The High Society ladies gasped.

"Please, my dear!" said Mrs. Westfield. "There's no need to speak so scandalously. We have merely decided to *befriend* the pirates and assist them in their mission. You yourself gave me the idea!"

"Well," said Hilary, "I didn't truly think you'd take it!"

"It *is* rather unconventional." Mrs. Westfield spoke as though she were admitting to leading a life of crime. "When I first read your letter urging me to become a pirate, I had to employ one of the maids to play soothing melodies on a harp for nearly three hours before I regained my composure. I spent the rest of the evening calming my nerves in a lukewarm bath. All sorts of peculiar thoughts run through one's mind when one is in the bath, however, and while I knew I could never take up piracy as a career, I realized that I would very much like to help you if I could. Someone needs to put an end to your father's foolishness, and if I can't do it myself, the least I can do is lend you Mrs. Cathcart's cannon." She lowered her voice to a volume better suited for gossip. "Mrs. Cathcart and the other ladies traveling with me have been snubbed and scorned by Georgiana Tilbury for years. They'd like nothing more than to see you spoil her plans."

The ladies behind her nodded modestly.

Hilary could hardly believe her ears. "What about the good Westfield name?" she asked. Her mother was always going on about how Hilary was tarnishing it; surely she couldn't have changed her mind so completely. "What will High Society say if they find out you're helping me in battle? What will *Father* say?"

Mrs. Westfield sighed. "Despite my best efforts, you and your father have damaged the good Westfield name far beyond repair. There's not much more I can do to destroy it. And High Society is simply abuzz about the battle. With Miss Pimm lending her students' services and the queen serving as referee, how improper could it possibly be?"

"You'd better not answer that," the gargoyle murmured to Hilary.

"As for your father," said Mrs. Westfield, "I expect he'll be furious with me. I was hoping you might be able to put him back in the Dungeons—for good this time." She frowned. "You can manage that, can't you, dear?"

Mrs. Westfield seemed to think that sending someone to the Dungeons was no more complicated than setting a dinner table. Hilary tried to explain that this wasn't exactly the case, but as far as her mother was concerned, the matter was settled. "You must tell me how else we can assist you," she said. "Mrs. Farnsworth owns a ship she is willing to lend, and Mrs. Inglenook has an extensive magic collection. Her family used to own mines in the Northlands, you know; their set of magic gardening tools is simply exquisite."

"That all sounds very useful," said Hilary, "but

actually, what I need most are five more people to support me against Captain Blacktooth. I know you don't intend to live the rest of your lives as pirates, but would you and your friends be willing to join my crew, just for the day of the battle?"

Mrs. Westfield spent a few moments in thought. "I suppose that would be possible," she said at last. "We could bring a picnic!"

"We'll bring the ship and the magic pieces, too," Mrs. Cathcart added, "just in case cucumber sandwiches alone aren't enough to defeat Captain Blacktooth."

After a few minutes of discussion, Miss Pimm's coachman agreed to deliver the borrowed cannon to Little Herring Cove, and the High Society ladies and their servants removed themselves to a nearby guesthouse. The gargoyle seemed awfully disappointed that nothing had exploded, but he hopped back inside with the schoolgirls. "You did a very good job with the shouting," Hilary heard him say to them. "What do you think of my cape?"

Miss Pimm and Hilary remained by the gates and watched as the carriages squeaked away down the lane. "I'm not entirely sure what just happened," Miss Pimm remarked. "The only thing I'm sure of, in fact, is that I've never seen anything like it."

"I'm awfully sorry about all that," said Hilary. "I encouraged Mother to help me, but I never dreamed she'd show up with a cannon."

"There's no need to apologize, Terror," said Miss Pimm. "Now that my school is no longer under siege, I'm perfectly content. If I'm not mistaken, you've just enlisted your two hundredth supporter—and the Mutineers' jaws are sure to drop when they meet her."

A LETTER FROM ROYALTY!

HER ROYAL HIGHNESS

Queen Adelaide of Augusta

Miss Eugenia Pimm, Enchantress of the Northlands
City of Pemberton
Augusta

Dear Miss Pimm:

I know you are anxious for me to select the kingdom's new Enchantress, and I have given the matter a good deal of thought during my travels to the southern kingdoms. While Miss Dupree is still my preferred candidate, Miss Tilbury is supported by both the VNHLP and the Coalition of Overprotective Mothers. As you know, such influential advocates simply cannot be ignored. The pirates are still threatening to attack, and the mothers refuse to give my royal advisers a moment of peace until their demands

are met. I have discovered over the past few months that both pirates and mothers can be remarkably tenacious!)

I am currently traveling home from my goodwill tour, and I do not plan to make a final decision on this matter until I return to Augusta. While playing badminton last week with the Duchess of Trumbley, however, I had a thought that caused me to become so distracted that I nearly crashed into the net. You have told me that Miss Claire Dupree will be supporting Hilary Westfield in next week's pirate battle, and I am sure Miss Philomena Tilbury will be on hand to support Captain Blacktooth. I, of course, will be present to judge the contest! These fortuitous circumstances will allow me to observe both girls' talents and determine which young lady is better suited for the position of Enchantress.

Since I know you favor Miss Dupree, I suggest that you encourage her to perform her best magical work on the day of the battle. If she is bested by Miss Tilbury, I will not be eager to appoint her to the post, no matter how friendly you may feel toward her.

Fondly,
The Queen

CHAPTER TWELVE

ON THE EVENING before the pirates departed for battle, Jasper and Miss Greyson hosted a massive feast at Little Herring Cove. Sailors and schoolgirls sipped lemonade in the back garden, while the members of the Royal Augusta Water Ballet instructed the northern pirates on the finer points of treading water. Even Miss Pimm was present, giving Mr. Flintlock a wary look as he carved the roast with his cutlass. The air was full of conversation about the best routes to Queensport Harbor and the cleverest ways to defeat the Mutineers.

Hilary had learned all of this from the reports Alice Feathering had been bringing her throughout the evening.

She sat in one of the bungalow's hammocks with her feet up on a grog barrel, staring at her notebook while Alice twirled around her in her best lavender dress. "It's a lovely party," Alice told Hilary for the sixteenth time, "and you're foolish to miss it. Won't you come outside?"

"I'd like to," said Hilary, "but the battle's only a few days away, and I don't feel entirely ready." She frowned at the crinkled scraps of notebook paper that littered the floor beneath her boots.

"How much more ready can you be?" The gargoyle hopped in circles around Alice's skirts. "The ships are seaworthy, the cannons are loaded, the galleys are stocked, your supporters are trained, and I haven't tripped over my cape in hours. I can't think of anything else we need to do, so can we please go outside and eat?"

"I believe Jasper's going to play his concertina," said Alice. "If we don't hurry, we'll miss the performance."

"I'm sure I'll be able to hear it through the window," said Hilary. All the residents of Little Herring Cove knew well that Jasper's concertina was neither quiet nor melodious.

The gargoyle squinted up at Hilary's notebook. "Is that what's got your hat feathers all ruffled?" he asked. "The Buccaneers' Code?"

Hilary sighed and set down her pen. "Yes," she said, "if you must know, that's exactly what it is. I'm nearly out of time, and I don't have any idea what to say. Every time I try to write down how a pirate should behave, I end up tearing the whole page out."

Alice picked up one of the discarded notebook pages and smoothed it out. "'A good pirate should never be overtaken by hiccups during a duel,'" she read aloud. "I suppose it's not exactly *bad* advice."

"It's terrible," Hilary told her. "I believe I still have a bit to learn about leading the VNHLP."

"You'll learn quickly enough once you're holding the presidential cutlass," said the gargoyle, "and you won't earn *that* unless you get out of that hammock. Come on, Alice; help me get the Terror on her feet."

For her size, Alice proved to be remarkably strong. She took hold of Hilary with her good arm and tugged her out into the garden as the gargoyle nipped at their heels. Hilary had fully intended to keep worrying about the Buccaneers' Code, but Mr. Flintlock handed her a glass of lemonade, Jasper struck up a tune on the concertina, and she soon found herself caught up in the cheerful throng of pirates. They were feasting and singing and dueling, and Hilary was happy to see that none of them had been overtaken by hiccups.

Hilary made her way to the edge of the crowd, where Claire was using a magic coin to light a row of lanterns before the sun set. "It's not too difficult once you get the hang of it," she was saying to Charlie. "I tried using a larger magic piece at first, but three of the lanterns melted. Would you like to try lighting one?"

Claire held out the coin to Charlie, who touched its edge as though it might burn him. "I'd better not," he said hastily. "Maybe I'll try it tomorrow. Or Tuesday—I hear Tuesdays are very good for magic."

"Tomorrow," said Claire firmly. "Do I have your word as Scourge of the Northlands?"

Charlie stepped backward, nearly bumping into Hilary. "Sorry about that, Terror!" he said. "It's just that I'm not the Scourge of the Northlands—not yet, anyway. There hasn't been a Scourge since my pa died."

"Then it's high time we had one again," Claire told him. "I saw you disarm seven Mutineers in a row last summer. Isn't that something the Scourge of the Northlands would do?"

"I—well, I suppose so," said Charlie, "but—"

"Besides," said Claire, "it seems to me that the only real requirement for being a Scourge is saying that you are one."

Charlie stared at her. "I hadn't considered that."

"I should consider it right away if I were you." Claire tucked away her magic coin and turned to Hilary. "What have you been up to, Terror? Were you charting our course to Queensport? Or coming up with a new trick to play on the Mutineers?"

"The Terror doesn't need tricks," said Charlie. "She'll defeat them fair and square. Isn't that right?"

Hilary swallowed. "Of course," she said quickly. "Fair and square. It's all part of the plan." Truthfully, Hilary's plan didn't extend much further than that, but she didn't see any reason to alarm her mates.

"I wish I felt half as confident as you do," Claire said, gathering up as many lanterns as she could carry. "I'm sure you'll do splendidly, Hilary, but Miss Pimm just told me that the queen herself will have her eye on me. She wants to know if my magic's as strong as Philomena's. Miss Pimm tried to be cheerful about it, but she looked as panicked as à fish in a bucket."

Hilary took one of Claire's lanterns and hung it from a tree branch. "If the queen doubts you for an instant," she said, "the Scourge of the Northlands and I will set her straight."

"So will I," said the gargoyle, hopping up to them. "We gargoyles can be very persuasive."

Jasper had finally put the concertina out of its misery, and all the pirates clapped, probably out of relief. "Thank you all," said Jasper, bowing more times than was strictly necessary. "Now, for my encore—"

From somewhere in Little Herring Cove, there came an enormous splash that sounded very much like a cannonball landing in the shallows. Mrs. Westfield and her High Society friends gasped, a dozen pirates drew their swords, and Mr. Partridge's nephew Godfrey—the one who didn't care for loud noises—leaped into the air and landed hard in the vegetable patch.

"Oh, drat!" someone cried from the water. "Help!"

By the time Hilary reached the shore, a group of schoolgirls and water-ballet performers had already swum out into the cove. Now they towed a shivering and sodden young man back through the waves and dragged him onto dry land. "He's not dressed for swimming, Terror," one of the water-ballet performers said, "and he's not much good at it either. We think he might be a spy."

"Then he mustn't be a very smart one." Hilary glared down at the young man. Salt water dripped from his tail-coat, his cravat, and his nose. "Nicholas Feathering," she said, "you've got seaweed on your head."

Nicholas spit out a mouthful of waves and brushed off as much of the seaweed as he could. "I'm sorry," he said. "I swear I didn't intend for any of this to happen. I asked my magic piece to transport me here, but I wasn't strong enough to travel all the way to land, so it dumped me into the sea instead."

The gargoyle gave him a dubious look. "You certainly arrived with a splash."

"And he can leave with one too, for all I care!" Alice ran down to the water's edge, waving her sword in front of her and leaving clusters of nervous pirates in her wake.

"Are you going to slice off his ears, Terror? I'll do it if you won't."

Alice's sword was shaking in her hand, but she looked perfectly serious. "Wait a moment," said Hilary, stepping between Alice and Nicholas. "Before anyone does anything rash, I'd like to know what's going on. Alice, you'd better put down your sword; Miss Greyson looks ready to throw a fit."

Alice scowled. "Fine," she said at last, placing the sword on the ground. "Will you at least let me yell at him?"

"Someone certainly should," said Charlie. "What in the blazes is that Mutineer doing here?"

"Spying on us, I assume," said Hilary, "and lying, and telling his traitorous friends about everything we do."

"You've got it wrong!" Nicholas scrambled to his feet. He looked wet and unfortunate, and he smelled even worse than he looked. "Why haven't you replied to my letters?"

All two hundred of Hilary's mates had gathered around them by now; some still clutched their glasses of lemonade. "Letters?" said Alice. "What's he talking about?"

Mrs. Westfield stepped forward. "You mustn't be too upset, young man. My daughter has many talents, but I'm afraid correspondence isn't among them."

Hilary ignored her mother. "I threw your letters into the fire," she said, "and I'm glad I did. You swore you'd help me, and then you ran home to your beloved Mutineers and told them all about my plans."

"I didn't!" Nicholas brushed a drop of seawater from his nose. "I had no idea Captain Blacktooth was coming here, and I certainly didn't know he'd threaten the gargoyle. It doesn't seem like a very sporting thing to do."

"There's an awful lot Nicholas doesn't know," said Alice. "Perhaps that explains the strange whistling noise his head makes when the wind passes through it."

Hilary studied Nicholas's face. "Then how did Blacktooth find out I'd been recruiting schoolgirls to be pirates?"

"Oh, my dear," said Mrs. Westfield, "everyone in High Society knows that! Mrs. Grimshaw's daughter Nellie wrote home to say she was preparing to become a pirate, and Mrs. Grimshaw told her dear friend Mrs. Larimer, and Mrs. Larimer is no good at all at keeping secrets. If she stumbles across an item of gossip over breakfast, she'll spread it to every soul in the kingdom by teatime."

"The *Scuttlebutt* ran a few articles about you as well," said Nicholas. "I sent you a clipping in one of my letters."

Hilary could feel her cheeks growing warm enough to burn a year's worth of correspondence. Miss Greyson was always reminding her to keep up with the news of the day, and she supposed this was what came of ignoring Miss Greyson's advice. "If that's true," she said, "then I shouldn't have called you a black-hearted double-crosser after all. I'm sorry."

"I'm not," said Alice fiercely. "He's still a Mutineer, and he still hasn't explained why he magicked himself here in the first place."

"I agree," said Charlie. "He'd better have a good reason for dripping all over Jasper's garden."

Nicholas lifted his chin, looking as dignified as a High Society gentleman could under the circumstances. "I told the Terror I'd bring her information about Blacktooth's plans, and I've done exactly that." He nodded at Hilary. "In exchange for your protection, of course."

Hilary looked around at her mates. "What do you say?" she asked them. "Do you think it's a fair trade?"

"That," said Jasper, "depends entirely on what he's got to tell us."

"I don't mind helping Sir Nicholas," Claire said after a few moments. "Anyone who's betrothed to Philomena needs all the help he can scrape together."

"Aye," said Cannonball Jack. "If yer not givin' up yer life, yer limb, or yer gunpowder, 'tis a better trade than most pirates are likely to get."

Alice scuffed her boots in the dirt, sending a cloud of dust over the hem of her party dress. "I'm not sure I want to help him," she said at last, "but if you think we should, Terror, I'll do my best not to slice off his ears."

Nicholas looked so pleased by this that Hilary worried he would try to embrace them all on the spot. "Very well," she said before his sentiments had a chance to overwhelm him. "If you tell us what you've learned, we won't toss you back into the sea."

"Thank you," said Nicholas. "I'll begin at once." He reached into the pocket of his coat and pulled out a folded sheet of paper so soggy that it threatened to dissolve entirely. "About two weeks ago, Captain Blacktooth and Admiral Westfield both sailed up to the Northlands to make plans with Mrs. Tilbury. Philomena and I weren't allowed to join the meeting; we were supposed to take a stroll with that tiresome Oliver person."

"You don't like Oliver either?" the gargoyle asked. "Hmm. Maybe there's more than wind between your ears after all."

"I knew I wouldn't get a chance to overhear Captain Blacktooth discussing his plans if I was on a forced march around the mansion. At first I thought I'd pretend to be ill, but Mrs. Tilbury simply wrapped a scarf around my neck and pushed me out the door. She said there was no better cure for a fever than a bracing gust of cold air." Nicholas shivered a little just speaking about it. "Before I knew it, I was trapped outside with Oliver and Philomena. They're both very fond of long, wintry walks—or at least they claim to be. Truthfully, I think Philomena is too frightened of her mother to disobey her."

"I can't believe Philomena is frightened of *anything*," said Claire.

"Just be glad you're not a Tilbury," Nicholas told her.

"I walked nearly two miles through Nordholm, trying to come up with a plan. The others still thought I was ill, so they didn't seem to mind that I was lagging behind. I was just about to make a run for it when the postal courier hurried up behind us and gave me a letter—a furious one from Pirate Westfield, as a matter of fact."

Hilary bit her lip. "I apologize for that."

"Anyway," said Nicholas, "I told Philomena that the letter was from Alice. I said she'd changed her mind about fighting the Mutineers, and she'd agreed to pass information about the Terror's plans to us instead."

"I'd rather eat slugs!" said Alice. "Why would you say such a thing? They couldn't have believed you."

Nicholas shrugged. "They seemed to," he said. "I told them you'd sent me some news that I had to share with Captain Blacktooth immediately, and I ran back to the house as quickly as I could. The Mutineers were meeting in the drawing room, and I tried to listen at the door, but I couldn't make out most of the words. I'm fairly sure Queen Adelaide was mentioned more than once, though."

"Please tell me you heard more than that," said Jasper, "or I'll be tempted to throw my concertina at your head."

"Sorry." Nicholas gave the concertina a nervous sort of look. "The eavesdropping wasn't going as well as I'd hoped, so I summoned my courage and went into the drawing room. Captain Blacktooth was saying something about a new ship he was building in Summerstead, but I'm afraid he stopped talking as soon as he noticed me. I don't think anyone was terribly pleased to see me, and I still had to pretend I was delivering news from Alice."

Hilary crossed her arms. "What did you tell them?"

"Well," said Nicholas slowly, "I had to make something up, so I said that the Terror of the Southlands had ordered some fancy long-range cannons from the next kingdom over." He hesitated. "And Captain Blacktooth decided to order some fancy long-range cannons himself in response."

"Of course he did." Hilary sighed. "Now he'll be even more difficult to defeat."

"Mr. Feathering may have good intentions," Miss Pimm said from the crowd, "but he's the worst spy I've ever met."

"But I haven't told you about my triumph!" said Nicholas. He held up the soggy square of folded paper; it didn't look much like a triumph to Hilary. "While Blacktooth was talking about the cannons he wanted to order, I got a look at the plans for the ship he's having built. I don't understand it myself, but I know he thinks it's his secret weapon—the thing that's going to ensure his victory in battle. I memorized as much as I could and drew up a copy of the plans as soon as I'd left the room." Nicholas grinned and unfolded the paper, which was already tearing at the creases. "This," he said, laying the sketch on the grass, "is Captain Blacktooth's secret weapon."

Charlie fetched a lantern, and everyone gathered around to study the paper.

"Is it a fearsome galleon?" asked Twigget from the back of the crowd. "Has it got masts as tall as a thousand men, and a gun deck as vast as the southern sea?"

The gargoyle hopped over to Hilary's side and examined the drawing. "It doesn't *look* all that fearsome," he reported. "It only has one cannon, and—well, what do you know? Blacktooth's put a Gargoyle's Nest on the front."

"That's odd." Hilary looked from the ship's plans to Jasper and back again. "I may be mistaken, but . . ."

"You're not," said Jasper. "Are you sure this is the design you saw, Mr. Feathering?"

"Entirely sure. Is something the matter?"

"Not exactly," said Hilary. "I don't understand why this ship is Blacktooth's secret weapon, though." She looked around at her mates. "This ship is the *Pigeon*."

Kingdom of Augusta
OFFICE OF THE ROYAL RECORDS KEEPER

FORM 118M: INTENTION TO SET SAIL
INSTRUCTIONS: Please write legibly in ink. Forms
completed in blood will be rejected upon receipt.
All questions are mandatory.

NAME OF CAPTAIN: *Hilary Westfield,*
Terror of the Southlands
NAME OF VESSEL: *The Pigeon*
TYPE OF VESSEL: *Pirate ship (small)*
HOME PORT: *Wimbly-on-the-Marsh,*
The Southlands
DESTINATION: *Queensport, The Southlands*

GENERAL PURPOSE OF VOYAGE
(please check one):
☐ BUSINESS   ☐ PLEASURE   ☒ PIRACY

If PIRACY is checked, the Kingdom of Augusta
reserves the right to send the Royal Navy to attack
your vessel if necessary. Do you accept these terms?
As I expect to be attacked by an entire army of
pirates, I'm sure it won't be necessary for the
Royal Navy to attack me as well.

NUMBER OF CREW MEMBERS: *There are two hundred pirates in our fleet.*

NAMES OF CREW MEMBERS (please list):
Various freelance pirates, schoolgirls, governesses, gargoyles, Enchantresses, tradespeople, water-ballet performers, reformed villains, High Society ladies, parrots, and mothers—far too many to list here.

PRIMARY OBJECTIVE OF VOYAGE: *To defeat Captain Blacktooth in battle and win the presidency of the Very Nearly Honorable League of Pirates*

NUMBER OF FLOTATION DEVICES ON BOARD:
Fewer than I'd like

NUMBER OF WEAPONS ON BOARD:
Fewer than we'll need

If you PERISH AT SEA, would you like a MEMORIAL PLAQUE installed in your honor at the Royal Palace?
☐ YES ☒ NO
If it's not too much trouble, however, my gargoyle would like someone to dedicate an ornamental fountain in his memory.

Thank you for complying with the rules and regulations of the Kingdom of Augusta, and enjoy your voyage!

PIRATES AND ONLOOKERS
GATHER FOR THRILLING BATTLE

QUEENSPORT, AUGUSTA—With only one day remaining until the High Seas confrontation between Captain Rupert Blacktooth and Pirate Hilary Westfield, swashbucklers and spectators alike are making their way toward Queensport Harbor. Taverns and groggeries are stuffed to the seams with pirates from across the kingdom, and guesthouses are filled with holidaymakers, many of whom have traveled for days to witness the battle.

"I came all the way from Otterpool to cheer for the Terror of the Southlands," said farmer Peter Scattergood. "She and her mates gave me a magic piece of my own last summer, and I'm grateful for it." Though the queen has vowed to remain neutral during the battle, it is rumored that she hopes the Terror will emerge with the victory. Others, however, will be rooting for the Terror's opponent to win the contest. "I wouldn't want to say a word against Captain Blacktooth," said Cecil Theodore, manager of the Ornery Clam boardinghouse. "All of my guests support him, and their swords are frightfully convincing."

Captain Blacktooth's ships have already gathered on

the western side of Queensport Harbor, and the Terror's ships have recently set sail from Wimbly-on-the-Marsh. Eyewitnesses report that while the Terror has assembled a fascinating and unusual pirate crew, her mates are greatly outnumbered by those pirates fighting alongside Captain Blacktooth. "I'm sure it will be an exciting battle," said parlor maid Bess Millet, "but I'm not sure it's going to be a fair one."

Queen Adelaide, the judge of tomorrow's contest, is still traveling back from the southern kingdoms. In a message sent by postal courier from HMS *Benevolence*, however, she promised to arrive as promptly as possible. "I wouldn't dream of missing such a historic occasion," she wrote. "Furthermore, because I know my citizens will want to enjoy viewing the battle as well, I hereby declare that tomorrow shall be a holiday throughout the kingdom. I wish all the competitors the best of luck, and may the bravest pirate win!"

THE ROYAL GUARDS
KINGDOM OF AUGUSTA
THE FIRST NAME IN VIGILANCE

WARNING!

It was discovered today that convicted criminal Georgiana Tilbury has escaped from her home in the Northlands. After serving her guard a cup of tea mixed with sleeping powder, Mrs. Tilbury slipped away from Tilbury Park and left for parts unknown. Citizens who encounter her should proceed with caution: this criminal possesses both a sharp wit and a sharp tongue, making her a dangerous adversary.

CHAPTER THIRTEEN

HILARY HAD NEVER seen a more unusual procession of ships than the one that sailed in front of her on the way to Queensport. Leading the fleet was the *Blunderbuss*, with dozens of pirates standing at attention behind its rows of cannons. Lucy Worthington had only sent the ship in the wrong direction twice, and Cannonball Jack had planted new flowers in the window boxes especially for the occasion. The *Dancing Sheep* sailed close behind, captained by Miss Pimm and crewed by a multitude of schoolgirls wearing golden crochet hooks behind their ears, cutlasses on their belts, and colorful feathers in their new hats. Then came Mr. Stanley's vessel, and Mr. Twigget's, and Captain

Wolfson's second-best longship, all doing their best to stay in line. Hilary's mother and her friends had already spread out their picnic blanket beside the antique cannon on the deck of Mrs. Farnsworth's ship, where Flintlock served as captain and the Pemberton baker as first mate. A gramophone at the stern played Handel's *Water Music* for the members of the Royal Augusta Water Ballet, who swam in the ship's wake with legs extended above the waves and toes pointed toward the sky. Last of all came the *Pigeon*. A warm spring breeze filled her sails, and the Terror of the Southlands stood at her helm.

"Terror," said Alice, "Nicholas is poking me again." She rapped her knuckles against the side of the treasure chest she was sitting on. "If he doesn't stop, may I push him overboard?"

"I'm only poking you because you're sitting on my air holes," Nicholas said from inside the chest. "You're supposed to protect me, not smother me. Can I come out now?"

"Why don't you climb up to the crow's nest and keep a lookout?" Hilary said to Alice. "As for you, Sir Nicholas, you're welcome to come out of the chest as soon as you're prepared to face the Mutineers and fight them alongside us. If you don't want them to know you're here, though, you'd better try to get comfortable."

There was a moment of silence from the chest. "On second thought," said Nicholas, "it's very nice in here."

"I could turn him invisible," Claire suggested, patting the magic coatrack that Jasper had brought out of storage. "I'm not entirely sure it would work, though. When I tried it on the mouse that lives in our dormitory staircase, he only went *mostly* invisible. If you looked closely enough, you could still make out his whiskers."

"You'd better not try it on Nicholas," Hilary said. "You'll need all your strength for the battle, and besides, it would be awfully inconvenient to have an invisible person wandering about the ship. We'd all keep bumping into him."

The door to the captain's quarters swung open, and Charlie, Jasper, Miss Greyson, and the gargoyle filed out, each looking more exhausted than the last. "We've done it, Terror," said Jasper, rubbing his eyes in the sunlight. "We've thought of every possible reason why Captain Blacktooth might build an exact replica of the *Pigeon*."

"And it only took us an entire day," Charlie added.

"That's wonderful!" said Hilary. "May I hear your results?"

Jasper nodded. "Eloise shall do the honors."

Miss Greyson looked down at the piece of paper she was holding. "First possibility: Captain Blacktooth so admired the *Pigeon*'s elegant design and sturdy construction that he simply had to have a copy of his own." She looked sideways at Hilary. "Jasper came up with that one."

"So I did," said Jasper. He let out a tremendous yawn. "You're quite welcome."

"Second possibility: Captain Blacktooth wants the battle to be as fair as possible, so he has abandoned the *Renegade* for a smaller, less powerful ship that happens to be identical to his enemy's."

Miss Greyson looked proud of this suggestion, but Jasper shook his head. "My dear," he said, "you're entirely too optimistic."

"Oh, very well. I admit it's not likely. Third possibility: Captain Blacktooth believes he will win the battle, and he is preparing to take ownership of the gargoyle by building a ship with a Gargoyle's Nest on the bowsprit."

Hilary frowned. "That doesn't make much sense."

"I'll say," said the gargoyle. "If he thinks he can win me over with a Gargoyle's Nest, he'd better think again."

Miss Greyson cleared her throat. "Our fourth and final possibility is that Captain Blacktooth has a nefarious plan we know nothing about, and that plan somehow involves the *Pigeon*."

"That was my idea," said Charlie proudly.

"To summarize our findings," Miss Greyson said, folding up the paper, "we have absolutely no idea what Captain Blacktooth is going to do, but whatever it is, we assume it won't be pleasant."

Claire applauded politely, and the gargoyle bowed.

A true pirate would never admit how worried she felt, so Hilary held her tongue. "Thank you for trying," she told the others instead. "We'll just have to do our best to thwart Captain Blacktooth's plan when he unveils it."

As the *Pigeon* drew closer to Queensport Harbor, Alice called down from the crow's nest that she could see the crowds gathering along the shore. "They've got flags," she said giddily, "and banners as well. I think the black ones are for Captain Blacktooth, but the red ones must be for you, Terror. There's a stall selling flowers, and a few others selling food, and—my goodness! Is that the Otterpool Royal Orchestra? I can't imagine how they expect to be heard over the cannon fire."

"Really?" Hilary fanned herself with her hat. The air was beginning to feel thick and uncomfortably warm around her, like a woolen bathing costume she couldn't wriggle out of. "I didn't realize we were going to have such a large audience."

"Can you see Blacktooth's ships?" Charlie asked. "Has he brought his secret weapon and his two hundred pirates?"

Alice raised her spyglass. "The *Renegade* is at the far side of the harbor," she said. "I don't see any ship that looks like the *Pigeon*, but as for the other pirates . . ." She looked down at Hilary. "It looks like there are a good deal more than two hundred of them."

"Oh dear," said Hilary. "I was afraid of that."

Claire tightened her grip on the magic coatrack, and Charlie tugged at his collar, but the gargoyle simply rolled his eyes. "There's nothing to be afraid of," he said.

"Blacktooth may have more supporters than you do, but I'm sure they're nowhere near as good-looking."

When they reached the spot where the coastline bent northward toward Queensport Harbor, the gargoyle shouted out to the other ships to halt. Hilary clambered up on a storage crate, and Miss Greyson handed her a speaking trumpet that had been hiding somewhere in the depths of her carpetbag. Aboard the *Dancing Sheep*, Miss Pimm clapped her hands to quiet her students, and on Mrs. Farnsworth's ship, Hilary's mother hushed the gramophone.

"Hello," said Hilary to her mates. "Before we sail into the harbor, I've got something I'd like to confess. I'm not sure what will happen to us when we face Captain Blacktooth and his supporters. Some of us haven't been pirates for very long, and most of us haven't been in a battle before—not a battle like this one. Blacktooth's mates are fearsome; they've got shiny gold teeth and nicely polished hooks, and they've probably just sharpened their cutlasses. They'd like nothing more than to sink us as quickly as they can."

"Um, Hilary?" said the gargoyle. "Is it traditional for a pirate captain to scare the pants off her crew?"

"If it's tradition you want," Jasper murmured, "you're on the wrong ship."

Hilary grinned at him. "I used to think that pirates weren't afraid of anything," she said, "but I'm starting to believe I was wrong about that. Captain Blacktooth's mates are only supporting him because they're afraid of him, aren't they? And I'm quite sure Blacktooth is afraid of *us*. He wouldn't be hiding behind his threats and his magic pieces if he weren't."

Mr. Partridge raised his hand. "I'm a bit frightened myself," he said.

"Good!" said Hilary. "So am I. But the difference between us and the Mutineers is that the Mutineers are fighting *because* they're frightened. We're frightened too, but we're fighting in spite of it. Any pirate can find a treasure or wave a sword, but hardly any are brave enough to face the things they're truly afraid of. That makes all of you the bravest pirates I know." The stifling air had started to fall away around Hilary, and she set down the speaking trumpet; she believed she could shout halfway to the Northlands at the moment. "What do you say, mates?" she called. "Are you ready to show Captain Blacktooth what it truly means to be a good pirate?"

"Absolutely!" said Charlie.

"More or less," said Miss Greyson.

"Not really," said Claire, "but I suppose it's too late to do anything about it."

"Shiver me timbers!" cried the gargoyle. "Let's bite some villains!"

The pirates let out a rousing cheer as, one by one, their ships sailed toward the harbor and the seaside streets of

Queensport. First went the *Blunderbuss* and its rows of cannons; then went the *Dancing Sheep*, looking for all the world like a fine pirate galleon. When the final water-ballet performer had disappeared around the bend and the tinkling notes of *Water Music* had faded on the breeze, Hilary stepped down from her crate and steered the *Pigeon* into the harbor.

Or at least she started to. Before she could guide the ship around the bend in the coastline, however, a strong gust of wind caught its sails and began to push it toward the cliffs. Hilary pulled at the ship's wheel as hard as she could, but it made no difference: although the sea around them was calm in every direction, the *Pigeon* was being driven into the rocks. "What's happening?" she called to her mates.

"Magic!" Charlie shouted back. He was holding on to his hat to keep it from flying away. "It can't be anything but that."

"But the battle hasn't even started yet! Does Blacktooth think he'll win by wrecking us against the rocks?"

"He won't wreck us," Claire said fiercely. The wind was howling around them now, and the cliff face cast shadows across the *Pigeon*'s bow as Claire wrestled with the golden coatrack. "Magic," she shouted, "please——"

The wind stopped blowing as abruptly as it had started. At first, Hilary thought Claire had calmed it, but Claire's mouth had dropped open in mid-sentence. Another shadow hung over the *Pigeon* now——the long, dark silhouette of the naval ship anchored next to her.

"What a curious magic piece you've got, Miss Dupree," said Admiral Westfield from its deck. "Unwieldy, but utilitarian." Hilary wasn't sure what was most alarming—her father's smile, the large golden urn he was holding, or the gleaming swords his mates were pointing toward the *Pigeon*. "I'm afraid, however, that if you value your life, you mustn't say another word."

THE *AUGUSTA BELLE* was the fastest ship in the Royal Navy's fleet, freshly painted in blue and gold, with polished wooden decks that smelled faintly of lemon juice and vinegar. None of this, however, made it a pleasant place to be held captive. "I'd rather be stashed in the Dungeons," Hilary said as two naval officers pushed her against the *Augusta Belle*'s mast and a third tied her to it with a long coil of rope. "At least the jailers there don't spend their holiday afternoons yanking pirates off their ships."

"Then I pity them," said the officer holding the rope, "for it's one of my favorite pastimes." He pulled a knot tight around Hilary's middle, and she clenched her fists. "I've still got molasses in my boots thanks to you."

"You navy types are remarkably good at holding grudges, aren't you?" asked Jasper from the other side of the mast. The entire crew of the *Pigeon* was tied to it by now, though Hilary could only see Claire on her left, boiling over with fury, and the gargoyle on her right, squirming in the ropes that held him a few feet above the deck. There hadn't been time to fight against Admiral Westfield's men; they'd swarmed the *Pigeon* in a whirlwind of weaponry before Hilary had even unsheathed her cutlass. Now that their prisoners were secure, the naval officers were hauling armloads of treasure from the ship's storerooms onto the *Augusta Belle*. Two of them had retrieved the treasure chest that held Sir Nicholas Feathering, though at least he'd had the good sense to stay quiet.

"If you truly wanted to get your revenge," said Jasper, "why didn't you send us to the bottom of the sea at once and avoid this whole production? It would have been much more efficient."

"Don't give them any ideas," said Charlie.

"I'm only following orders," the naval officer replied. "If Admiral Curtis wants you pirates tied up, then I'm happy to oblige."

"I doubt Admiral Curtis wants anything of the sort," said Hilary. "Let me guess. Did those orders come through his adviser?"

The officer glared at her. "This one's getting cheeky, sir," he called over his shoulder. "I can't say I like the look of her."

Admiral Westfield turned from admiring the gleaming piles of treasure he'd looted from the *Pigeon*. "What else would you expect from a notorious scallywag?" he asked. "She's exactly the sort of pirate that Admiral Curtis has asked us to eliminate from the High Seas." He sifted a pile of gold coins through his fingers. "As for why we didn't sink you, Mr. Fletcher, as hard as it may be for you to believe, I want nothing more than to keep you all alive."

"How charitable of you," Hilary said. "You're not usually so kind to your enemies, Father."

"But I've reformed!" said Admiral Westfield. He looked about as sincere as a sneak thief. "Quite frankly, Hilary, I'm disappointed that you haven't done the same. There was a time when I thought you'd grow to appreciate the comfortable life I've given you, but I've abandoned all hope that you'll ever return to your proper place in High Society. If you insist on acting like a pirate, then I shall treat you like one."

"I'm glad to hear it." Hilary would have crossed her arms if they hadn't been lashed to her sides. "If you wanted to capture me, though, you should have chosen a more convenient time. We've got a battle to attend, and if we don't arrive soon, our mates will come looking for us." She hoped very much that this was true. No spectators stood nearby to send a warning; the entire kingdom was gathered around the harbor a mile away, and no passersby were likely to glimpse the *Augusta Belle* anchored in the shadows below the cliffs. Even Fitzwilliam couldn't deliver a message to the others: one of the naval officers had tied his wings together with a spare bit of rope.

"What a frightening thought," said Admiral Westfield.

"Your schoolgirl friends will attack us with curtsies, I expect, and your mother will dump a pitcher of lemonade on my head." He chuckled. Once he'd given the nearest naval officers a quick jab in the ribs, they quickly joined in. "No, I'm afraid you won't be appearing at today's battle—and while I'm required to keep you all more or less unharmed, I can't say the same for your ship."

Miss Greyson gasped, and Jasper cursed. "Don't you dare," said Hilary, but her father had already bent down to retrieve the golden urn that lay at his feet.

"Captain Blacktooth loaned this to me from his personal treasure trove. Isn't it remarkable? I suppose pirates are good for something after all." Admiral Westfield held the magic piece in front of him as though it were a trophy he'd won at a sporting match. "Magic," he said, "sink the *Pigeon* at once."

As Hilary watched, her father took three enormous breaths, each more labored than the last. His legs trembled, his knuckles tensed, and his shoulders shuddered until Hilary felt sure he would collapse under the magic's strain. For a moment, he nearly looked frightened.

Then waves began to break over the sides of the *Pigeon*. They swamped the deck and battered the Gargoyle's Nest until it was nothing more than flotsam. The sea poured into the captain's cabin, flooded the galley, and overturned Miss Greyson's bookshelves. Rows of leather-bound novels splashed into the water like doomed sailors walking the plank. As the ship's bow tipped toward the sky, chairs and crates and compasses bobbed at the surface for a moment or two before disappearing entirely. With a final creak of wood and a damp rustle of sails, the faithful *Pigeon* descended beneath the waves.

"Oh, Hilary," the gargoyle whispered. "How can we be pirates if we don't have a ship?"

Hilary couldn't answer. Instead, she stared at the spot where the *Pigeon* had been and willed it to come back, though it stubbornly refused to resurrect itself. She had promised Jasper she'd take good care of his ship, and now it was lost for good.

Admiral Westfield relaxed his grip on the golden urn. He wiped his brow with a trembling hand and bent over to catch his breath. "That's better," he said. "I can't imagine why you pirates look so glum. Your vessel was practically a wreck already."

Hilary couldn't see Charlie tied to the other side of the mast, but she was sure he was shaking. Claire, however, had suddenly become still. "Your father's used more magic today than most people use in a month," she whispered to Hilary. "I'm sure he doesn't have much strength left. Isn't there anything we can do to overpower him?"

Hilary did her best to search her pockets, but the naval officers who'd taken her cutlass and plucked up her magic pieces hadn't missed a single coin. The knots that bound her to the mast were impressively tight, and there was no room to squirm out from under the coils of rope. She tried to imagine what the heroes in her favorite books would do if they found themselves in such a dire situation, but that only made her think of the floating bookshop and all the stories that were drifting down to the ocean floor, with only snails and sea horses to turn their pages.

A trumpet fanfare rang out from the direction of the harbor, and Admiral Westfield clapped his hands. "It must be time for the battle to begin. How fortunate we all are to have a front-row seat."

"But there won't *be* a battle if we're not there to fight it," said Alice.

"I don't know who you are, little girl, but you show a surprising lack of imagination." Admiral Westfield raised a finger. "Now be quiet, and pay attention."

MR. GULL MUST have been using a magic piece to strengthen his voice, for although Hilary couldn't see him around the bend in the shoreline, she could hear him all the way from the *Augusta Belle*. "On behalf of the Very Nearly Honorable League of Pirates," he said, "I welcome you, one and all, to this afternoon's battle. I am your humble servant, Horatio Gull, and I will serve as the announcer for today's festivities." A ripple of applause floated over the waves. "The pirate who emerges victorious in this contest will win the presidency of the VNHLP, while the losing pirate will be forced to leave the kingdom of Augusta immediately and forever. The contestants will try not to blast, behead, or otherwise injure the spectators, but if you fear for your life or safety, I recommend scampering away as quickly as possible."

Miss Greyson clicked her tongue. "How impractical."

"I agree," said Jasper. "Why run away from a battle when you could run into it?"

"It's hard to run anywhere when you're tied to a mast," Charlie pointed out.

Admiral Westfield glared at them. "Quiet!"

"The contest," Mr. Gull continued, "will be judged by none other than our beloved monarch. Queen Adelaide, would you please step forward?"

Hilary waited for cheers to erupt from the spectators, but there was only silence.

"Well," said Mr. Gull at last, "it seems the queen hasn't yet returned from her travels, but I'm sure she'll be here shortly. In the meantime, why don't we introduce our contestants? On the starboard side of the harbor is Captain Rupert Blacktooth: the most fearsome pirate in Augusta, the owner of the finest beard in sixteen kingdoms, and my personal employer. Please give three cheers for Captain Blacktooth!"

A round of huzzahs rose up from the crowd, but none of the prisoners on the *Augusta Belle* joined in. "I'd rather eat my boot leathers," said Hilary.

"So would I," said the gargoyle. "I hear they're good

with marmalade. Do you have any marmalade, Admiral Westfield?"

"I do not," said the admiral icily.

"And on the port side," said Mr. Gull once the huzzahs had faded away, "is our challenger, Pirate Hilary Westfield, the Terror of—pardon me." He paused. "Where is the Terror? And where are the rest of her supporters?"

"I suppose this is Blacktooth's grand plan," Hilary said to her father. "If I don't show up at the battle, I'll be forced to forfeit, and Blacktooth will win without even having to raise his cutlass. Is he really too cowardly to face me?"

Admiral Westfield's mouth conspired with his eyebrows to create an expression that looked something like amusement. "Blacktooth *is* a coward," he agreed, "but I assure you, Terror: that's not his plan." He looked hastily at his officers. "Not that I would know anything about the captain's intentions, of course."

"This is most unusual," Mr. Gull was saying. "My assistants have taken a count of the Terror's supporters, and six are missing, not to mention the Terror herself. Her mates assure me that she is on her way, and her mother has graciously offered me a glass of lemonade. If Pirate Westfield does not appear within the next few minutes, however, she will have to surrender her gargoyle and travel at once to the Pestilent Home for—" He broke off. "What's that on the horizon? Where did I put my spyglass?"

Just beyond the harbor, a tall ship decorated with

pennants and ribbons was approaching with tremendous speed. "It's the *Benevolence*!" said Mr. Gull. "Queen Adelaide has arrived!"

The spectators cheered, and Claire twisted her neck to get a better view. "Can you see her, Hilary?" she asked. "Is it really the queen? I ought to curtsy if it is, but being tied up by villains makes it difficult to bend one's knees."

"I'm sure the queen won't mind about that," said Hilary. "It does look like her ship, though it's flying navy flags along with the royal pennants. Admiral Curtis must still be traveling with her."

"Another naval officer?" said Charlie. "Don't we have enough of them to deal with already?"

"This one might actually be willing to help us," Hilary pointed out. A good pirate would rather snap her cutlass in two than ask for help from the Royal Navy, of course, but Hilary wasn't sure she had any other choice. "If they sail close enough to us, we might be able to get the admiral's attention—or even the queen's."

The cheering grew louder as the queen's ship approached. Hilary could see Queen Adelaide now, standing at the bow of the *Benevolence* and turning her cupped hand back and forth to wave to her subjects. The sleeves of her gown billowed in the breeze, and her crown sparkled where it caught the light. All the naval officers on the *Augusta Belle* removed their hats out of respect as the *Benevolence* sailed closer—all but Admiral Westfield.

As Hilary tried to think of a way to capture the queen's attention, another ship sped across the waves. It was smaller than the *Benevolence*, but a good deal faster; it moved so quickly, in fact, that Hilary wouldn't have recognized it if she hadn't spotted the Jolly Roger flying from the mast and the Gargoyle's Nest lashed to the bowsprit. "Well, shiver me timbers," said Mr. Gull. "The Terror of the Southlands has finally arrived in her ship, the *Pigeon*!"

"What?" cried Jasper.

Hilary stared at the new ship. It looked exactly like the *Pigeon* in every detail, but she certainly wasn't its captain. In fact, she had no idea who was standing at its helm. The gargoyle looked equally befuddled. "Is this part of Captain Blacktooth's plan?" he asked.

"It must be," said Hilary, "but it doesn't make a bit of sense! Why would the Mutineers go to so much trouble to sink our ship if they were going to bring a new ship in to take its place?"

Then a cloud of smoke bloomed in front of her, an earsplitting bang drowned out the roar of the crowd, and a cannonball sailed from the false *Pigeon*'s deck, tracing a long, lazy arc across the sky before it smashed into the *Benevolence*.

The notorious pirate Hilary Westfield has just blasted a hole in the side of the queen's ship. Onlookers gasp. Infants cry. I fumble my handful of magic coins; they clink to the deck of the *Renegade*. In short, chaos reigns!

Chaos may, however, be transformed into order through the talents of an effective secretary. Sensing that a record of this historic event might be useful in the future, I retrieve a pen and parchment from my satchel. The following conversation transpires.

MR. GULL: Captain Blacktooth! The Terror of the Southlands has attacked the queen! I'm quite sure the guidelines set forth in *Leading the League* don't allow anything of the sort. Would you like me to consult them, sir?

CAPTAIN BLACKTOOTH: Never mind the guidelines, Mr. Gull.

MR. GULL: You don't seem very alarmed, sir. This entire situation is highly irregular, and—

CAPTAIN BLACKTOOTH: (*Interrupting, as pirates often do*) Of course I'm alarmed. The Terror has opened fire on Queen Adelaide, and the whole kingdom has seen her do it. She certainly won't be the president of the League now, will she?

MR. GULL: I sincerely doubt it, sir. But I've got to say I'm surprised. I thought the Terror was fond of the queen.

CAPTAIN BLACKTOOTH: You must have been mistaken.

MR. GULL: I can't believe she would act so recklessly.

CAPTAIN BLACKTOOTH: (*Looking irritated*) I imagine she wants to seize control of the kingdom and rule Augusta herself.

MR. GULL: Are you sure? She doesn't seem like the treasonous sort.

CAPTAIN BLACKTOOTH: That's enough, Mr. Gull.

MR. GULL: And sir, doesn't the *Pigeon* look awfully similar to the ship you commissioned in Summerstead?

CAPTAIN BLACKTOOTH: I said enough!

MR. GULL: If I may make an observation, sir, you're remarkably quick-tempered this afternoon.

CAPTAIN BLACKTOOTH: (*Glaring daggers at his secretary*) I am simply concerned about the queen's welfare. I'll send my most fearsome ships to fight off the Terror of the Southlands and assist Queen Adelaide. Then all of Augusta will see how I protected the kingdom from a dangerous and dishonorable scallywag.

MR. GULL: It will make an excellent story in the *Gazette*.

CAPTAIN BLACKTOOTH: It had better. (*Under his breath*) I wish Georgiana had never dragged me into this mess.

MR. GULL: Pardon me, but would you mind speaking up? It's for the transcript.

CAPTAIN BLACKTOOTH: (*With great vexation*) Mr. Gull, if you don't put that pen down at once, I shall throw it into the sea, and you won't be far behind.

MR. GULL: Yes, sir. Of course, sir. Shall I keep announcing the battle, sir?

CAPTAIN BLACKTOOTH: Please do.

CHAPTER FOURTEEN

THE CREW OF the *Augusta Belle* was in a panic. "The queen's ship has been hit!" cried the naval officer who'd been complaining of molasses in his boots not half an hour before. "It won't stay afloat for long, from the looks of it. We must rescue Her Majesty at once!"

"Steady, mates," Admiral Westfield boomed. All of the officers stopped chattering. "I am just as distraught as you are to see our beloved monarch so rudely attacked. I'm confident that Admiral Curtis has the matter well in hand, however, and we must not place ourselves in his way. Our task is to guard our prisoners and prevent them from doing any more damage to the queen or the kingdom."

"But we haven't done any damage in the first place!" said Hilary. "How could we have possibly attacked the queen? We've been far too busy getting tied to the mast and watching our ship sink!"

Admiral Westfield walked across the deck and stopped so close to Hilary that she could have counted every bristle in his beard if she'd wanted a way to pass the time. "Of course you have," he said quietly enough that his officers couldn't overhear. "I know that as well as you do. But the queen herself surely believes you've fired upon her, and so does Admiral Curtis. So, for that matter, does every person watching from the Queensport coast—including your own crewmates."

"They'd never believe any such thing," said Hilary, though she had to admit the circumstances didn't look good.

"When Captain Blacktooth's mates fight off the false *Pigeon*," Admiral Westfield continued, "and when I deliver you criminals to the Dungeons, we shall be national heroes! Then, of course, I shall have to do away with Blacktooth somehow. Do you think an unfortunate fishing accident would do the trick? It will be an enormous hassle, but I don't want to have any competition when the wise citizens of Augusta choose their new ruler."

Perhaps the ropes that held Hilary fast had tightened themselves, for it was suddenly much more difficult to breathe. "What do you mean?" she said carefully.

"He means they're going to let the *Benevolence* sink." Charlie sounded as though he might be running out of air himself. "They're not going to rescue the queen."

"That friend of yours is rather clever." Admiral Westfield reached around the mast to pat Charlie on the shoulder. "It's a pity you're not well-bred, my lad, or you could have joined the navy."

Charlie drew in his breath, and Hilary gave her father her sharpest glare, though it was nowhere near as sharp as her cutlass. "I can see you're thoroughly enjoying yourself," she said, "but you're not nearly as good a villain as you think you are. Your plan is absurd! There's no way it's going to work."

Admiral Westfield looked pointedly at the spot where the *Pigeon* had sunk. "It seems to be working wonderfully well so far," he said, "and all thanks to you. We've wanted to remove the queen from her throne for ages, but we couldn't settle on someone to frame for the crime. When you issued your challenge to Captain Blacktooth, however, all the pieces of our plan fell into place." He brushed his hands together, as though he were dusting away something he didn't care for. "I admit I'm not thrilled about sending my own daughter off to the Dungeons—but of course you know exactly what it feels like to betray one's relations, don't you, Terror?"

The rope grew tighter around Hilary's middle.

"Don't answer him," the gargoyle whispered. "He's just trying to make you mad."

"In that case," said Hilary, "he's succeeding."

"If I may ask a question," Miss Greyson said from the other side of the mast, "won't these charming naval officers unravel your plot? They know perfectly well that Hilary didn't attack the queen."

Admiral Westfield's shoulders stiffened, the way they often did around governesses. "You have an inquiring mind, madam," he told Miss Greyson. "I can't say I care for it. As for my mates, I'm sure they'll piece things together sooner or later." He glanced behind him, where the officers were taking turns peering through a spyglass at the sinking *Benevolence*. "They're only half as dull-witted as they look. I expect, however, that a few crates of magic from the Royal Treasury will convince them to keep their ideas to themselves. And if they don't—well, the sharks aren't *too* terribly hungry this time of year. With a bit of luck, these fellows might survive for weeks!"

"Did you hear that, gentlemen?" Alice called to the officers. "Admiral Westfield plans to feed you to the sharks!"

A few of the officers frowned at her, and the others didn't even bother to turn around. "Don't waste the air we've granted you, scallywag," one of them said. "Pirates lie; everyone knows that."

"You'd think they'd be more concerned," the gargoyle remarked. "Sharks are the second most fearsome beasts in the kingdom."

"After sea monsters?" Claire asked.

The gargoyle rolled his eyes. "After *me*."

Hilary looked over her father's shoulder and out toward the sea, where a large portion of the queen's ship had already sunk below the surface. Admiral Curtis was returning the false *Pigeon*'s fire, and a number of other vessels of all shapes and sizes had sailed into the fray. Although most of them belonged to Blacktooth's allies, Hilary spotted Captain Wolfson's longship as it bounded over the waves toward the *Benevolence*, followed closely by Marrow, Slaughter, and Stanley. All the thick rope bonds in the world couldn't hold her back from smiling at the sight of them.

Admiral Westfield removed his hat and fanned himself with its brim. "Why do you look so pleased with yourself, Terror?" he asked. "You can't be enjoying this."

"I'm not," Hilary assured him. "I'm simply wondering what will happen if my mates are able to rescue the queen. That will put a cramp in the Mutineers' plans, won't it?"

"It will never happen," said Admiral Westfield. "Mr. Sanderson is at the false *Pigeon*'s helm. He happens to be the most talented young sailor on the High Seas—and why wouldn't he be, when I trained him myself?"

Of course Oliver was the villain sailing the *Pigeon*;

Hilary should have guessed. "He does excel at treachery," she said, "but Admiral Curtis is delivering a good defense. Doesn't that worry you?"

"Hardly." The very corners of Admiral Westfield's eyes twitched. "Trust me, Terror: Admiral Curtis doesn't worry me at all."

When Hilary was growing up in Westfield House, her mother had warned her not to provoke her father, most especially not when his jaw was tight and his eyes prone to twitching. In all those years, she had never dared to disobey. Now, however, Hilary's magic piece was out of sight and her cutlass was out of reach. A good pirate had to use any weapon in her possession, she reasoned, and provocation was the only weapon she had left. She stood up a little straighter against the mast.

"I've heard people say that Curtis is the finest naval admiral this kingdom has ever seen," she said, more boldly this time. "Who knows? He might even be the finest admiral in *any* kingdom!"

The twitch returned to Admiral Westfield's eyes. "Who says that?"

"Oh, everyone," said Hilary. "The queen. The Enchantress. Most of High Society."

"Nonsense," said Admiral Westfield.

"It's true!" Claire chimed in. "Curtis seems very impressive to me. I'm sure he'll win this battle."

"You can't even see him!" said Admiral Westfield.

"You're facing the wrong way!"

"We don't need to see him to be impressed," Jasper said calmly from behind the mast. "That's how talented he is."

"The *Pigeon* has fired its cannon once more," Mr. Gull was shouting over the din of the battle, "but Admiral Curtis has dealt another blow to the attackers! Will he manage to save the queen from peril?"

"Of course he won't!" said Admiral Westfield. His voice had grown louder, and a few of his officers turned to stare at him.

"Even if Admiral Curtis doesn't save the queen," said Hilary cheerfully, "even if he only puts up a very good fight, he'll still be the most famous hero in Augusta. They'll install a plaque in his honor on the palace wall."

"They'll build a statue in his likeness," said Charlie.

"They'll name a dessert after him," said Jasper, "or perhaps a type of cheese."

"They'll hold parades in his honor!" the gargoyle cried. "They'll sing songs and ballads!"

"Yes!" said Hilary. The twitching had spread from Admiral Westfield's eyes to the rest of his face; she could hardly stop talking now. "Everyone will speak for years to come about brave George Curtis, the finest naval admiral the kingdom has ever known."

"They'll do no such thing!" cried Admiral Westfield. "That Curtis fellow is as useless as a horse in a railway carriage! He's as spineless as a sponge! Why, he can hardly think for himself! Who do you think has been giving orders to the navy these past few months? Who's been directing Curtis's every move? Who's been plucking freelance pirates off the High Seas like fleas off a mutt? Who had you scallywags captured?"

The gargoyle thought about this. "You?" he asked.

"Exactly! All the naval officers in the kingdom answer to me, and there's not a thing George Curtis can do about it. He's far too frightened to challenge me. When the Mutineers have sunk him, he'll be forgotten within the week, and everyone will know who is *truly* the finest admiral in Augusta!"

From behind Admiral Westfield came the distinctive swishing sound of six naval officers drawing their swords.

Admiral Westfield put a hand to his mouth. He cleared his throat. He spun around to face his mates. "Gentlemen," he said, "what I meant to say—"

"We know exactly what you meant to say." The officer with molasses in his boots pointed his sword at Admiral Westfield's coat buttons. "You're plotting against our admiral and our queen."

"That's treason," said another officer, "not to mention bad manners."

"You've misunderstood!" Admiral Westfield protested as the officers gathered around him. "The pirates tricked me into saying those things! I love Admiral Curtis! He's as delightful as a daffodil, as charming as a chickadee—"

"You know, Father," said Hilary, "I don't believe your mates are quite as dull-witted as you said they were."

Admiral Westfield looked from port to starboard and back again. He reached for his sword, then seemed to think better of it and picked up the golden urn from the deck. "Stand back, men," he said, "or I'll enchant you all overboard, and the sharks shall have you for lunch!"

The officers' swords wavered. Their eyes grew wide, and their feet hesitated.

"He's lying through his teeth," Claire called to them. "He can't possibly have enough strength left to use all that magic. Don't let him frighten you!"

The officers exchanged glances. They began to lower their swords.

"Blast it all," said Hilary, "what are you doing? A true pirate never backs down from his enemies!"

"But we're not pirates, miss." At least the officer who said this had the good sense to look embarrassed. "And I don't care to be a shark's luncheon."

"I knew you'd see sense," said Admiral Westfield. Drops of sweat gleamed on his brow as he edged over to the treasure chest he'd stolen from the *Pigeon*; he clearly didn't trust his mates enough to turn his back on them. "Why don't I give you each a handful of magic coins, and we'll forget about this awkward conversation once and for all." Still looking at his men, he reached over with one hand and opened the treasure chest.

"Step away, you pickle-hearted scoundrel!" cried Sir Nicholas Feathering.

With a shout worthy of any pirate, he launched himself out of the chest where he'd been crouched for hours, tumbled through the air, and crashed to the deck, bringing Admiral Westfield down with him. The admiral's magic urn slipped from his hands, and Nicholas grabbed hold of it. "Release my sister and her friends," he said, "or I'll blast you into the next kingdom."

Admiral Westfield blinked up at him. "But, my lad, you're a Mutineer!"

"Actually," said Nicholas, sitting back on his heels, "I've discovered I'm not." He nodded to Hilary. "I'm a pirate."

In a matter of minutes, the naval officers released the pirates from their bonds and used the long length of rope to tie up Admiral Westfield instead. He had turned purple with rage, reminding Hilary strongly of a tinned beet. "Please sail us into the harbor, officers," she said, rubbing the lines along her arms where the ropes had bitten into her skin. "As you probably know, we're running late for a battle. Once you've dropped us off, you can take the admiral to the Dungeons—but tell the guards there that he's not to bribe his way out again."

The officers practically fell over one another in their eagerness to agree. "Of course, Terror," they said. "We'd be happy to. Thrilled! Delighted!"

"Oh, for heaven's sake," said Hilary, "you needn't look so petrified. I promise you I'm nothing like my father."

As the *Augusta Belle* sailed into Queensport Harbor, the smoke from the battle grew thicker. The shore was a scramble of spectators, who peered through opera glasses, wrung their hands, and hurried away from the docks whenever a cannon blast shook the air. At the near edge of the harbor, the *Dancing Sheep*, the *Blunderbuss*, and most of Hilary's other crewmates floated in a confused knot. "Ahoy!" she called to them. "Can any of you take a few more pirates on board?"

"Hilary?" Cannonball Jack squinted at her over the side of the *Blunderbuss*. "Be it really ye? I knew ye couldn't have been firin' at the queen! Mateys, come quick; the Terror be here at last!"

Worthington's head appeared next to Cannonball Jack's. "But why are you all on board a navy ship?" she asked. "And who's sailing the *Pigeon*?"

"I'd love to explain," said Hilary, "but I'm not sure this is the best time. For now, we'd be grateful if you'd throw over a rope."

By the time Hilary and her mates had scrambled onto the *Blunderbuss*, her supporting ships had gathered around the houseboat. "Captain Wolfson and Mr. Stanley have taken their crews across the harbor to assist the queen," Rosie Hatter reported from the *Dancing Sheep*, "and Miss Pimm's gone with them to lend a hand with the magic.

The rest of us are ready to follow you into battle, though." She hesitated. "That is, if you're still planning to fight Captain Blacktooth."

"Of course she's planning to fight Captain Blacktooth!" The gargoyle flapped his wings so eagerly that he nearly rose off the deck. "Aren't you, Hilary?"

Truthfully, Hilary suspected she'd already had enough adventure to last her at least the rest of the week. Most of her mates seemed to feel the same: Jasper had sat down on the deck of the *Blunderbuss* without even bothering to look for a chair, and Miss Greyson kept looking over her shoulder at the sea as though she hoped a few bedraggled books might float up to the surface. Still, Hilary couldn't take her eyes off the tall black galleon that skulked near the edge of the cannon smoke. "Captain Blacktooth and his Mutineers have sunk my ship," she said. "They've blackened my name, turned the pirate league against me, threatened my gargoyle, and attacked the queen. If I don't try to stop them, I might as well toss my pirate hat into the sea." She turned to Cannonball Jack, who was polishing his hook rather nervously with a handkerchief. "Lead our fleet to the *Renegade*, please—and sail as quickly as you can. If we're going to save the kingdom, we can't lose another second."

A curious fleet approaches the *Renegade*. I study it through my spyglass and take up my pen and parchment once more, for I anticipate that my employer's response to this sight is likely to be noteworthy.

MR. GULL: Captain Blacktooth! A houseboat approaches!

CAPTAIN BLACKTOOTH: A houseboat?

MR. GULL: Yes, sir. It's got daffodils in its window boxes, sir, and lovely checkered curtains. Aside from that row of cannons, it looks remarkably cozy—

CAPTAIN BLACKTOOTH: Get to the point, Gull!

MR. GULL: Of course, sir. (*With trepidation*) I'm not entirely sure how this is possible, but if I'm not mistaken—and I may be mistaken—Hilary Westfield is on board.

CAPTAIN BLACKTOOTH: What? Give me that spyglass!

MR. GULL: I thought she was on the *Pigeon*, sir. Didn't you say she was on the *Pigeon*?

CAPTAIN BLACKTOOTH: It's impossible. She's supposed to be tied to a mast somewhere, blast it all!

MR. GULL: Pardon me?

CAPTAIN BLACKTOOTH: (*Throwing the spyglass to the deck, showing a surprising lack of regard for VNHLP property*) Georgiana! Philomena! Come here at once!

CHAPTER FIFTEEN

HILARY HADN'T EXPECTED that she and her mates would receive a polite reception at the *Renegade*, but the Mutineers who looked down at her from the galleon looked even less pleased to see her than she'd imagined. Mrs. Tilbury wore a strand of pearls and a permanent frown, Philomena clutched the ship's rail, and Captain Blacktooth sighed heavily as the *Blunderbuss* passed into the *Renegade*'s shadow. Next to him, Mr. Gull was fanning himself with a piece of parchment. "This day has been a disaster!" he said. "The queen is under attack, the Terror is in two places at once, and no one has paid an ounce of attention to the rules! Am I the only pirate here who has even bothered to read *Leading the League*?"

Captain Blacktooth ignored this. "I'm surprised to see you, Terror," he called down to Hilary. "Why aren't you on your way to the Dungeons?"

"Because Father is on his way there instead." Hilary grinned up at the Mutineers, whose faces had fallen like cold soufflés. "You should be pleased about that, though. He wanted to arrange an unfortunate fishing accident for you."

Philomena leaned farther over the rail of the *Renegade*. "Nicholas!" she called. "Is that you? Oh, I just *knew* those horrid pirates had captured you! I told Mama—"

"Er, actually," said Nicholas, "I've decided to be a pirate myself."

"A pirate?" Philomena blinked. "Have you lost your wits? I can't marry a pirate!"

"And I can't marry a Mutineer." Nicholas edged closer to Alice, who nodded up at him. "Sorry about that."

Philomena began to shake, but her mother laid a hand on her shoulder. "Focus, my dear!" she said. "This is hardly the time for emotions. If you must cry, you may do it when the queen's ship finally sinks."

Hilary's own mother gasped into her glass of lemonade. Even Captain Blacktooth flinched. "There's no need to sound so eager about it, Georgiana," he said.

"Do you regret attacking the *Benevolence*, then?" Jasper called up. "I wish you'd felt half as regretful about sinking the *Pigeon*."

"That wasn't my idea," said Blacktooth. "I don't know why you pirates are looking at me so reproachfully. I did everything I could to keep you out of this battle! If you'd gone quietly into exile, Terror, there would have been no need for us to sink your ship, and we could have taken over the kingdom in a far more civilized fashion." He shrugged. "Even this morning, I hoped you'd stay away, but James warned me you weren't likely to give up so easily."

Hilary stared at Blacktooth. If what he said was true, her father had nearly paid her a compliment. She would have been less astonished if a sea monster had emerged from the harbor and invited her over for a bowl of porridge. "Well, he was right," she said, "at least about that. Was attacking the queen his idea, too?"

Blacktooth nodded, and Mrs. Tilbury aimed her frown in his direction.

"I thought so," said Hilary. "Now that he's off to the Dungeons, though, I'm sure he'll try to blame you for the whole affair. Why don't you tell Oliver Sanderson to stop blasting cannonballs at the queen and surrender yourself to the royal guards?"

"Surrender?" Blacktooth formed the word carefully, as though he'd never spoken it before.

"Yes," said Hilary firmly. "I don't think you're entirely heartless."

Captain Blacktooth stepped back from the rail.

"Don't be a fool, Rupert," Mrs. Tilbury snapped. "Now

that James is in the Dungeons, we won't have to worry about sharing our magic with him—and no one will believe his tales in any case. Haven't you always wanted to do what is best for the pirate league, and for your family?" She gestured to the sinking *Benevolence*. "Didn't we agree that this is what's best?"

"It seems an awful lot like *worst* to me," said Charlie.

But Captain Blacktooth was nodding his head. "I'd rather sink my own ship than surrender, Terror," he said. "I'm a pirate, after all, and pirates don't simply give up."

Hilary sighed; she'd expected as much. "In that case," she said, "we'll stop you."

"That's right!" cried the gargoyle. "We'll roast you nicely, carve you up, and serve you on a bed of lettuce!"

"Oh my," Miss Greyson murmured.

Mr. Gull stopped fanning himself with his parchment. "Are you ready to begin your battle, then?" he asked. "I thought this moment would never come!" He hurried away and reappeared a moment later with his thick copy of *Leading the League*. "Since the queen is busy with other matters at the moment," he said, "I shall judge the competition. The usual rules apply, of course: the winner of this battle shall be president of the VNHLP, and the loser shall go into exile, et cetera. The winner shall also be granted ownership of that curious creature." He pointed to the gargoyle, who hopped closer to Hilary's feet. "And if I understand what you all have been chattering about, if Captain Blacktooth wins, he is likely to seize control of the kingdom, though I'm absolutely certain League rules don't permit anything of the sort."

"When my daughter is Enchantress," Mrs. Tilbury said to him, "perhaps she'll turn you into a lamppost."

Philomena crossed her arms. "I don't see why any of this is necessary," she said. "If anyone should be surrendering, it's Miss Westfield and her friends. Do you really think you can defeat my uncle, Hilary? Do you truly think you'll be able to lead an entire league of pirates?"

Hilary didn't answer right away. She looked over at Charlie, with his wrists sprouting from the sleeves of a pirate coat he'd been swimming in only last year. She looked at Claire, who was meeting Philomena's gaze without blinking, and at Alice, standing in front of Nicholas to shield him from the Mutineers. Jasper had drawn his cutlass, Miss Greyson had drawn her crochet hook, and Cannonball Jack had brought out a plate of homemade shortbread for the crew to munch on during the battle. The finishing-school girls let their hair ribbons blow defiantly in the wind on the deck of the *Dancing Sheep*, the water-ballet performers pointed their toes, the High Society ladies raised their forks, the gargoyle ground his teeth, and Mr. Twigget's men sharpened their swords. All of them waited for Hilary to speak.

"There are plenty of things I can't do," she said to Philomena. "I can't sew a neat embroidery sampler, I can't remember which spoon to use when I eat soup, I can't bring my ship back from the bottom of the sea, and I can't stop you from being cruel. But I do believe I can lead an entire league of pirates."

"I, for one, am relieved to hear it," said Mr. Gull. "Please take your places, pirates, and let the battle begin!"

HILARY HAD SPENT most of the previous night lying awake in her cot on the *Pigeon* and imagining each of the things that might go wrong during the battle. After all, no pirate clash in Augustan history had ever gone entirely smoothly. Cannons misfired; ships sprang leaks. Magic pieces slipped out of hands. Peg legs washed up on the shore, missing their owners.

In all those wide-awake hours, however, Hilary had never imagined that everything might go wrong at once.

From the moment Mr. Gull waved a Jolly Roger above his head to signal the start of the battle, all the pirates in Queensport Harbor were swept up in a raucous mess that not even the queen's own housemaids could have tidied. Dozens of Captain Blacktooth's men tossed ropes down to the *Dancing Sheep* and began to storm the ship, mocking the schoolgirls as they went. Their parrots flew in a feathery swarm over Hilary's head, clawing at sails and pecking at ropes. One burly pirate swiped a tray of cucumber sandwiches straight out of Mrs. Westfield's hands. Partridge accidentally started a small fire in the *Blunderbuss*'s galley, and Worthington nearly fell overboard when she ran too quickly in the wrong direction. Even the gargoyle kept getting tangled up in his cape.

"Get me out of this thing, Hilary!" he yelped. "I think it's trying to eat me!"

As Hilary wrestled with the gargoyle's cape, Claire ran up to her. "Most of our treasure is still on board the *Augusta Belle*," she said anxiously. "The magic coatrack, the sacks of coins—nearly everything useful. I did manage to swipe this from the pile, though." She held out the golden gravy boat. "I'm sure it won't be as impressive as whatever the Mutineers have brought with them, but at least it's something."

"Something *dangerous*," the gargoyle said, hopping free of his cape.

Hilary stood up, keeping her distance from the gravy boat. "The gargoyle's right," she said. "That magic piece is entirely unreliable—but if it's all we've got, we'll have to use it until we can find something better." She squeezed Claire's hand. "Please promise me you'll be careful."

Claire laughed. "I'll do nothing of the sort," she said. "I am a pirate, after all."

Hilary wished there were time to search the *Blunderbuss* for more suitable magic pieces, but some of Blacktooth's pirates were already climbing over the houseboat's rails, and it would have been thoughtless to keep them waiting. She drew her cutlass and rushed over to join Charlie and

Alice, who were already entangled in sword fights with two of the most fearsome pirates. "Thank you for entertaining our guests," she called over her shoulder to them. "My mother would be proud of your hospitality."

The pirate she was dueling scowled at this. "Is your mother the woman with the lemonade?" he asked between parries. "She tossed a pitcher of the stuff at me a few moments ago, and now I'm chilled to the bone."

"Perhaps Captain Blacktooth will lend you a spare coat," Hilary suggested, slicing a button from the pirate's lemon-scented sleeve.

"Ha!" The pirate clipped the top of Hilary's hat feather. "The only thing Blacktooth ever willingly lends is his poor opinion."

Hilary dodged the pirate's sword, hurried around behind him, poked him in the breeches, and watched with satisfaction as he jumped several feet into the air. When he crashed back down on the deck, she stood over him, holding her cutlass to his nose.

"Well played, pirate," he said in a quavering voice. "Are you going to send me off the plank?"

Hilary glanced over at the *Blunderbuss*'s plank, which Cannonball Jack had transformed into an herb garden. Anyone who tried to walk it would have to step gingerly over the potted rosemary and mint. "I don't think that would be wise," she said.

The pirate looked skeptical. "Captain Blacktooth would send me off the plank."

"I'm sure he would," said Hilary, "but I'm not that sort of pirate. I'd rather lock you up inside the houseboat until the end of the battle."

"So you'll take me prisoner?" The pirate nodded, being careful to avoid the cutlass. "That sounds suitable. Taking prisoners is enthusiastically endorsed by the League."

Hilary pulled the pirate up by his arms and dragged him into Cannonball Jack's living quarters. "Don't let this scallywag escape," she told the greengrocer, who was carrying a sack of onions to throw at the Mutineers.

"Aye, aye, Captain!" he boomed, waving an onion rather menacingly in the pirate's direction.

As the battle wore on, Cannonball Jack's cabin took on more and more prisoners. Charlie defeated eight pirates in a row so convincingly that one of them asked him for swordplay lessons if they both survived the battle. Alice's arm wasn't entirely healed, but that didn't prevent her from chasing several more pirates all around the *Blunderbuss* in a swirl of ruffles and lace. Most of the pirates Hilary faced were handy with a sword, so it was fortunate that the gargoyle had offered to bite their ankles whenever she found herself in a tight spot. By the time she'd fought off five or six pirates, she had nearly perfected the swordplay figure she'd used to slice up the drapes in Westfield House.

One pirate had made the grave mistake of insulting

Miss Greyson, who was now employing her crochet hook to dangle him upside down until he had learned his lesson. Fitzwilliam busied himself by pecking the enemy's ears, Nicholas proved to be surprisingly handy with a borrowed sword, and Jasper ran through the crowd waving a net and shouting something about a parrot. Even Mr. Partridge and Miss Worthington were fighting admirably: Partridge confused two of the ship's ropes and accidentally lowered the boom on top of half a dozen of Blacktooth's men, and Worthington sent several others in confused circles by giving them poor directions. The crew of the *Dancing Sheep* was still locked in battle, and cannonballs from the *Renegade* were flying uncomfortably close to Hilary's head, but she was beginning to wonder if it might be possible to beat the Mutineers after all.

"Horsefeathers!" cried Claire.

She stood behind the *Blunderbuss*'s long row of cannons—or, at least, what used to be cannons. "I should never have used that gravy boat," said Claire miserably. "I wanted the enchantment to stick to the *Renegade*'s cannons, but it seems to have stuck to ours instead."

Hilary looked down at the things that had been cannons. They looked back up at her. Then they ruffled their wings. "I don't mean to be insensitive," she said to Claire, "but why did you ask the magic to turn them into chickens?"

"I didn't! All I wanted was to stop Blacktooth from

firing on our mates, so I told the gravy boat to make sure the pirates' cannons couldn't be used." Claire stared at the chickens. "I suppose I should have been more specific."

"What's going on?" said the gargoyle, coming up behind them. "Why are all these feathery things here? I don't like the look of them."

One of the chickens made a noise very much like a cannon being fired.

"What do we *do* with them?" asked Claire. "We can't launch them at the *Renegade*!"

"Never mind the chickens," said Hilary. At her feet, one of them had laid a small, perfectly round cast-iron egg. "Run as quickly as you can and ask the others if anyone has a magic piece you can borrow. And for heaven's sake, toss that gravy boat into the sea!"

Claire nodded and ran off, nearly crashing into Jasper, who was running in the opposite direction with a large red parrot tucked under his arm. "Eloise!" he shouted as he dashed past. "I need a pen and an inkpot!"

The gargoyle shook his head. "This battle is entirely too full of birds."

Hilary brushed the chickens out of the way and hurried to the stern of the houseboat. "Mr. Twigget!" she called. "How are you faring?"

"Not too well, Terror," Twigget replied from his ship. "One of Blacktooth's cannonballs grazed us, and I think we're takin' on water. What should we do?"

Hilary rolled up the sleeves of her pirate coat, breaking six different rules in the League dress code in the process. "Keep your cannons firing as long as you can," she said, "and then climb aboard the *Dancing Sheep*. They should have room for you there."

"Thank you, Captain," said Twigget. "We'll get Blacktooth yet. Just you wait and see."

The air at the far end of the harbor had become so thick with smoke that Hilary couldn't make out the queen's ship or the ships her mates had taken to offer their assistance. She had no idea how their battle was progressing, but then again, she could barely keep track of the pirates who were fighting all around her. Blacktooth's men were still tossing ropes over to the *Dancing Sheep*, but the schoolgirls on board were cutting the ropes with sewing shears and waving politely as their attackers splashed into the sea. Several girls confronted the remaining pirates with cutlasses and crochet hooks, while others bandaged up scrapes, mended torn breeches, and shouted loudly enough to crumble the walls of any finishing school.

Aboard the *Renegade*, Philomena had gathered an entire armful of magic coins, and now she was conjuring up more problems than Hilary could count. A tiny whirlwind spun across the deck of Mr. Twigget's ship, a respectably sized crocodile floated in the middle of the harbor, and a flurry of regretfully declined party invitations fell on Mrs. Westfield and her High Society friends.

But Claire had found a magic piece in Cannonball Jack's storeroom, and she hastily unwhirled the whirlwind, sent the crocodile home to warmer waters, and changed all the declined invitations to joyful acceptances. Philomena created a thick gray storm cloud; Claire ordered it to rain rose petals. Claire made Blacktooth's mates trip over their bootlaces; Philomena made Hilary's crew lose their boots altogether.

"Doesn't she ever stop to breathe?" Claire said as Philomena changed the Royal Augusta Water Ballet's music to a furious tarantella. The performers, who had been mounting an attack on one of Blacktooth's smaller ships, suddenly lost their rhythm and flailed helplessly in the waves. "I'm not sure I can keep thwarting her much longer."

"Don't worry, my dear!" called Mrs. Westfield from the next ship over. "We've concocted a marvelous plan." She turned to one of the other ladies, who stood at attention behind the antique cannon. "Fire away, Mrs. Cathcart!" she cried.

With a triumphant bang, Mr. Flintlock exploded out of the cannon's barrel and flew through the air, landing heavily on the deck of the *Renegade*. Before Philomena could step away, he had picked himself up and begun to pluck the magic coins out of her arms.

"Don't touch me, you horrid pirate!" Philomena shouted. "I am a High Society lady!"

"And I," said Flintlock, "am a human cannonball."

As Flintlock tossed handfuls of magic coins into the sea and Philomena conjured up a swarm of hornets to sting his ankles, Hilary turned her spyglass toward the far end of the harbor. The glass had cracked during the battle, and she felt as though she were squinting into a spider's web. "I still can't see much through all the smoke," she said to Claire, "but . . ." She lowered the spyglass and blinked. "Look! Isn't that the *Benevolence*?"

Claire hurried to her side, and both of them looked out across the waves, where a badly battered ship was limping toward them. It sat perilously low in the water and looked as though it might fall to bits at any moment, but its singed flag bore the queen's emblem. Behind it sailed two pirate ships captained by Mr. Stanley and Captain Wolfson. The smoke had begun to clear, but the false *Pigeon* was nowhere in sight.

All of Hilary's mates were staring in the same direction now. So were all the Mutineers. Even Mr. Flintlock, who had dived into the sea to avoid the hornets, kept his head above the water to watch. The crowd on the shore had begun to cheer, but most of the pirates grew silent. "What's this?" shouted Mrs. Tilbury from the *Renegade*. "How has the queen survived? It's impossible!"

"Where's that fool Sanderson?" Captain Blacktooth scanned the horizon.

"He's gone home," said Jasper happily. His hands were

splattered with ink, and bright red parrot feathers clung to his sleeves. "But you mustn't blame him. He was only following your orders."

Blacktooth glared at Jasper. "I never gave any such orders."

"And I didn't expect you to," said Jasper. "That's why I had to capture your parrot, forge a letter in your handwriting calling off the battle, and convince the parrot to deliver it to Mr. Sanderson. You should know that your Polly's loyalties can be bought for only three pieces of shortbread."

As the Mutineers looked on in disbelief, Jasper took a bow. Miss Greyson appeared to be in danger of kissing him right then and there.

"I don't think the queen is likely to be pleased with you when she finds out what you've done," Hilary called up to the *Renegade*. "What do you say now, Blacktooth? Will you turn yourself in?"

Captain Blacktooth buried his head in his hands.

"What are you doing, Rupert?" said Mrs. Tilbury. "Of course we won't turn ourselves in! We deserve to rule the kingdom!" She turned to Philomena. "Your uncle may be useless, but perhaps you're still good for something. Hurry up and sink the queen's ship once and for all!"

Philomena looked down at the coins she'd managed to keep from Mr. Flintlock. "But I don't have enough magic—"

"Never mind that," Mrs. Tilbury snapped. "Use the cannons, then!"

Hilary grabbed Claire's shoulder. "Can you stop her?" she asked.

Claire had turned pale. "I'm nearly out of strength."

"Magic . . . ," said Philomena. Her voice trembled over the word, and she paused. "Magic, please . . ."

"Wait a moment!" said Hilary. "You don't have to sink the queen just because you're told to!"

Philomena hesitated. She looked from her mother to Captain Blacktooth and back again. Then she glared directly at Hilary. "There are plenty of things I can't do," she said, "but I can do this." She straightened her spine, lifted her chin, and walked up to the *Renegade*'s long row of cannons. "Load these weapons," she said to her magic coins, "and prepare to light the fuses when I give the word."

"Hurry!" Hilary shouted to her mates. "Sail in front of the queen's ship! Block the *Renegade*'s line of fire!"

Cannonball Jack nodded and began to steer the houseboat toward the *Benevolence*. "Won't Philomena just sink us too?" Alice asked. "There's got to be something else we can do!"

The shouts from the crowd rang in Hilary's ears, and the gargoyle was nudging her foot with his snout, but she didn't have time to think about anything other than the queen and Philomena's cannons. "If we scraped together a few magic pieces," she said, "then maybe—oh, very well, gargoyle! What do you want?"

"I can do it," he said quietly. "I can save the queen."

Hilary wasn't sure she'd heard him correctly. "But you hate to protect people!"

"I do," the gargoyle agreed.

"It hurts you!"

The gargoyle nodded. "It's certainly not pleasant."

"And I promised you I'd never let anyone use you."

"Much appreciated," said the gargoyle, "but if some-one doesn't hurry up and do something heroic, we'll all be belly-up in the harbor as soon as those cannons go off. It wouldn't be a very nice fate for the kingdom's most intrepid gargoyle."

Hilary had an uncomfortable feeling that he was right. "If you're sure about this," she said, "I'll get Claire to do the wishing, or perhaps Miss Greyson, and—"

But the gargoyle was shaking his head. "They're both exhausted," he said, "and anyway, I'd feel much safer if it were you. Please, Hilary, can't you do it?"

Hilary looked down at her toes in their wet socks; her boots still hadn't reappeared after Philomena's enchant-ment. "I'll try," she said at last. "What's the worst that can happen?"

"Well," said the gargoyle thoughtfully, "we might both explode."

Hilary swallowed. "A good pirate doesn't mind exploding," she said. "Or at least she doesn't complain about it afterward."

Charlie had been watching them from across the deck, and now he came over to join them. "What are you doing?"

"Saving the kingdom," said Hilary. She picked up the gargoyle. "You'll probably want to stand back."

"Light the fuses, magic!" ordered Philomena. There wasn't even a trace of hesitation in her voice any longer. A dozen flames sparked to life on the *Renegade*, and Hilary stared down the barrels of a dozen cannons. Somewhere in the distance, a chicken squawked.

"Gargoyle," she said, holding him so tightly that she thought he might crumble, "please protect Queen Adelaide from the Mutineers—and protect the rest of us, too. The pirates, I mean, and Admiral Curtis, and all the spectators on the shore."

The gargoyle's eyes widened. "Hold on!" he said. "You want to protect *everyone*? Not even the Enchantress is strong enough to do that!"

But the magic was already pulling Hilary's breath away and knocking her backward against the houseboat's rails. It crashed through her arms and rolled out of her fingers; she nearly dropped the gargoyle.

"It's not working!" he cried. "We're doomed!"

Hilary tried very hard not to think of cannon fire, or

sinking ships, or the Pestilent Home for Foul-Tempered Pirates. She tried not to imagine the queen's flag washing ashore, or how pleased Captain Blacktooth would look when he plucked the gargoyle from the wreck of the *Blunderbuss*. "We'll just have to find a way to be stronger, then," she said. "We're pirates, aren't we?"

"Of course we are," said Charlie.

Before Hilary knew what was happening, he'd placed the palm of his hand on the gargoyle's back. Then he sucked in his breath as though he'd run straight into somebody's cutlass. "Pirate Dove," Hilary said, "whatever are you doing?"

"Helping you save the kingdom." Charlie's teeth were gritted, but he smiled at her. "It's my duty as the Scourge of the Northlands." He took another long breath and raised his voice. "Claire!" he called. "Miss Greyson! Jasper! Come here and help the Terror!"

Claire and Miss Greyson gathered up their skirts, and Jasper skidded across the deck in his stocking feet. "Hold on to the gargoyle," Charlie ordered them, "and think protective thoughts."

Hilary thought she could feel the magic beginning to pull at the others as they placed their hands on the gargoyle, but it kept on tugging at her, too. "Do you really think this is going to work?" she said in between breaths.

"Honestly?" said Charlie. "I've got no idea."

"Are you crazy?" the gargoyle cried. "This is no time for experiments! We're about to be turned into gunpowder soup!"

Then the cannons went off.

A DOZEN CANNONBALLS soared through the air. They passed over High Society ladies drinking lemonade, water-ballet performers with their arms extended upward, pirates lifting their eye patches to get a better view, and Miss Pimm's girls with their hands clasped to their chests. Then they curved toward the sea, toward a houseboat with cheerful checked curtains and a royal ship with tattered sails.

In Hilary's arms, the gargoyle blinked.

"Well," he said, "what do you know?"

As the pirates onboard the houseboat watched, the air above their heads began to shimmer. A noise like a thunderclap echoed over the harbor as the cannonballs collided with the shimmering stretch of air. For a moment, they seemed to stop entirely. Then, as gracefully as waltzing schoolgirls, the cannonballs reversed their course and curved back toward the *Renegade*, picking up speed as they flew.

"Oh, blast," said Mrs. Tilbury.

THE QUEEN'S INSPECTORS
KINGDOM OF AUGUSTA
DILIGENCE, LOGIC, DISCRETION

Report to H.R.H. Queen Adelaide regarding
THE ADVENTURE OF THE MUTINEERS

Report No. 1
FIELD INSPECTOR: *John Hastings*
LOCATION: *Queensport, Augusta*
CASE STATUS: *Closed*

Inspector's Comments: *Your Highness, I was
summoned to Queensport Harbor last week when
our agency received word of a vicious attack on
your royal person. Though eyewitnesses originally
reported that the attack was launched by the pirate
Hilary Westfield, I soon discovered that the real
attackers were a group of villains known as the
Mutineers. (Miss Eugenia Pimm, who is watching
over my shoulder as I write this report, says that she
has been trying to warn me about these Mutineers
for nearly a year now. I admit that I may have
ignored her warnings, but my natural talent for*

the deductive arts has allowed me to close this case nonetheless.) Thanks to the efforts of Pirate Westfield and her crew, the Mutineers have now been captured, and Your Highness's safety has been secured.

I believe the Mutineers were intending to take control of the Royal Navy, the Very Nearly Honorable League of Pirates, the office of the Enchantress, and, indeed, the throne itself. One leader of the nefarious group, former admiral James Westfield, was seized by a brave crew of naval officers; he is currently locked in the Royal Dungeons, where he stands accused of plotting to overthrow the kingdom, unlawfully sinking a pirate ship, mocking an officer of the queen, and pretending to reform himself. A second Mutineer, Oliver Sanderson, was chased across the High Seas and eventually caught by a band of northern pirates. Pirate captain Anders Wolfson is currently transporting Mr. Sanderson to the Dungeons.

The remaining Mutineers were more easily apprehended. When their ship, the Renegade, was pelted with cannonballs, it splintered into pieces before sinking in the waters off the coast of Queensport. My men found Captain Rupert

Blacktooth, Mrs. Georgiana Tilbury, and Miss Philomena Tilbury clinging to floating scraps of wood and plucked them from the sea. Mrs. Tilbury, who had escaped from a royal guard, is now awaiting trial in a triple-barred cell in the Dungeons, which she shares with her daughter, Philomena. Captain Blacktooth, however, was sent to the southern kingdoms immediately after the battle. He will live in exile at the Pestilent Home for Foul-Tempered Pirates and must never return to Augusta.

As for the rest of Blacktooth's crewmates, my investigations have convinced me that they had no knowledge of the Mutineers' treacherous plans. I believe they are loyal Augustan citizens who should be given a chance to redeem themselves under the leadership of a less villainous captain.

I hope you are feeling well, Your Highness, and I trust the singed edges of your royal hairstyle will make a full recovery.

Signed
John Hastings
Captain, Queen's Inspectors

A ROYAL DECREE!

LET IT BE KNOWN THAT TODAY

IN THE CITY OF QUEENSPORT,

∽

IN RECOGNITION OF HER MAGICAL TALENTS

AND HER SERVICES TO THE KINGDOM,

∽

Miss Claire Dupree

HAS RECEIVED THE TITLE OF

Enchantress of the Marsh.

∽

A LUNCHEON WILL BE HELD AT THE ROYAL PALACE

IN MISS DUPREE'S HONOR.

TEA AND FISH STICKS WILL BE SERVED.

HER ROYAL HIGHNESS

Queen Adelaide

of Augusta

WITH GREAT REGRET,

Miss Philomena Tilbury

AND

Sir Nicholas Feathering

ANNOUNCE THE

CANCELLATION OF THEIR WEDDING.

WEDDING FUNDS WILL BE USED TO

PURCHASE FURNISHINGS FOR MISS TILBURY'S

CELL IN THE ROYAL DUNGEONS.

GIFTS WILL NOT BE RETURNED.

THE PESTILENT HOME FOR FOUL-TEMPERED PIRATES
Where Scallywags Itch to Stay!

Dear Rupert Blacktooth,

Welcome to the Pestilent Home! We look forward to serving very few of your needs and attending to none of your whims during your years in exile. As a resident of the Pestilent Home, you will make new enemies, take up dull and unpleasant hobbies, and develop mysterious, incurable illnesses. There is so much to look forward to!

Please be advised that the Pestilent Home is a parrot-free lodging. Sheets, blankets, and pillows are not provided by our housekeeping staff. We do, however, furnish each room with one lumpy mattress and plenty of bedbugs. Gruel is served promptly at five o'clock every morning. On Thursday evenings, the entire Pestilent Home community gathers to share hardtack, conversation, and regrets. A small library of Improving Works is available for you to browse at your leisure.

We are confident that in no time at all you will feel uncomfortably at home here, and we are thrilled to count you among our residents.

Most sincerely,
Miss Vitriola Barnes
Manager

From
The Picaroon
BEIN' THE OFFICIAL NEWSLETTER OF THE VERY
NEARLY HONORABLE LEAGUE OF PIRATES

VNHLP WELCOMES NEW LEADER. Polish your
boots and groom your parrots! All scourges and scallywags
from every corner of Augusta are cordially invited to attend
the investiture of our new League president, Pirate Hilary
Westfield. The ceremony will take place this Saturday
afternoon in Gunpowder Square, with Scourge of the
Northlands Charlie Dove and Enchantress of the Marsh Claire
Dupree rumored to be planning appearances. A rollicking
pirates' ball will follow the ceremony, featuring Cannonball
Jack's famous chocolate mousse, fireworks over the bay, and
special performances by the Otterpool Royal Orchestra and
the VNHLP Chantey Chorale.

❧

**TREASURE FOUND IN QUEENSPORT
HARBOR.** A large collection of books washed up last night
on the Queensport shore. The books themselves are damp,
sandy, and inhabited by sea creatures, but the stories within are
still thoroughly enjoyable. If you are the owner of these fine
volumes, please contact the Picaroon to collect your treasure.

❧

WILDLIFE SANCTUARY PLANNED. The lawn behind VNHLP headquarters will soon be transformed into a permanent home for ten fortunate chickens. Until recently, these chickens served as cannons on the pirate ship *Blunderbuss*, but a plan to return them to their original state was thwarted when the birds rose up in protest. They will now spend their days grazing on the green pastures of Gunpowder Island and laying free-range cannonballs, which pirates may purchase from the League by the dozen. Former presidential secretary Horatio Gull has been chosen to serve as head of the VNHLP Cannon Chicken Initiative.

CHAPTER SIXTEEN

THE GUNPOWDER ISLAND roses had just come into bloom, and the rented rooms above the Sword and Seahorse groggery bustled with pirates. Jasper hurried through the hall in search of his cuff links, Charlie grudgingly ironed his best shirt, and Miss Greyson tricked the gargoyle into a washtub, where, against his wishes, she proceeded to give him a bath. "Hilary!" he cried from the washtub. "Rescue me! I feel very undignified."

"I'm afraid there's nothing I can do," said Hilary. "Miss Greyson made me bathe too, you know."

"So I did." Miss Greyson took up a soapy cloth and scrubbed lichen from the gargoyle's wings. "Not even the president of the pirate league has a chance of defending herself against a determined governess."

"I'm only *nearly* the president," Hilary reminded her. "And I can't imagine what my fellow scourges and scally-wags will think when I arrive at the ceremony with soap behind my ears. Most pirates are fairly crusted over with dirt."

"This," said Miss Greyson, "is a special occasion. I'm sure everyone will be looking their best." She lifted the gargoyle out of the washtub and wrapped him in a fluffy towel. "Now, if you'll excuse me, I've got to dress for the ceremony. We don't have much time before the carriage arrives."

Hilary had been dressed for ages already, but she cleaned her boots, braided her hair three times in a row, and chased Fitzwilliam down the hall to retrieve the gold hoop earring clasped in his beak. Waiting to leave the Sword and Seahorse, she decided, was almost as torturous as a long grammar lesson on a beautifully blue day. She poked her head into Claire's room. "Are you ready to leave?" she asked.

"Mostly," said Claire. She'd put on the golden gown Miss Pimm had bought her for formal Enchantressing events, but she wore only one pearl earring and only one shoe; her hair was already falling out of its elegant twist. She sat on the floor with an enormous and ancient book spread open in front of her. "I believe you're more anxious about this ceremony than you ever were about going into battle."

Hilary nodded. "Half the pirates in the League were fighting against me less than a month ago," she said, "and some of them still won't look me in the eye. I don't think they'll be entirely pleased to follow my orders."

"I know just how you feel," said Claire, pulling on her other shoe. "A few days ago, one of those horrid ladies from the Coalition of Overprotective Mothers walked up to me in the street and said she didn't think I was well-bred enough to be the Enchantress. I demonstrated my excellent breeding by not kicking her in the shins." Claire tried to pin her hair up, but it immediately fell down again. "We'll simply have to win people over with our charms."

"Or your cutlasses," said the gargoyle, coming in from the hallway. He held his pirate hat in his mouth, and Hilary helped him place it over his ears. "What are you reading?" he asked Claire. "Is it a thrilling pirate romance?" He hopped closer hopefully.

"It's Augustan history, actually," Claire told him. "I believe Charlie was onto something when he ordered us all to grab hold of you. Ages ago, before the kingdom started running out of magic, people used to work together to use magic pieces for the strongest enchantments. They didn't try it very often, though, and it didn't always work." She leaned over the book once more. "I'll have to do some experiments when I get back to Pemberton. There's still a huge amount we don't know about magic, and I'd like to do more than simply scold people while I'm Enchantress."

When the carriage arrived at last, all the pirates climbed inside and set off down the lane to Gunpowder Square. It was fortunate the trip was a short one, for the carriage wasn't quite large enough for half a dozen pirates in their finery: Miss Greyson's elbow settled itself in Hilary's ear, Fitzwilliam was forced to perch on the roof, and Charlie was squashed between the window on one side and Claire on the other, though truthfully, Hilary didn't think he looked all that miserable about it.

As they squeaked down the lane, Jasper told them all about the sketches and plans he'd received the previous day from the pirate shipbuilder on the other side of the island. "I can't imagine the new ship will measure up to the *Pigeon*," he said, "but it will have extra storerooms for treasure, plenty of bunks for visitors, and a whole series of cabins for Eloise's floating bookshop. It's fairly massive, actually. I have no idea how we'll manage to sail the blasted thing."

"I'll help you whenever I come to visit," Hilary promised, "and so will Charlie, I'm sure."

Charlie nodded. "When the Terror and the Scourge aren't performing daring deeds or marching around VNHLP headquarters, they're surprisingly good at selling books."

"I'll help too," the gargoyle said, "as long as there's a Gargoyle's Nest."

"Never fear," said Jasper. "If the day ever comes when

I captain a ship without a Gargoyle's Nest, I'll toss myself overboard in shame."

When the carriage rolled to a halt, the others went to take their places in the crowd, and Hilary made her way to the edge of Gunpowder Square. Cannonball Jack was waiting for her there in his best coat and hat; he bowed to Hilary when he caught sight of her. "Thanks for askin' me to do the honors, Terror," he said, "an' for lettin' me rejoin the League."

The VNHLP had been flooded with applications from the pirates who'd fought alongside Hilary in Queensport Harbor, and she had instructed the League officers to approve each and every form without delay. One-Legged Jones had seemed slightly scandalized by the prospect of sending membership cards to several dozen finishing-school girls, but to Hilary's relief, he'd done as she'd asked. "You're very welcome," she told Cannonball Jack. "It was the least I could do, especially considering what happened to your cannons."

"I just paid 'em a visit up at headquarters." Cannonball Jack brushed a fluffy white chicken feather from his lapel. "But that be neither here nor there. What have ye got in yer hands, Terror? Be it yer rules of conduct?"

Hilary nodded and passed him the rolled-up paper. "It's called the Buccaneers' Code," she said. "I should tell you, though, I had a bit of help writing it."

Cannonball Jack unrolled the paper, and Hilary read it over his shoulder.

The Buccaneers' Code

- Pirates are practical (most of the time).
- Pirates are brave, even if they're also terrified.
- Pirates should not climb trees.
- Pirates can learn a lot from finishing school.
- Pirates don't let their spirits sink when their ship does.
- Pirates look excellent in hats.
- Pirates are loyal to their friends.

Cannonball Jack gave Hilary an approving nod. "'Tis a good Code," he said. "'Specially the bit about hats."

By the time the ceremony began, Gunpowder Square was packed with pirates standing shoulder to shoulder. A few duels were breaking out at the edges of the crowd, but that was common enough at any League gathering when the members were in good spirits. Cannonball Jack led Hilary to the front of the square, where someone had placed an empty grog barrel for her to stand on. As she greeted the crowd, she spotted several of the pirates she'd defeated in battle and a large group from the Ornery Clam, though the scallywag who'd threatened to slice off her fingers hadn't bothered to attend. Miss Pimm had given her students a holiday, and several schoolgirls were sprinkled throughout the audience, clapping politely as Hilary read her Buccaneers' Code aloud. Even the Royal Augusta Water Ballet troupe had gathered at the back of the square, all looking uncomfortably dry.

The ceremony didn't take long, for pirates are hardly ever patient. Still, it seemed to Hilary as though no time at all had passed before Cannonball Jack was handing her a jewel-handled cutlass far too fancy to be useful, draping a Jolly Roger over her shoulders, and pinning the presidential skull-and-crossbones badge to her coat. Then a round of blasts echoed from the cannons along the beach, and the Very Nearly Honorable League of Pirates gave three huzzahs for their new president, leaving Hilary so lightheaded that she had to step down off her grog barrel.

The crowd of pirates seemed to swirl around her as they marched her out of the square and up the hill to VNHLP headquarters. They kept swirling as Cannonball Jack served his chocolate mousse, Mr. Marrow gave a toast, and the Otterpool Royal Orchestra launched into a rousing series of jigs. Finally, halfway through the Chantey Chorale's performance of traditional Northlands sailing tunes, Hilary shrugged the Jolly Roger from her shoulders and set down the jewel-handled cutlass. She got up from her seat as quietly as she could, picked up the gargoyle, and slipped out of the ballroom.

From the rocking chair on the headquarters' front porch, Hilary could see halfway across the island. She could see the sun setting over the bay, the statues standing in Gunpowder Square, and the strange walled garden where Miss Pimm's family estate had stood before the days of pirates. A new cottage stood there now, for Miss Pimm was leaving her finishing school in the nimble hands of the embroidery mistress and moving back to the island to enjoy a thoroughly proper retirement. The gargoyle had already promised to bring her a plate of spiders as a house-warming gift.

"Is everything all right?" the gargoyle said. He frowned up at Hilary. "Didn't you like your fancy cutlass?"

"It's lovely," said Hilary. "So were the songs, and the dances, and the chocolate mousse, but I still feel like something's not quite right." She looked out at the waves. "What's the opposite of seasick?"

"Landlocked," the gargoyle said knowingly. "I felt that way the whole time I was stuck on my wall."

The porch door swung open, and Claire burst through it. "Here she is!" she called. Jasper, Charlie, and Miss Greyson all tumbled out the door after her. "We've been looking for you everywhere," Claire said, sitting down on the arm of Hilary's chair. "Jasper thought you might be practicing treading water in the swimming pool, and he dragged us all the way there even though I said you certainly *wouldn't* be practicing since you're already so good at it!" She took a breath. "Anyway, we've found you at last."

"And we've got a gift for you," said Jasper.

"A good one," said Charlie.

"A gift?" the gargoyle asked. "I don't know anything about a gift!"

"That," said Miss Greyson, "is because gargoyles can't be trusted to keep secrets."

The gargoyle sighed. "It's true," he said. "We can't."

"The gift can't come to you, Terror," said Jasper, "so we've got to bring you to it." He tipped Hilary's rocking chair forward until she slid out of it. "Come along, every-one. If we don't move quickly, I'll die of suspense."

"I can't believe you tipped the president of the pirate league out of her chair, Mr. Fletcher," Hilary said as she followed the others down the lane. "I'm sure *Leading the League* has quite a few things to say about that."

The pirates filed down the hill, across the square, and through a tangle of narrow cobblestone streets. At last they arrived at the wall that encircled the island. A small iron gate was hidden away behind a rosebush, and Jasper pushed it open.

Beyond the gate was the shore, beyond the shore was the sea, and anchored in the sea was a ship with battle-scarred sails, long rows of bookshelves, and a basket tied to the bowsprit just big enough to fit a gargoyle. For a moment, Hilary was sure she'd imagined it. "But the *Pigeon* sank!" she said. "I saw it happen!"

"It was thoughtful of the Mutineers to build us a replica," said Jasper, "and even more thoughtful of Captain Wolfson and his men to patch her up once they'd chased Oliver Sanderson halfway around the kingdom. I'm afraid you'll still need to give her a good scrubbing to get the villainy off her, though."

"She's a good size for setting out in search of buried treasure," said Charlie.

"And for visiting friends," said Claire.

"She's perfect," Hilary said. She set down the gargoyle and ran across the sand to the dinghy that sat ready to take her out to the *Pigeon*. Waves lapped at her ankles as she dragged the dinghy into the water, climbed inside, and took up the oars. Gunpowder Bay was still cold enough to numb Hilary's toes, but even when she finally noticed the chill, she didn't mind it a bit.

Then she looked back at the others, who were still waiting by the gate. "Are you coming?" she called.

Her mates glanced at one another. "You want us to come with you?" Miss Greyson asked.

"Of course," said Hilary. "If we start right away, we'll have just enough time for a sail around the island before the fireworks begin."

ACKNOWLEDGMENTS

I'M HUGELY GRATEFUL, as always, to the people who guided this book into the world and made the experience so rewarding while they were at it:

To Toni Markiet, whose warmth, wisdom, and mastery of pirate jargon are unparalleled, and whom I can't wait to join on more adventures;

☙❧

to Abbe Goldberg, who's taken excellent care of these books since her first day on the job;

☙❧

to the entire team at HarperCollins: Amy Ryan, Gina Rizzo, Karen Sherman, Kathryn Silsand, Emilie Polster, Alana Whitman, Kate Morgan Jackson, and everyone else who worked in large and small ways over the past four years to bring this series to life;

☙❧

to Pétur Antonsson and Dave Phillips, who draw the worlds I can only imagine, and to Katherine Kellgren, who makes it all sound even better;

☙❧

to agent/miracle worker Sarah Davies and the whole wonderful crew at the Greenhouse and at Rights People;

☙❧

to my foreign publishers, who have guided Hilary around the world with great talent and enthusiasm;

🙰

to Hannah Moderow, who always has the right words;

🙰

to the multitude of writers who've given me advice, encouragement, company, and sanity in equal measure;

🙰

to the parents, educators, librarians, and booksellers who have shared these stories with the young readers in their lives;

🙰

to my friends and family, who are the finest of their kind anywhere in the known world;

🙰

to Zach, who makes all challenges less fearsome;

🙰

and to the gargoyle, who came to visit one day and decided to stay for a while.

Caroline Carlson's newest novel,
The World's Greatest Detective,
is bursting with hilarity, high jinks, murder,
and mayhem. It would be a crime to miss it!

Dear Reader,

For twenty years I have tried to uncover the truth of every circumstance, unravel the most tangled of plots, and bring even the most dangerous criminals to justice. It is why I earned the title as the World's Greatest Detective. However, it is time for me to pass on my good fortune to one of you!

I would like to invite you to a friendly competition I am hosting at Coleford Manor. Food will be served, games will be played—and a crime will be committed. Who will the guilty party be? That is for you to deduce. You must work quickly, though, for whoever is first to solve the crime will win a monetary prize, my personal recommendation, and the title of World's Greatest Detective.

I hope you will join me in this contest of wits, and I look forward to seeing you soon.

Yours,
Hugh Abernathy

SAIL THE HIGH SEAS WITH ALL THREE SWASHBUCKLING ADVENTURES!